30 DAYS IN

JUNE

Chris Westlake

For Elizabeth, who has always believed in me

DAY ONE
1ST JUNE 1988

Removing his foot from the pedal, John Watts flicks the full beams of his Austin Allegro so that the figure up ahead - the *only* figure - illuminates like an actor in the spotlight.

Red-brick buildings cast a shadow on the road. Black smoke spouted from the chimneys a decade or so ago, but now the factories are shut, the buildings abandoned. Moss fills the cracks, and wood fills the square windows. This is a forgotten street. No light. No life.

Squinting at the clock on the dashboard, John inhales the early morning breeze blowing through the open window. The car edges closer. He can hear the heels clicking on the bumpy tarmac. His eyes follow the zip running the length of the black leather boots, stopping just north of the knee. Closer. A glimpse of pale white flesh separates the boots from the pencil skirt, clinging to the thighs. Thrusting his head out of the window, John recalls the intoxicating perfume he inhaled when he brushed close to the figure in the club, just hours earlier.

The head outside remains high, eyes focussed on the

monotonous, unchanging road ahead, seemingly oblivious to the car, now just feet away. The fake eyelashes do not blink. There is no sideways glance. Could be on the catwalk. The narrow hips swish from side to side. A black handbag dangles from the right shoulder.

John beeps the horn. Like a click of his finger; the figure is awakened from the trance. Long fingers on hips. Swivels to face the car. The lips remain a full, red line. No cracks in the painted face.

Plumping his cheeks, John keeps his lips pressed tight together; a thirty-a-day habit has left his teeth yellow and rotting. "Don't want to be out here on your own at this time of the morning," he says. "Never know who might be lurking with bad intentions now, do you?"

His face burns as the almond eyes unblinkingly evaluate him. The long legs bend at the knee as the pelvis is thrust forward. John's upper lip quivers as silence fills the air. His jaw drops as the scent of the perfume grows more alluring. Click of the heels. The door is pulled open and then pushed shut. Bloodshot eyes glance in the mirror, as the legs unfold and then part to allow enough room in the back seat. John blows air from his puffed cheeks.

Not usually this easy.

Pushing his fingers inside the pocket of his jeans, John digs out an oval mint; it disappears inside his waiting mouth.

Only has a few left and so he decides against offering one. Taps the steering wheel. His rapid thoughts rebound off each other like a pinball. Important to get the balance right, he thinks. Important to be interesting and interested, but not appear too keen, too eager.

"Gets cold this time of morning, doesn't it?" he says. "And it's been such a hot day, too. Difficult to know what to wear when you go out, don't you think?"

His eyes flicker in the mirror, notices the rise of the skirt, that it barely covers the curve of the buttocks. Forces his eyes to rise. *Needs to get the balance.* Catches the shrug of the shoulders. They are lean and broad: swimmer's shoulders. The head turns, stares at the blank canvas out of the window. John seizes the opportunity. Eyes narrow into slits as they scan every muscle and contour of the beautiful body in the back of the car. In the back of *his* car. The thighs are slightly parted. His eyes focus on the straight line that divides the leather boots from cold, naked flesh. His eyes are ready to continue their journey, keep moving higher, keep continuing all the way to the top, but the head turns away from the window and catches him looking. John is sure he saw the briefest of smiles. He strains against his jeans, digs into the hardness of the steering wheel.

John turns to his wife in the passenger seat. *Forgot she was there.* He idly wonders what she makes of this sudden -

incredible - development. Will she be jealous? Will she give him a hard time? Her puffy cheeks are flushed, and her glasses have left red indents on both sides of her nose. The street lights bring focus to her oily, pockmarked skin, like moon craters. Her tight, shapeless top is just another layer over rolls of belly. John wonders what the beauty in the back of his car thinks of his sexless wife? They've been together a long time; they are partners in crime. John is blissfully aware he is lucky to have found somebody with the same mindset. She is even worse than he is. Sure, she might be bristling with jealousy, but John knows that underneath that outsized skirt, his wife's drab panties are soaked from thinking about the events that are about to unfold.

John turns around. "Let me apologise for my lack of courtesy," he says, momentarily exposing his teeth before slamming his mouth tight. "How rude of me. No introductions. My name is John, and this lovely lady here is my wife, Valerie."

Silence.

They'd discussed giving false names, but they both agreed: what was the point? They never met for a second time. They had rules, and the first rule was that they never broke the rules. John shakes his head as Valerie shuffles in her seat and gives a limp wave. Did she think she was the Queen? He waits for a return introduction. None comes.

John fiddles with the radio button, keen to fill the void. Turns the volume up. The male voice is calm and monotone.

"The news today, 1st June 1988. London prepares for the visit of President Reagan tomorrow. The President, who has been in meetings with General Secretary Mikhail Gorbachev over the last few days, is scheduled to meet both the Queen and the Prime Minister, Margaret Thatcher..."

John mutters under his breath. Changes the station. Bops his head back and forth to the blaring music. *Won't you take me to funky town?*

Glances in the mirror. Decides it is time to pick up the pace, that it is finally time for the train to leave the station. "Did you have a good night, darling? Busy, wasn't it? Especially for a Wednesday..."

The nod is slow and mechanical. Much better than John anticipated. All the encouragement he needs to keep talking, to introduce his charm offensive. "That club sure is an odd place, isn't it? Full of freaks. Present company excluded, of course. We both saw you in there, didn't we, Valerie?"

"We sure did, John."

"There were some proper sights, weren't there?" John shakes his head and chuckles, pulls back an involuntary snort. "Still, each to their own and all that. We're liberals. Very open-minded about these things. But you were different, darling. You were special. Stood out in a good way.

We both said so, didn't we, dear?"

"We sure did, John."

John moves the car from second to first as they pull up on the drive of their semi-detached house in the quiet cul-de-sac they'd lived in for over fifteen years. He'd mowed the lawn over the weekend and taken the opportunity to chat with his neighbours, who were mainly out washing their cars. It was a nice little community. John was part of the Neighbourhood Watch scheme and they'd baby sat for a couple of the younger families. Unplugging his seatbelt (John still wasn't used to the damn things), John swivels his hips to properly face their young victim for the first time. "Nightcap?" he asks. John raises his eyebrows, flecked with silver.

This was where they were going to face objections, of course. Hadn't even asked for an address from their beautiful young guest, just headed straight to their house like it was a perfectly natural thing to do. John squeezes his wife's clammy hand. They were in this together.

The eyes in the back seat have returned to staring out of the window. The head turns. John's cheeks prickle as the eyes fix on his own. Ready for the onslaught, the protests. The dark hairs on his arms straighten. Valerie rearranges the position of her ample backside on the seat next to him. John's jaw is heavy and numb as the long legs in the back unravel. The door opens and shuts. His eyes are like saucers as the legs make their way up his drive and then stop outside his front door. Turns. The hands are on the hips. Again. The shoulders shrug.

What the fuck are you waiting for?

John struggles to keep his tongue in his mouth and his dick in his trousers as he hurries out of the motor and dangles his keys in the door. His poor wife waddles somewhere behind him, just as keen, but lacking his natural athleticism. Inside, their guest sinks into the depths of the sofa without waiting to be asked. John returns from the kitchen with three glasses of red wine. Valerie gulps and snorts and stains the rim with lipstick. She rests her hand on one of the long legs for just a few moments too long, daring to be outrageous.

"Why don't you go and change into something a little more comfortable, Valerie?" John asks.

His wife looks up at him from the sofa and wolfishly grins. "Something more *comfortable*, you say?"

John felt there was no need for his wife to raise her eyebrows quite so many times; it looked like she was having a funny turn. Valerie struggles up out of the chair and, blowing her husband a kiss, says, "I'll be back in just a few minutes. Don't go anywhere."

John barely waits for his wife to leave the room before

occupying the space she vacated on the settee. "Bless her," he says. He shuffles, reducing the gap between them. "I love her to bits, of course. Who wouldn't? Such a kind heart. But we are very used to each other. Fish and chips is all very well, but sometimes it is nice to have steak, isn't it? I hardly know you at all and that makes you so much more interesting, don't you think?"

The plump lips sip the wine. The body stretches at the waist and places the glass on the living room table. Hair falls down to the chest. The brown eyes fix on John. "I know *exactly* what you mean, John."

The voice is deep and husky, like it belongs to a completely different body, and John instantly twitches. He brushes his fingertips down the nape of the neck.

"You do?"

"Oh yes. I certainly do..."

"So what should we call you?" John asks.

"You can call me Samantha..."

John's hand rests on the shapely naked thigh, in precisely the same spot his wife rested her hand just moments before. His fingertips are teasing at first, like a feather, and then he massages more firmly. The legs widen. An invite. His hand rises, continues higher...

The door pushes open. His wife enters the room. John removes his hand, not quite sure why. He bites his lower lip;

blood trickles on the tip of his tongue.

"Why, don't you look sexy?" their guest slurs, looking up at Valerie.

Valerie does a twirl, transformed into a giggly sixteen-year-old-girl trying on her frock for the Prom. Only, Valerie is not sixteen: she is forty-three. She is not trying on a frock: she is clad in a black leather bodice, and she holds a whip in her right hand. Her fleshy pink bosom spills and jiggles. She places one hand on her hip and gazes challengingly at their guest.

"As you can probably see, neither Valerie nor myself are prudes. I guess you might call us broad-minded. We are into some pretty interesting things..."

"No shit."

John watches from the pit of their sofa as their guest stands up and towers over his wife, now in four-inch heels. John arches his neck to look up the skirt. He has been a good boy for long enough. Now it is time to be a bad boy.

He pulls himself up. He can't control his hands any more. They disappear inside the skirt, frantically reaching for what has been playing on his mind all night. The legs part a few inches more. This time he won't be stopped. This is what he is really interested in. His hand continues rising, all the way to the top. There you go.

His hand cups the balls, squeezing them like a limpet, and

then they grab hold of the dick. So much thicker than his own. So much longer.

"We sure have found ourselves a big boy here, Valerie," John says to his wife, his mouth wet with saliva.

John is aware of his own tiny erection, hidden away somewhere under the overflow of his belly. Glancing at his wife, he suddenly resents the look of wanton desire on her thin lips. *She* is comparing their young, athletic guest to *him*. He squeezes hard on the dick. *He* is in control. John straightens his back but still he looks up at the young man, pale pretty face partly hidden by a frizzy, brunette wig. John is aware that his wife is dressed up because she wants the young man inside her. She wants to be fucked by a r*eal* man for a change, not by him.

The guy puts his hand inside the skirt and snaps John's hand away. The hold on John's wrist is strong. John couldn't resist, even if he tried. His wife is right: ironically, there is only one man in the room now.

"Let me have some fun with that beautiful wife of yours before you get what you want, *John*," he says.

John is taken aback by the forcefulness of the command. How old is this lad? Old enough - for sure - but still, barely out of school. And yet, here he is, ordering him about in his house, demanding to do whatever he wants with his wife. Blood flows to his dick.

Fanning thin air and twirling her middle finger, Valerie says, "Come here, you naughty boy."

"Pass me that whip," the boy says.

"Ooh, I love it when a man takes control," Valerie coos, thrusting out her monumental bosom. It does look magnificent, John thinks. She passes him the whip. She does exactly as she is told.

"Bend over."

John watches as his wife obediently bends at the waist. Her breasts finally spill out of the bodice, two gigantic mounds of flesh dangling towards the floor. Her plump bottom points to the ceiling, the skin rippling. John slumps back onto the sofa, disappears into the background. Unzips his fly.

The young man, still dressed in a short skirt and thigh-length black leather boots and who, until a few hours ago, was a complete stranger to John and Valerie, pulls back his hand and smacks the naked buttocks. Valerie yelps with pleasure. John's trousers are down by his knees. The young man pulls back with the whip and slashes it down against the rippling flesh. John listens to his wife screaming.

"Turn around," the boy commands.

Valerie turns around. John notices that her eyes are watery and red. Tears trickle down her pink cheeks. She holds out her hands. What does she want? Help? It serves her right. John looks down pitifully at his own limp cock.

The whip slashes down against her naked breast, leaving a red mark, like a jolt of lightning.

"No!" she shouts. "Stop! You're hurting me!"

The boy slashes harder. John notices the sinewy muscle in his arms. The boy's face is distorted with glee. He turns to John challengingly. *What are you going to do about it?* John looks up at the boy. He takes his hand away from his crotch. "I think maybe you are being too rough with her?" John says.

The boy looks him up and down. He says nothing, but the look says it all. John has never felt so pathetic, so dirty.

"This is what she wants," the boy says. He pulls back his hand and then whips Valerie with such force that even John flinches. John gets up. No man is going to treat his wife like this, not his darling Valerie, his partner in crime. John clenches his fists, tightens them into tiny, knotted balls. His trousers are down by his knees. He cannot keep his balance. The lad swipes at him with the back of his hand, hitting him flush on the mouth. John plunges towards the edge of the coffee table. He rolls over onto his back. His head leaks. He stares up at the lights, which are bright and yellow and nauseating.

He realises that the deafening noise in the room is the sound of his wife screaming. The side of his face presses against the carpet. Saliva trickles down his chin. He reaches out at the black leather boots, but as he does so the boot moves out of reach and the heel stabs down against his mouth. Again. And again.

There are just shapes and colours as the world goes in and out of focus. John has a perfect view up the skirt from this angle. The boy kneels down. Unzips one of the long leather boots. Pulls something out. John squints. The bright light reflects from the sharp object in the boy's hand. Just what is it?

John only realises that it is a stainless steel cut-throat razor when it is far, far too late to do anything about it.

The boots move away from John. The boy stands over his wife, lying motionless on the floor with her bodice pulled down by her midriff. The boy slashes the razor in a straight line down her bosom. The boots move back towards John. He stands over him.

"Look at me."

John closes his eyes.

"*Look* at me."

The grip on his throat is so strong that John foams at the mouth. John opens his eyes. Looks at the boy, sees the saliva glistening his perfect, white teeth. John keeps looking at the boy, his body limp and lifeless, as the boy carves the razor down his chest. He keeps looking - just as he is told - as the boy pulls back the razor and then claws it down his chest again.

John is aware of screaming in the room. He knows it no longer belongs to Valerie, that his wife is no doubt dead by now. He knows that, this time, the screaming is his own.

DAY ONE
1ST JUNE 2018

"We are going to put that incredible imagination of yours to good use. I urge you to maximize its full potential," he says. Definitely a *he*. Undisputedly masculine. "Imagine you've organised a party. The party is in your house - your home - and therefore it is *your* party. The party belongs to *you*. It is your possession. It is the most fantastic party that your imagination will allow. And remember, the power of your imagination, unlike the real, predictable world, is limitless. Can you imagine that?"

"I can imagine that."

"You've created a guest list. It is *your* guest list, and so the only people included on the list are the people *you* want to be there. Some people who don't make the list might be offended. Frankly, this isn't your problem. You have heard that lyric: "*It's my party and I'll cry if I want to.*"? Well, it is *your* party, and so *they'll* be doing the crying if need be, not you. Can you create that guest list?"

Nod my head.

"But what if somebody else turns up at your party?"

"Who?" I ask. "Who turns up at my party?"

"You *know* who."

Remain silent. Tap my feet on the floor.

"He turns up at your house uninvited. You didn't invite him because you didn't want him to be there. He brings out the worst in you. The *very* worst. A side of you that is best buried away. So what happens if this person turns up uninvited at your house?"

I rub my fingertips in straight lines up and down my forehead, digging into the bone. "How can I answer that? You haven't told me who this person is..."

Long, drawn out sigh. "You *know* who this person is. Please don't humour me. There is no need for me to answer that question and, quite simply, I don't intend to. He is outside *your* house, knocking on *your* door, demanding *your* attention. So what are you going to do about it?"

"I'd open the front door..."

"You would? That means that you'd come face to face with him. Is that what you want? Do you really think you could cope with *that*? Why would you do that?"

"Think about it. Otherwise he'd keep knocking on the door. My guests would be upset. It would negatively impact my party."

"Your guests can't hear the knocking. Only you can hear the knocking," he says.

My fingertips move upwards, tugging at loose hairs from my scalp. "Even so, the knocking will become louder, you can't deny that. I'm not a magician. The knocking will become a barking dog keeping me awake when I'm exhausted and desperate to sleep. I'll have no choice but to answer that door - to face *him* - just to put a stop to the unbearable noise..."

"You know you are wrong," he says. "You pay attention to a fly, for example, and it becomes a nuisance. A damn *fly*. You focus on something else - *anything* else - and your subconscious no longer has room to give that damn fly any importance. It might remain in the room; who cares? It will disappear from your mind and you'll get on with your life. I'll ask the question again: what are you going to do when your greatest fear comes knocking on the door, demanding to be let in?"

Pause. Need to put the correct words in the right order. "I'd ignore the knocking on the door. And then I'd return to my invited guests. I'd do everything I can to make them feel welcome, to ensure it is the most fantastic party they've ever been to. And the knocking would just become some distant, irrelevant noise. Eventually, I won't even notice it is there. Just like that damn fly you talk about."

"Fantastic. I'm certain your actions are the right ones to take. Let me just play devil's advocate for one moment, though, if you don't mind? Let me put another question to you: how do you think he'll react to you ignoring him?"

I blow out hot air. "I can't try to control how other people react," I say. "You told me that."

"You're right. I did. And you can't. But I'm not asking you to. I'm just asking you to tell me what his likely reaction will be. You're ignoring him. He is stood on your doorstep. You are humiliating him. Aren't you just going to make him angry?"

I nod. I'm smiling. "But like you said: I can't control that. Let him get angry. Let him tear his shirt off and turn green for all I care. If I don't open the door then he has nowhere for that anger to go. He'll get bored of the situation. He'll get bored of the anger. He'll get bored of *me.*"

Silence. Fingers tapping. They're mine.

"Fantastic," he says. "Tell me, what is the most important aspect of your world?"

"My mind," I say. No hesitation. The words slip off my tongue. He's asked the question countless times before.

"Exactly. Your mind is a precious commodity. So how should you treat your mind, this precious commodity?"

"Like I treat my house."

"Precisely. You control who enters. You tell any uninvited guests to leave. If they do not listen, then you just ignore them. They will eventually get bored, and *nobody* likes boredom. They will leave. They will no longer even *want* to come to your party. *He* will no longer want to come to your party. If you remember that golden rule, then everything will be absolutely fine."

I nod. Smile.

"Splendid. Absolutely splendid," he says. "I think that is enough for today, don't you? Now. Slowly, and in your own time, please open your eyes again..."

****

I lean forward in my swivel chair and focus my eyes on the young girl sat the other side of the mahogany table. The girl brushes her hand through her long auburn hair and tries - in vain - to focus on somebody - anybody - so long as that somebody is not me. The crimson flush highlights the sprinkling of brown freckles on her cheeks. I briefly scan the rest of the table: five men in designer shirts rolled up at the sleeves; five women in prim, white blouses. Nice round number. All ten are twenty years younger than me, twenty years keener than me. Yet it is me they all turn to, anticipating the next words that come out of my mouth.

"Janine," I say, "the last thing I want to do is to put you under any unnecessary pressure, my love; but shall we cut to the chase? This is your moment in the spotlight. All eyes are on you. Make the most of it..."

A couple of the (braver) guys snigger. One has suddenly developed an irritating tickle in his throat. Pressing her hands against the edge of the table, Janine tentatively rises to her feet. Her chair rolls backwards. Glancing over her shoulder she decides - wisely - not to chase after the chair. Upper lip rising, she displays a row of acceptably straight teeth. The tips of her fingers never leave the edge of the table. Rotating her head, her eyes work the table. Janine reaches me. I deflect her gaze.

We're on the 11th floor of this pristine, modern office building, and the wall to ceiling glass window provides a picturesque view of the Thames. I look around: there are three jugs filled with water in the middle of the table; everybody has written their name in black felt tip on a white placard, even though, as far as I can tell, they all already know each other; green plants, which look like they are watered daily, overflow from impressively expensive vases in all four corners of the room. The air conditioning is working overtime. The Beast from the East is a distant memory. It has been the warmest May in a hundred years, and June doesn't appear to be letting the side down, either.

"We have five teams in five different locations who all, essentially, do the same job," Janine begins. I raise my hand. Clearly, Janine is aware that I have raised my hand but she chooses to ignore it. Everybody else in the boardroom swivels their chairs and chooses not to ignore my raised hand. Janine releases a tired sigh. "Yes?"

"Last thing I want to do is to interrupt you when you are in full flow, Janine," I say, examining my fingernails. "Would you agree that the key word in what you've just said there is 'essentially'?"

"Sorry?"

"No need to be sorry, Janine. I'm not sure you've actually done anything wrong. I just want clarification, that is all. You say that the five locations are essentially doing the same job. 'Essentially' allows considerable flexibility. Are you saying that essentially they all do the same job, but in reality, they do different jobs?"

Janine wrinkles her forehead. "No, I am not saying that. What I am essentially saying - sorry, what I am *saying* - is that they all do the same jobs, only with some inevitable, trivial differences. Does that clarify my use of the word?"

"It does. And thank you for the clarification."

Janine maintains equal eye contact with the rest of the room. "Or at least, the teams *should* be doing the same job. But because the teams do not communicate with each other either regularly or effectively, they do *not* do the same job. Each team puts their own individual spin on procedures and this leads to inconsistency and - ultimately - inconsistency leads to unfairness to our customers."

She has quickly gained confidence, and this confidence has quickly gained momentum. Janine is no longer so aware of the round sweat marks under her arms, or of her glowing, burning cheeks. Her shoulders are no longer hunched. Janine is ready to continue the flow but is unable to do so, because I interrupt her.

"With all due respect, Janine," I say, gazing at the round circles underneath her armpits and then at her glowing, burning cheeks, "but all I am hearing at the moment are problems. The world is full of problems. We are sick of problems. We don't need any more problems, dear. Your negativity is spreading like wildfire in the room. What I am more interested in are the solutions. Do you actually *have* any?"

"Yes," Janine says, bravely holding my eye for just a millisecond. "I was just about to come to that. I was merely setting the scene first. I apologise if I came across as negative. I would like to think that I was being realistic, but there you go. My solution is to migrate the five teams into one team, in one location, with one leader, all doing one, consistent job..."

"Sounds absolutely fantastic," I say, jutting my neck out. There is plenty of room inside my pink shirt to do so. The other, younger and more athletic men in the room all wear ties. I don't. "So that means that four teams will be out of jobs. These employees will lose their livelihoods and, with no money or hope coming into the household, they will presumably end up living on the streets, begging for food with the ducks down by the Thames. As if that wasn't enough, the company will lose their invaluable experience and expertise. And that is only the beginning of our problems: the company will need to recruit their replacements. Recruitment costs money; what other cuts will need to be made to meet this? I'm not sure I share your undoubted enthusiasm for the proposal, Janine..."

One guy around the table, the one with muscled arms and a shirt that has been rolled up higher than any of his compatriots, buries his head in his hands. Janine clears the frog from her throat. Her voice croaks, then rises. But she still manages to talk. "Thank you for your contribution," she says. Her smile could be drawn with a ruler. "*Naturally,* I have already considered all of these objections. I reassure you that none of our valued colleagues will lose their jobs. Other teams are keen to utilise their experience and skills in roles at the same grade. And colleagues in the core location have expressed an interest in joining our team. They will require limited training and will, I am confident, be an asset to our unit..."

Janine's eyes fix on me; they are wide and glaring and

challenging. In fact, all eyes are on me. The rest of the room expect me to throw a grenade back at Janine. They expect it to explode, and to cause maximum disruption.

"Well I don't know about you," I say, glancing around at each and every face, "but I think Janine deserves a round of applause for that delivery..."

The tension disappears with the metaphorical click of a finger and is replaced with laughter. I lead the way, loudly clapping my hands. The others quickly join in. Janine fans her pretty face and then does a curtsey, which, in turn, gets a laugh. She gladly returns to her seat, relieved that the drama is over. I wait for the adrenaline to die down.

"That was fantastic, Janine," I say.

"You really were such a horrible little man," Janine says, laughing. "I wanted to throttle you."

I hold the palms of my hands up in surrender. "I do get carried away sometimes, I confess," I say. "But unfortunately, it is the name of the game with these workshops. The better you do, the more I test you. Take it as a compliment that I was heinous. I am here to play your very worst nightmare. And these people do exist, although - admittedly - usually in more subtle guises. The worst ones are those in sheep's clothing. You've picked up everything I covered on this workshop, though, and that is a credit to you. You were prepared for each of my objections and confrontations and you responded with logical and reasoned arguments. I'm sorry that I was hard on you," I say, and this is met by knowing laughter, "but for you I upped the tempo somewhat. I'm just glad that you didn't bite and tell me where to go, because that would have ruined the effect somewhat."

I've been running these workshops for about five years now. I mainly deliver them to large corporations across the city with deep pockets and plenty of learning and development boxes to tick to keep the regulators off their backs. The topics range from Leading and Communicating to Building Resilience and they vary in length from two hours to five days. This session started just mid-morning, just after my appointment. Sometimes I even need to pack my suitcase and travel to cities as far afield as Birmingham, Manchester and Leeds. I'm self-employed, and I can choose whether or not to accept a job. I don't need the money and I don't need the work. I'm aware that this is an enviable position to be in. I don't even view it as a real job. All of this suits me fine. It is a deliberate arrangement. I see it as a hobby. I only do it to keep my mind sharp and to maintain regular contact with other human beings. I actually quite enjoy it. Sure, I could get bored and walk out halfway through a session and, realistically, my life wouldn't change much.

I wrap up the session and exchange standard farewells. The room clears. It is Friday afternoon and everybody is keen to escape the cesspit and jump head first into the weekend. I am left in the conference room with just my papers to tidy up. I am not in any hurry. I don't have any workshops booked next week. Nearly every day is the weekend to me.

I shut the door and wave to a few faces I saw on my way into the building, just before lunch. This is not my office. I don't have an office. I go wherever I am booked. I push open the doors and stand in the corridor, staring at the carpet. I am alone. My mind drifts. Do any of my school friends now work at the steel plant in Port Talbot, the heartbeat of the town? Will the steel works will be affected by the import tariff Trump has imposed? I don't know, because I'm not in contact with any of them. My mind drifts to the counselling appointment I had this morning: Richard was on fine form. My days are not usually this busy, but then they do say you wait ages for a bus and then two turn up at the same time.

The doors to one of the lifts are closing. Picking up my pace, I begin walking briskly. Hopefully whoever occupies the lift will notice me and hold the doors open. There will always be another, though, just like the bus. The doors continue edging closer together. There is a voice from inside the lift. I hear it just before the doors meet in the middle.

Have a nice weekend, Jeffrey Allen. See you in 30 days.

My legs buckle. Bile fills my throat. My fist slams against the button to the lift. I look up. The lift is going down. Tenth floor. Ninth floor. Eighth floor. It stops. Somebody is getting in.

I thrust open the door to the stairwell. I clamber down the wide marble stairs, three steps at a time. Pushing through the middle of a couple of guys in suits idling down the stairs, talking on their mobiles, I leave a trail of swear words and obscenities. The floor numbers reduce, one by one, until finally I'm on the ground floor, sprinting past reception and out of the rotating main entrance.

I look left, right and forward. I spot somebody in a long cream raincoat pull a hood over his head and then quickly disappear inside the narrow entrance to the tube station. That is my target. The heat and pollution of the underground makes my skin tight and clammy. I don't care. There he is - navigating past innocent commuters on the escalators. I push people out of the way, uttering meaningless apologies as I do so.

I'm at the bottom of the escalators, running left and then right, not sure which direction he went in. There he is - on one of the trains - his face covered by the hood. I've never ran so fast but - just as I get within touching distance of the train - the doors shut. He is just inches away from me, on the other side of the glass, his face hidden away by the hood. I slam the palm of my hand against the button, but the doors remain shut.

The train moves away. The man in the cream overcoat raises his hand. Waves at me.

The light on the underground feels amazingly - *painfully* - bright. I sit on a bench to gather my bearings, maybe to stop myself from toppling over. I push my face in my hands and close my eyes. My breathing starts to slow.

I have no idea what just happened.

All I know is that it has been nearly thirty years since anybody called me Jeffrey Allen.

DAY TWO
2ND JUNE 2018

This, I muse, is like wrestling a crocodile.

The early morning sun filters through a tiny crack in the curtain, dusting the cabin gold. The air is so dry it feels like the moisture is being sucked from my body, leaving it weak and limp. I pull the duvet up over my chest, protecting me; then I push it away and lie on my back, naked and exposed. Staying in bed is only going to make my active mind more rampant. Accepting my fate, I unroll my sleep crumpled body and place a reluctant foot down onto the hard, unwelcoming wooden floor.

I know it only takes twenty-five (huge) steps to walk from one end of my long (not so long) boat to the other end, because I counted it. This morning, though, I don't reach more than five steps before I stub my big toe on the kitchen skirting board; I then hop the other twenty steps cursing under my breath. I put on my pink, fluffy dressing gown and glance down at my legs, exposed from the knees. It should have been put in the trash years ago, but then a sane man would never have purchased it in the first place. I pick up a packet from the working top and slip it inside the chest pocket. Pull the belt tight. Nobody deserves to see one of my balls unexpectedly popping out, even if - personally - I'd find it hilarious. Glass in one hand, a bottle in the other and a box of matches balancing between my teeth, I open the (only) door of my boat, my home.

Sure, to the bystander it isn't much, but this life is my choice. Besides, who gives a damn what a bystander thinks? I had much, much more - once - but I gave it up. The boat suits me just fine.

Stretching my legs onto the uneven, grassy bank, I inhale the familiar odour of the canal. Pull out my deckchair. Clasp my hands behind the nape of my neck. Close my eyes. Breathe in slowly through the nose. Pause. Exhale out through the mouth. Normally this routine is sheer bliss, one of the simple pleasures in my life. The rhythm is off this morning, though. Unwanted thoughts bang on the door, demanding to be let in. Telling them to fuck off just doesn't do the trick. Not this morning.

Opening the bottle and pouring myself a sherry, I stir the glass and observe the drink before taking a sip. What is the time? Who knows? Who cares? The cool breeze that slips beneath the opening to my dressing gown suggests that it is still early morning. When was the last time I had a drink? Days? Weeks? I try not to count. I don't tend to follow a routine. I don't, for example, open a bottle on a Friday and Saturday night just because it is deemed socially acceptable to do so. Who makes these rules, anyway? Are the rule makers regulated? As far as I'm concerned, they can all go and do one.

I light my cigar and extend my legs. This is another simple pleasure. This one seems so much easier this morning.

A couple with a young boy and a dog walk along the bank and past my boat. This is all unhealthily healthy. Shouldn't the boy be stagnating in his room, trying to beat his top score on Minecraft? They're set for a trek, with rucksacks and bulky walking boots that pick up the mud. The dad's red shorts and yellow raincoat is surely preparing for all eventualities. *Fail to prepare, prepare to fail.* Fuck off. I take a long swig of sherry as my mind flicks back to the cream raincoat from yesterday afternoon. Was it really just yesterday? It was a long night. Yesterday was the first day of June. Odd. May had been glorious, bar the odd thunderstorm here and there; but then, what is more delightful than the occasional sprinkling in spring? Yesterday was a bright, hot day. The clear clouds gave no indication of rain. Irritated commuters on the tube wiped sweat from their foreheads with their bare arms. The cream raincoat stood out.

Every member of this walking party, not excluding the dog, jerk their heads backwards as they pass me. The boy's mouth drops, able to catch a fly. Dad checks his watch. I hold my hand up and wish them good day. The jolly family jerk their heads back to the front in perfect synchronisation. Mum clips the back of the boy's head (presumably) for gawping. I smile and take another sip of my sherry. There aren't many sips left till I reach the bottom of the glass.

I pull my mobile phone out of the chest (and only) pocket. No messages. No surprise. I tap away with my index finger.

Miss you, Princess x

Although I try to avoid technology wherever I can, and I seriously fear robots will bring down the world, perversely it still fascinates me. I just try not to tell anybody that it does. The idea that I can send a message on my phone that instantly pops up on somebody else's phone (miles away) is just mind-boggling. And that is just texting! It feels like only seconds before my phone starts vibrating. How are other people so quick? Do they use more than one finger? How do they manage that?

Aww watch you. I miss you too Dad x

I tap away, trying to impress my little girl with my speed. I am caught out by the predictive text, and so I delete what I've written and start again. She isn't going to be impressed at all. I consider writing a long message but think better of it.

Give my love to your mum x

Another vibration.

Will do. But you can speak to her yourself the next time I see you!
x

I consider sending her another message, but think better of it; I'm sure Emma doesn't want to spend her Saturday morning texting her dad, does she?

I think back to when I met her mum, the mother of my only child: I was nineteen in December 1989 and I'd been working in the city for just over a year. When I say I had been working in the city, what I really mean is that I had a junior administrator job that was *located* in the city. Friday evening. Pay day. Naturally I felt like the richest kid on the planet, even though I was paid just above what my employer was allowed to pay me without getting into trouble (remember, there was no minimum wage then). And yet, despite my sudden wealth, I was still the invisible man at the bar as I waved my crisp ten-pound note in the air with one hand and hid my identification in my pocket with the other. I'd been shaving for at least six months but, with no confirmed sightings of hair, it had merely brought a flush to my cheeks. I looked up and caught the eye of a pretty young lady with ash blonde hair next to me.

"Oh hello," she said, smiling.

My shaven cheeks probably turned two shades redder. And then I spoke my first word to my future wife, and mother of my child, Jenny. It was a very simple, unoriginal word. "Hello," I said.

A lady brushed my shoulder, her back appeared in my peripheral vision and then she embraced the girl I'd just said hello to. Damn. So she wasn't speaking to me after all. I waved my ten-pound note even more elaborately as the two women exchanged pleasantries. The intruder left. I hoped that the girl hadn't noticed me speaking to her. And yet I could still sense her eyes on me. I dared to glance up. I noticed that she was smiling. I glanced over my shoulder. Once is unlucky, twice is careless.

"You're a charming young man, aren't you?" Jenny said. "Saying hello to random people at the bar, completely unprompted?"

I smiled. It wasn't forced. I found it funny because she only looked a year or so older than me. She had the perfect opportunity to make me feel small, but she chose to do the opposite. Suddenly, I was standing head and shoulders above the other people at the bar still waiting to be served. I was instantly and unusually comfortable speaking to her. Still, she ignored me for a few moments as she ordered her drink (even though I was sure I was at the bar before her). "Less of the young, please," I said. "I'm old enough to drive, although I can't. I'm old enough to drink, although I can't do that very well. I'm old enough to do plenty of other things that, surprisingly, I *am* very good at..."

Jenny raised her eyebrows and laughed. My last statement could very well have been true: I was still a virgin and so, for all I knew, I could turn out to be the greatest lover in the world. I longed to pull the photograph out of my wallet, just give it a quick glance, make me feel stronger, but I couldn't. I knew I had to do this on my own.

"Well, it sure is a shame you can't drive," Jenny said. "I was looking for somebody to chauffeur me around, to be Clyde to my Bonnie."

"I'm not sure Clyde was best known for his driving skills," I said. "Do you come here often?"

"Is that a chat up line?"

"Depends..."

"On?"

"How well you respond to it."

Jenny glanced over my shoulder, smiling. I yanked my head and was met by a group of girls waving in our direction. Jenny fumbled in her handbag. She pulled out a pen and a strip of white paper. She used the bar to write on the paper. "Listen," Jenny said, "I've got to go back to my mates. But you seem nice, and harmless enough. Not openly weird. If you fancy meeting up for a drink sometime, give me a call."

I was numb as I returned back to my boisterous group on the other side of the pub. They were young guys in suits, mainly traders on the floor who all earned a multitude of my salary. Traditionally, I faded into the background.

"Where you been?" one of them asked, arm stretched over the back of the chair.

"The bar," I replied.

"Where's your drink?"

I looked down at my empty hands. "Oh for..."

I was interrupted by a chorus of raucous laughter. This was the first time I'd been the centre of attention. It was a good night.

Now, nearly thirty years later, I return to the boat smiling. The dry, claustrophobic cabin is of startling contrast to the fresh air outside. I crack eggs on the frying pan and lay bacon under the grill. Cooking is usually therapeutic. Any distraction that is even remotely interesting usually is. The thoughts invade my mind, though. I want to swat them, like an annoying fly - just like the one Richard talked about - hovering with intent around the fried food; I know this merely makes the thoughts stronger. I need to ignore them. It is painfully difficult, however, to avoid the metaphorical elephant in the room.

Who was it who called me Jeffrey Allen? And why, thirty years to the day since the first killing?

Fortunately - thank *God* - there *is* a close and welcome distraction. I don't even need to go looking for it. There is a gentle rustling of sheets on the bed. I observe movement underneath the duvet, like a mole furrowing beneath a lawn. A long sigh. And then a yawn. Smiling, I pour two cups of coffee and perch on the edge of the bed.

A hand appears from under the duvet and grazes along my thigh. The hand didn't need to wander, to search for me; it instinctively knew where I was, where to find my naked leg. Erica knows my body like it is her own. I imagine Erica under the duvet. She sleeps on her front. She sleeps naked. Her face will be buried deep in the pillow, her black hair nestling on the nape of her back, just above her pert buttocks, curved like a ski slope.

Her naked body remains motionless. Her hand, though, continues stroking my thigh. Continues rising. She takes me in her hand. I stiffen.

Momentarily, at least for the next five minutes or so, the overwhelming compulsion to find out more about what happened yesterday afternoon vanishes, just like *I* did, thirty years ago.

DAY THREE
3RD JUNE 1988

Yvette nurses her cup of tea in her dressing gown and slippers at the round, oak kitchen table, early morning daylight just beginning to fill the room. Glancing at the clock, she momentarily wonders whether young John King had slept in again, bless him; she wasn't sure that an early morning paper round suited the young boy in the village who carried a sleepy demeanour with him wherever he went. Still, it was Friday morning and so he could have a lie in tomorrow, couldn't he? The thought passes; the rustle at the front door and the thud indicates the paper has safely dropped on the mat.

The morning paper is delivered at about seven and then the South Wales Echo is pushed through the letterbox at about four in the afternoon. Yvette was more than happy to walk up to the shop in the afternoon, stretch her legs, but the last thing she wanted was to deprive the paperboy of some extra pocket money, put the kid out of a job. On the other hand, the Echo was a bulky paper, and maybe David Williams would welcome a little less weight on his shoulders, one less paper to worry about? Maybe she would discuss it with Joyce in the shop next time she popped in.

Yvette unfolds the paper and then flattens it down on the table, removing the crease in the middle. This is her time of the day. She sits back in her chair and puts her slippers up on her husband's chair. Her eyes scan the front page. Her hand droops. Body goes cold. She is only awoken from her trance by the warm tea that trickles down her arm.

She wipes away the drink with her hand, then tugs at her hair, head bowed over the paper like she is praying.

"Morning, love."

Yvette springs up like she has seen a ghost. Where did he come from? Normally she hears her husband's footsteps as he comes down the stairs in the morning. Now he stands in their kitchen, crisp sky-blue shirt tucked into his slacks and tie straining his collar. He leans down and kisses her on the temple. She squeezes his hand. Yvette pushes the newspaper across the table. She wants to throw it in the bin. She has only read the front page.

"There has been a murder. A couple have been stabbed to death in their own home."

"In their home? How did he get in? Did he break in?" Gordon asks.

"From what I can make out, the newspaper is saying the couple likely invited the killer into their home to partake in -

you know - well, to have sex..."

"Oh. I see. *That* type of couple. Where did it happen?"

"Cardiff. Ely."

"Jesus," Gordon says. Yvette knew what he was thinking. This was the morning paper. The afternoon paper was supposed to provide the local news. This was *big* news. "It's one thing when these things happen on the other side of the world, another when they happen on your doorstep. When did it happen?"

"The early hours of Wednesday morning. First of the month. What a way to start June," Yvette says.

Gordon thumbs the words on the page. His silver eyebrows become one, the lines on his forehead form an upside down triangle.

"I know they weren't youngsters, that they were in their forties, but I still can't help but think," Yvette says. "Everybody has a story to tell, Gordon. Somebody has still probably lost a daughter and a son. What was the need? There *was* none. No need at all..."

Gordon rubs her shoulders with his long fingers. He knows exactly what she is thinking, too. They'd been a couple since school and he knows her thoughts before she even thinks them. He follows her eyes, fixed on the photograph on the windowsill. Two boys. One is ten and the other is eight. The older boy has his arm around his younger brother. Yvette dabs her eye with her finger. The best of friends. Went everywhere together. And Luke was so protective of his younger brother, always fighting his corner. Luke would have been twenty now had it not been for the leukaemia; had that wicked, wicked disease not taken him away. Not a day goes past without Yvette wondering what he would be like now. What would he look like? Would he have a girlfriend? A job? She knew, though - just knew - that the two boys would still be the best of friends.

His little brother had grown up, of course. Had only one year left before he headed off to university. They needed to talk to him about that. They needed to make sure that was what he really wanted to do. She didn't really mind what he did with his life so long as he was happy: she hated the thought that he could possibly be unhappy.

Yvette can't bear the silence in the room, the thoughts that fill both their minds."It gets worse," Yvette says, filling the void. "South Wales Police have put this detective on the case, DCI Baldwin. He thinks that this is likely to be only the beginning of the killings."

She watches her husband's reflection in the kitchen window, his face strained, searching for the right words. "He can't possibly know that, dear. They don't even know the motive. Maybe it was a personal vendetta? People don't kill for no reason. Besides, I'm sure the police will catch him before he can do any more damage."

Yvette looks up at Gordon and manages to smile.
"Anyway," she says, "any sign of that son of ours?"

Gordon shakes his head. "Not yet."

"That boy is getting up later and later. We can't let things
slip now. He spends too much time in that room of his. It
isn't healthy. We need to have a word with him."

"I'll speak to him, Yvette."

She squeezes his hand. She wants to see her little boy
more than ever this morning, just to know he is safe. She
worries when he is asleep, worries that he will never wake
up. Her husband leaves the room, stands at the bottom of
the stairs, gently shouts to Jeffrey that it is time to get up.

DAY FOUR
4TH JUNE 2018

The poster on the wall is split equally in two, cut in a straight line down the middle. The one side is blue and gives a list of incidents when you should call 101. The other side is red and gives a list of incidents when you should call 999. Both lists are extensive. I can't help but think that, by the time I'd decided which number to call, the burglar has probably already escaped with the jewels. I glance around the walls and hope to find mug shots of wanted villains. No such luck. There is not much else to do and the urge to look at the walls is instinctive. It is just like at the doctors. I go in because I have a cold, but by the time I actually see the doctor I'm convinced I must be dying of at least one disease. I glance at the vacant seats. Somebody has left a newspaper. Apparently Jeremy Thorpe's hit man isn't dead after all. Who would have guessed?

I stretch out my hand to pick up the paper, but I'm interrupted by another hand, dangling in my face, "DCI Reeves. It is a pleasure to meet you, Mr Clancy."

"Marcus," I say, rising to my feet. "Please call me Marcus."

His handshake is firm, but it feels natural, not like some of the Alpha males I meet in my workshops who try to crush the bones. The shoulders stretch his shirt and fill the doorway to his office, and yet his waist could belong to a ballerina. The effect is a V-shape that could grace the cover of *Men's Health*. I notice, with a hint of envy, that his jet-black hair, which is full and cropped short, has no hint of grey. I estimate him to be in his mid-thirties, but then it is likely the guy has a moisturising routine that would put Posh Spice to shame. "Thank you for seeing me at short notice."

The interview room is square and bland. Just a table separates us. It brings back memories; only last time, this was so much more bland, much more dire. DCI Reeves dabs at an imaginary stain with the tips of his two middle fingers. He sits with a straight back and his solid arms by his sides. Reeves looks like the type to take his online DSE training *very* seriously. "This deranged man goes on a killing spree in the month of June, beginning on the first day of the month. You were supposed to be the seventh victim, on the final day of the month. And yet you are the one that got away. The *only* one. It isn't every day we have a celebrity knocking on our door. So I was honoured to see you at short notice, Marcus."

This is a joke, of sorts, but it puts me out of sync. There is some logic in the madness of his statement, but really I am the literal opposite of a celebrity. I am a complete enigma.

"Before we get the ball rolling here, I just want to apologise on behalf of the force for the way you were treated all those years ago. We do not see the likes of DCI Baldwin any more. Our recruitment and training programme has seen to that. Thankfully, the force has progressed..."

DCI Baldwin. I divert my eyes. I dig my sharp nails into the palm of my hands. It has been a long time since I heard that name. DCI Baldwin is part of my past life, the life I escaped from.

"Is DCI Baldwin still alive?"

"Just about. Apparently, he is a reformed man, too. He lives a quiet, civilised life with his wife. Hard to imagine, isn't it? Of course, he is a man of advanced years now."

"I am glad DCI Baldwin is well," I say, looking away.

"I know that you didn't come here to just have a chat, Marcus," DCI Reeves says. "The short notice is quite ironic, isn't it? How long has it been since you were attacked, now?"

"Thirty years," I reply. "The 30th June 1988, to be exact."

I want to be exact, because the date feels relevant.

Reeves flicks through a slim paper file. I presume that he has printed off some basics from the system: I'm sure there must be an office brimming with files on the case somewhere, unless it has been transferred onto a computer. This is a digital age we live in. "Thirty years, and we haven't heard a word from you. *Nobody* has heard a word from you. We've heard more from Lord Lucan than we have from you. You're a ghost. This was quite advanced witness protection for the time-"

"It wasn't witness protection. I decided to change my identity, to move away. It wasn't really because of protection."

His eyes widen. "Of course," he says, "back in those days witness protection was the responsibility of the local police force. Things would have been much more official and stringent these days. I don't know the exact details, but it makes sense you changed your identity and moved away, regardless of why you did it. After all, you were the only witness, the only one who could give a description. I understand you've been a considerable success in the city? Quite astonishing, really..."

"It depends on your definition of success," I say. "Of course, I never made it to university. My life was all set up for that life - it was in the script - but then, of course, *it* happened. But I don't think it mattered really, not as much as it would now, anyway. There were more opportunities for lads like me in those days-"

"Lads like you? There weren't many like you out there..."

"The world was less censored. So long as you were willing to work hard then there were plenty of companies willing to give you a chance. These days you need a diploma before you're allowed to cut hair. I got in with a firm as a junior, passed the exams I needed to and, before I knew it, I was a trader. I didn't have a clue what I was doing but - luckily - neither did half the other people out there, but we sort of worked it out as we went along. I made it to partner, which I thought was hilarious. They trusted me to be a partner! But I lived that life for long enough. I deliver workshops now. It suits me much better."

Reeves raises a single eyebrow and then smiles from the corner of his mouth. "And you got married? You have a daughter? This was more surprising, considering the circumstances of how you were found..."

This is a dig. I don't mind that and, to be honest, I quite enjoy the challenge. Ducking and diving is all part of the fun and it is one of the reasons I enjoy my hobby; sorry, this is one of the reasons I enjoy my job. Having a go at Jenny is fair enough; she brought some of it on herself. There is no need to bring my little girl into this, though. Emma is the one innocent in this whole saga. Two can play at that game, I think. I wasn't necessarily intending to be difficult, but sometimes it is just much more fun that way.

I casually slide a cigar from the chest pocket of my polo shirt. "Do you mind if I smoke?"

Reeve's eyes widen. He leans forward, close enough for

me to smell his minty breath. "Smoking is illegal in public buildings, Mr Clancy," he states. "This is a *police* building. So, not surprisingly - yes - I *do* mind if you smoke."

"What are you going to do?" I ask. "Arrest me?"

He smirks. "I see what you're doing here," he says, playfully wagging a finger at me. "You're keeping me on my toes. So long as you don't start crossing and uncrossing your legs then we aren't really going to have a problem here. We'll keep this between ourselves, shall we?"

You rebel, I think. I protest my innocence with a smile. I put my cigar safely away in my pocket. I don't even fancy a smoke, not in the confined, stuffy surroundings of an interview room."What is life if you can't have a little fun, Inspector? But to answer your question: I'm divorced now. It's been five years. Everything surrounding the split and the divorce wasn't much fun, particularly - as you quite rightly pointed out - there was a child involved. It is fair to say that I've had more than one monumental transformation in my life. Everything changed - yet again - with that divorce."

"Quite." Reeves nods his head but then he quickly glances at his watch. "So why exactly are you here, Marcus?"

That, right there, is the correct question. "Friday afternoon I was delivering a workshop in an office in Monument, so smack bang in the middle of the city. This building has eighteen floors. My workshop was held in a board room on the eleventh floor. I've only ever been to this building a few times before, and I've never held a workshop in this particular room. In essence, I don't have a fixed place of work, DCI Reeves, and I haven't for five years now, but even if I did then this monstrosity of a building would not be it. There was no reason why anybody, apart from those connected to the workshop, would expect to find me there. And yet, just before five in the evening, after the session has finished, and as I'm waiting for a lift, somebody in the lift said to me, 'have a nice weekend, Jeffrey Allen...'"

DCI Reeves thinks about this for a moment. I can tell that he is thinking about it because he makes a big show of thinking about it: he puts his granite chin in his hand and then he rubs it with his thumb. It is as if he is doing an impression of Socrates, although I'm pretty sure the only Socrates this goon is aware of is the Brazilian footballer. "At least he was polite with it," DCI Reeves finally says, smiling. He looks at me for a reaction and, when I deliberately don't give one, he says, "Asking you to have a good weekend, you know?"

Kind of ruins it when you need to explain it, I think. I'm tempted to tell him that he is a proper comedian, that Frankie Boyle had better watch out, but I resist. It just wouldn't be constructive. "Do you know how long it has been since anybody has called me that?"

DCI Reeves apparently *does* know how long it has been since anybody called me that. "I'm imagining," he says, "that from the way the question is worded, you haven't been called Jeffrey Allen since you changed your identity and started calling yourself Marcus Clancy. So I'm fully aware that it must have been a shock. I sympathise with you. Did you get a view of the person in the lift?"

I'm encouraged. Slightly. Maybe he *is* taking me seriously? The question, though, isn't one I can properly answer. "Unfortunately, no. The lift doors were closing just as the person uttered the words. But I'm sure that was the plan. There was no coincidence here. He wanted to scare me. He didn't plan to engage in conversation with me-"

"Quite," DCI Reeves interrupts, with a knowing chuckle.

"I followed him out of the building and onto the tube, but he was wearing a cream raincoat that deliberately covered his face, and so I did not really see him."

"How did you know that the guy in the raincoat was your man?"

"It was the 1st June, and it wasn't raining. It was a hot day. The city of London wasn't exactly overloaded with people in raincoats. More significantly, I'm sure I saw an outline of his coat in the lift, just before the doors closed. I've been thinking about this over the last day or so, and I've concluded that he wore the coat because he wanted me to pick him out. He wanted to be seen. He wanted me to chase after him."

"The 1st of June?" I can see that Reeves is counting down the days in his head. It shouldn't be this difficult: it was only three days ago. The penny finally drops.

"Yes," I say. "The date of the first murder."

He smiles at this. "John and Valerie," he says, shaking his head. "Two of life's unfortunates." His mind drifts. He reins it back in. "As I said, I appreciate that this must have been a shock for you, especially after all of these years. And completely out of the blue. But the fact that you are sat here now indicates to me that you are more than shocked. What is it exactly that you are worried about?"

"He is a serial killer," I reply. "He has already tried to kill me once. What the *fuck* do you think I am worried about?"

Reeves apparently thinks I am joking, for he breaks into a belly laugh. The guy doesn't understand my sense of humour, or lack of. He has a prominent Adam's Apple. Momentarily I think about strangling him.

"So you think it was *him* then? You're in London now. He only killed in Wales. We haven't heard a thing from him in thirty years. Why should it be him?"

What? Is he looking for a rise? I count to three before replying. I am quietly confident, from his general demeanour, that he wouldn't respond well to being told to go fuck himself. I need to be more calculated than that. I decide to play him for the fool. "You don't think he could have a fucking Oyster card? You know how dumb that sounds?" I smile. His feathers are ruffled. "Listen, I have a fake identity. Nobody knows who I am. That is the whole purpose of the fake identity."

Reeves raises an eyebrow and holds my gaze for a moment, like he is sizing me up. "Oh come on, Marcus; you are an intelligent man, and I'm sure you can't be that naive. The news of your attack caused an international news frenzy. At the time, people were scared to leave their homes. The country hadn't seen anything like this since the Yorkshire Ripper. Only, Peter Sutcliffe targeted prostitutes. This guy wasn't so particular about who he targeted, was he? There are hundreds of books on the subject, not to mention that phenomenon that is social media. You can't possibly imagine that, just because you changed your name, lost some poundage and grew a beard, somebody couldn't work out who you *really* are if they wanted to? You're smarter than that; I'm sure of it. There are obsessive people out there. There are trolls. It could be the person who sits next to you on the train or the person who lives next to you. It could literally be *anybody*."

That was reassuring then, wasn't it? Maybe this guy had missed a training course or two? I was concerned when I entered his room, but I am petrified now.

"Is there anybody you have pissed off? Anybody you can think of who might want to rattle your cage?" he asks.

I think about this. I've met plenty of potential oddballs over the years, but I can't remember any I majorly pissed off. That person would need to care enough to actually find out who I was. They would need to have a reason to suspect I was once Jeffrey Allen. I tried to stay away from social media as much as I could, but sometimes our paths inevitably passed. Even I knew that it offered an endless avenue for crackpots. If this person wasn't him then it was most likely to be some obsessive from the internet with a penchant for serial killers.

I tell Reeves that there is nobody.

"Has there been any contact from this person since Friday, since 1st June? Anything that doesn't quite seem right?"

I shake my head.

He softens his tone. He probably has a form to fill in about my visit; I assume he relishes admin. He needs to tick all the boxes. Reeves pulls a card from his pocket and hands it to me. Clearly, he isn't going to get a result from me. It is best to get me out of the door as quickly as he can so he can concentrate on hitting his targets.

"Is the murder enquiry even open?" I ask.

"This was a very serious murder enquiry, involving a serial killer," Reeves says. "This wasn't just a domestic incident that went tragically wrong. I assure you that the enquiry will most likely always be open. We actively follow up any leads that we find."

"So South Wales Police are still busy on the case then?"

"As far as I'm aware, there haven't been any real leads for a long time. So I don't think they are actively doing *anything* on the case. But as I said, they will if they are given a lead."

"Hmmm."

"Listen, I do appreciate you coming here, and it was the right thing to do. At the moment, though, we have nothing to go on. This person hasn't committed any crime. He didn't threaten you and he didn't harm you. It was probably absolutely nothing, just some sad case who got a kick out of scaring you. You'll probably hear nothing again and it will all blow over. If you do hear anything - anything at all - then you promise to call me, you hear? I do hope I never speak to you again, though," he says, grinning. "And I mean that in the nicest possible way, of course."

Fuck you. He probably uses the line with every poor soul he wants to see the back of. I nod my head and join in with the joviality, thanking him for his time, for seeing me at short notice. I stop as I reach the door, though. I think I can hear him sigh. I know what he's thinking. *Oh, for fucks sake.*

He thought he'd got rid of me. I have one final question. It has been playing on my mind, vying for attention with all the other unwanted thoughts.

"So why don't you think it is him, then? After all, he was never caught. Why can't he still be out there? Why can't it be him?"

DCI Reeves takes his time before answering. He proudly pumps out his (substantial) chest. I half expect a button to pop off. "As a detective, you get a hunch for these things. Call it intuition. Rest assured, Marcus, I'm quite certain we will never see the likes of *him* again..."

DAY FIVE
5TH JUNE 2018

Normally I take in the world around me as I go out and about on my travels to destinations unknown. Follow my nose. Deliberately slow things down, you know. Make a conscious effort, just as I'm told to by Richard. I spent so many years in the fast lane, imperiously busy and yet utterly oblivious to everything that was going on outside my tiny bubble that I sometimes felt the outside world just passed me by. Now, though, I'm living in my mind, which is completely against doctor's orders. I took a stroll, just to get away from the boat, but as I head back, I'm aware that I've taken nothing in.

I know that what DCI Reeves said makes sense. Of course, he wouldn't want to get his hands dirty unless he absolutely had to. The police force has been cut to shreds: they don't have enough numbers to deal with real crimes, let alone imaginary ones. I had the same thoughts before I even set foot in the interview room; I just tried to ignore them. It could have been absolutely *anyone* in that lift. In this technological age it is possible to be a ghost. Maybe it was one of the delegates from the workshop? Perhaps the person has been following my every move and footstep for years? I should be counting my blessings that a serial killer might not be hunting me down after all - but *really* - what sort of consolation is that?

Reeves was in a hurry to make it clear that he, and the rest of the force, had nothing to do with the way I was treated thirty years ago. I had to smirk at that. Talk about not wanting to be tarnished by association.

I can still smell the hospital, like the scent has never fully washed away, like it will always be part of me. They placed me in a single room, away from the media attention and the prying eyes. I drifted in and out of consciousness for days. My dreams were bleak, and they were torrid, and I'm certain my desperation to escape them helped me to wake up. I first realised I was awake - and alive - by the foul, acidic taste in my mouth, like I'd been sucking on a battery. The sensation was so vivid that I knew it just had to be reality.

People were around me, moving quickly, acting with purpose. My hands tugged at the bed sheets, then gripped the metal bars that surrounded the bed. A refreshing breeze flowed through the open window. Traffic passed on the streets below, somewhere in the distance; occasionally a horn beeped. I spotted a fruit bowl and a plastic jug of water on a square table at the foot of the bed. Somebody tenderly brushed their hand through my hair. Was it her? I pushed the thought out of my mind: it couldn't be her. My neck creaked as I looked up. No, it wasn't her. It was the one person I wanted to be sat at my bedside more than any other.

"You've had a bit of a bad time, my dear," Mum said, squeezing my limp hand. "You're going to be just fine, though, there is no doubt about that. No doubt whatsoever."

"I'm sorry, Mum," I said, aware my cheeks were puffy, my face was wet.

"What on earth have you to be sorry about?"

I looked away, didn't answer.

Mum was by my side when I fell asleep, and she was still there when I woke up. Mainly our conversations comprised of checking I was comfortable, that I wasn't hungry or thirsty. I was comforted by the repetition, by the predictability. She never, ever asked what happened, why she was visiting her only remaining son in hospital.

Most of my stay was a blur. The blue, green and white of the uniforms merged into one. Voices began to sound the same. I clearly remember seeing him through the square window of the door, though. His body was not visible, but I could tell just by his immediate presence that he was a large portly man, shaped like a barrel. His black hair was plastered down to his scalp, and his bloated lips could barely conceal his wet tongue. His movements were sharp and erratic. I knew who he was from the newspaper articles I'd devoured, from his occasional, awkward television interview. I knew why he was here: he wanted to get to me, and he would push down the door if he needed to.

Three things cannot be hidden: the sun, the moon and the truth.

He entered the hospital room holding his badge by his chest. His crumpled, outsized grey suit belonged in the attic. As he moved closer I noticed that his nose was heavily pockmarked and red, like somebody had repeatedly stabbed it with a dart; his eyes were outlined with laughter lines that had long lost their sense of humour. The officer he was with bowed his head. I clenched the crisp, white bed sheets, felt an imaginary fist pummelling down against my chest.

"Good afternoon, Jeffrey. My name is DCI Baldwin," he said. He turned to my mother and smiled. "I'm sorry to learn of your injuries, but I'm pleased to hear you've been making a fantastic recovery. I don't plan to take up much of your time today, because I appreciate you are still recuperating. We're as keen to catch this animal as you are, though, and as you can imagine, the first couple of days and weeks after the incident are crucially important. Are you please able to give some basic information for me today, Jeffrey, to help us catch this killer?"

I nodded my head. His voice was so much softer than I

expected, his manner infinitely more gentile and polite. There was something else: he smelt fantastic, like he was straight out of the shower and had smothered himself in Brut. I was startled, because it was just unexpected. I wasn't sure if all of this was just more unnerving than if he'd barged into the room shouting and snarling and reeking like a dead dog.

"My colleague here will need to take some photographs of your injuries if that is okay with you?"

I caught the eye of the young guy; he smiled apologetically. There was silence for a few moments as I unbuttoned my pyjamas and he took photographs. He thanked me for my time. DCI Baldwin sat down on the edge of my bed. "Would you be able to describe the attacker?"

"I'd say he was maybe a year or so older than me, so nineteen or twenty or something, like. He was maybe a few inches taller than me, so probably just over six foot. The guy was kind of slim but - I don't know - he was sort of strong looking, you know? He was wearing faded blue jeans and a white tee-shirt."

"Any distinguishing features? Birth marks? Moles?"

I shook my head. Then I remembered something. *Was* it something? "His eyes. He had these distinctive eyes. I'm not really sure why they were so distinctive, but I really noticed them. They were grey, I know that..."

"Grey?"

"Yes."

"Right."

The other guy was writing it all down on a pad. He probably didn't notice me looking at him, for he pulled an array of faces as he scribbled away.

"Did he give you a name?" DCI Baldwin asked.

"He said he was called Sam."

"Do you think it was his real name?"

"Who knows?"

"Can you tell me what happened?"

I closed my eyes. I gripped the sheets tighter, but this was only to stop my trembling. My mum spoke for me. "Only do this now if you feel you can, son."

I took a deep breath and told DCI Baldwin everything. The words fired out of my mouth. My body was covered in a layer of cold sweat by the time I'd finished, but somehow I felt cleansed, and so much lighter.

DCI Baldwin had moved closer. I felt his knee pressing against my leg. He didn't speak for a few seconds; he just widened his blue, watery eyes. "So, you went down the back of the library to urinate?"

My cheeks burned. I didn't want to repeat that part because I knew my mum would not approve. "Yes," I replied. "I wanted to make sure it was away from the high street, completely out of view. I wouldn't have done it at all if I wasn't desperate."

DCI Baldwin held up his hands and smiled. I couldn't help but notice just how big his hands were. "Don't worry, Jeffrey," he said, dimple in one cheek. "We're not going to arrest you for urinating in a public place. We have bigger fish to fry. So you turned around and he attacked you with the cut-throat razor?"

"Yes."

"That's strange," he said, thumbing his chin, coated with black stubble.

"It is?"

"You're sure you went to the back of the library?"

I nodded my head. I knew it was a loaded question, though.

"It's just you were found at the front of the library, Jeffrey," DCI Baldwin said. "At the front font of the narrow walkway next to the entrance with the concrete steps."

I glanced at my mum. Her smile was reassuring, completely non judgmental.

"You know what I think?" DCI Baldwin asked.

I shook my head. I really didn't want to know what he thought. Not now. Not anymore.

"I think he dragged or carried you to the side entrance."

"You do?" I asked, sensing my stomach deflate.

"Yes. And you know why he did this, Jeffrey?"

I took another deep breath. "No."

DCI Baldwin pushed his hands against the edge of the bed, lifting his full bodyweight. He looked down at me. "Because he *wanted* you to be found."

My mum piped up now, with a high-pitched shrill. "You will catch him, won't you, Detective?"

DCI Baldwin turned to my mother and smiled. "Your son has done you proud today, Mrs Allen. I'm sure, with Jeffrey's cooperation, we'll catch this brute before he can do any more harm. He is the only witness we have, you see, and so he is vital to our operation. I'll be in contact for you to come down to the station to give a full report once you are out of hospital, Jeffrey, if that is okay with you?"

I told him that I would cooperate, we exchanged pleasantries and that was the last I saw of DCI Baldwin until I was out of hospital. To all intents and purposes, everything had gone swimmingly. The dread of meeting him again, though, intensified until the scars on my body felt trivial.

The month of May 2018 simmered but the cackle of thunder always threatened, yet the temperature in June is rising to boiling point. I've been walking in no particular direction for over an hour, just chewing the fat, and now my legs feel heavy, the heat clings to my body and the enjoyment has just disappeared; I decide to take a short cut and skirt through the underground supermarket car park. It is now the middle of the day - I am fairly sure of that without glancing at my watch - and most of the cars park up early in the morning and are picked up again at the end of the working day. There is nobody else around, and if I relieved myself against one of the concrete pillars, then a hot trail of piss would be the only evidence I was ever here. I think back to my mum's disapproval of me urinating in public all those years ago, and I know I could never do it even if I wanted to.

But, alas, I am not alone. My floating, wandering thoughts are interrupted by noises up ahead, where the sloping path leads to the supermarket on the first floor.

There is a group of them. I count five. You could throw a blanket over the lot of them. Only, it is not a perfect five: there is four, and then there is one. Those are bad odds for some poor sod, unless he happens to be Jean-Claude Van Damme. The four are tall and broad and they all look the same - white shirts hanging over grey trousers and crooked ties dangling over their chests. They circle like a pack of wolves: jaws dropped, mouths open, teeth coated with spittle. Their prey has his hands up by his face, hunched over at the shoulders.

Reminds me of when I was a kid, just a nipper, maybe ten years old. It was a grey Saturday afternoon in October. The zip of my coat was pulled high to my chin, leaving my neck warm but my cheeks rosy. The long, curved stick in my hand was prised, ready to cause havoc. I pulled back with my arm, ready to strike. It landed in the soggy, overgrown grass without even threatening its target.

I turned around, cowering like a dog that has been clipped around the ear.

"Won't hit any conkers if you throw like a girl..."

The three boys approached, hoods covering their ears. I knew their names, recognised their faces, but had never spoken to them. They were older, bigger, stronger. They were often laughing, but their laughter always threatened and mocked. Now, they stood in a straight line, forming a wall. They looked me up and down, mouths slanted. I dug my hands in my pockets, tried to hide that they were pink, that they were shaking. I wanted to show that I was friendly. I released a high-pitched giggle.

"Something funny...?"

One of the boys took a single step forward. He'd been eating prawn cocktail crisps. The other two boys took a single step forward. I longed to take more than one step backwards, and quickly, but I'd been taught not to.

"You three going in for a hug? Maybe a kiss...?"

I looked over my shoulder, and when I turned back to the three boys, I swear to God I felt ten feet taller. It didn't matter that there were three of them and two of us: I was with my big brother. We'd be fine. We always were.

"Come on, put one on my lips if you really must..."

Luke pushed his neck forward, elaborately puckered his lips. He, too, was shorter than the boys, but his shoulders spread wider, his bravado spanned further. The toughest boy grimaced. His heavy-set eyes clouded over. None of them were sure what to make of this newcomer. They didn't like the uncertainty. He turned around, held up his hand for the other two to follow suit.

"Couple of weirdo's," he said, picking up his pace.

Now, the lone guy is me as a ten-year-old. I *know* him. I often take this route. I always say hello (being the friendly guy I am) and he always nods his head. Sometimes he smiles. Usually he does not. He is always in the car park. That is his job, his life. He is paid to collect and put away the abandoned trolleys, of which there are many. He is probably a few years younger than me, but he looks a good few years older, partly because his face is lined and weather-beaten and partly because he walks with a limp, like he can't quite fully stretch one leg. His eyes are always glassy, like a punch-drunk boxer who isn't sure he'll make it to the bell.

He is, in effect, an easy target for four teenage schoolboys with time to kill.

Judging by their size and the sprinkling of angry red spots

on their foreheads, I estimate the boys to be about fourteen or fifteen years of age. It is, I think, probably the optimum age to be idly hanging around a supermarket car park in the middle of the day, bunking off school and causing strife.

"Here you go, Ken," one of the boys says. He dutifully wheels a trolley towards Ken, kindly gives him a helping hand. The boy halts the trolley just a few short feet away from Ken's black shoes. There is a pause. Ken considers his options. Stand still and wait, or reach out for the trolley? Ken is aware that he is damned if he does, and damned if he doesn't. He stands still, with his crinkled hands on his hips. The boy doesn't move. His eyes don't flinch. He dares Ken to move. Ken doesn't want to wait, for the humiliation builds with every passing second. He lunges for the trolley like Superman on incapacity benefit.

The boy swiftly pulls the supermarket trolley to one side. Ken stumbles past him, suddenly a befuddled Frankenstein. The boy kicks him on the backside. Ken loses balance and ends up with his hands grazing the floor and his face just inches from the tarmac. The boys are no longer wolves. They are hyenas. They jump around with bent legs and long arms, laughing hysterically.

I have time. The boys don't even know I'm here. Pulling my wallet from my pocket, I take a quick look at the photograph. Just a glance is enough. I pull back my shoulders, jut forward my neck, muscles tensing.

"You alright, mate?" I ask. Ken takes my outstretched arm and then he is back on his feet. He brushes down his shirt. The boys stop laughing. They straighten their backs and push out their chests. They keep walking, though, forming a circle. There are two of us now, right in the middle of the circle: Ken's odds have suddenly doubled, and theirs have halved.

I keep my head straight. I'm a lamb taking on a pack of wolves. If they decide to attack then I'll be torn to shreds. Underneath, I'm that scared little boy again; outwardly, I stare straight into each of their eyes as they rotate around me, neither flinching or blinking. The circle narrows. I smell warm beer on their breath. My eyes are large; my body is motionless.

The circle widens. The biggest boy, the one with the most fluff on his cheeks, turns his back. He walks away, up the slope, swaying his shoulders. He holds his finger up.

"You better watch yourself, old man!" he says.

The other three look at me with disdain, then scurry off after their leader.

Now it is just me and Ken, left in the darkness of the car park. I'm still contemplating that they called me an old man. I'm not *that* old, am I? But then I'm prone to distorted, irrational thinking. We've discussed this. Age is, of course, relative. To the ladies at my local Bingo club I am still a young pup with so much life still to look forward to. To these youths I am prehistoric, probably on my last legs, riddled with arthritis. And besides, they were trying to insult me. I'm encouraged by this. If my age - something that is completely out of my control and that affects each and every one of us - is the only thing they could find to mock me, then I can't be doing too badly, can I?

I become aware that these random, spiralling thoughts are a subconscious distraction technique. Ken's hands are trembling. I go to give him a hug, to give him some reassurance, to tell him that it will be okay.

But he turns away and busies himself by doing what he is paid to do. He hunts down the trolleys. I am left standing in the car park, just watching him as he edges away from me. I start to feel awkward and self-conscious, even though there is nobody left to watch me.

"See you then," I say, but my words are lost in the slight breeze that picks up dust and debris from the floor. If Ken heard me then he shows no acknowledgement. I turn and leave the car park, feeling slightly bewildered.

DAY SIX
6TH JUNE 1988

Gordon Allen taps gently on the door. There is no answer, so he taps harder. "Son?"

The door pushes open and Gordon peeks his head inside. It's only been a few hours since he sat next to his boy at the dinner table, but in the interim the colour has faded from his son's cheeks and his hair appears greasier and more fragile. "Can I come in, son?"

Jeffrey bows his head and smoothes down one of the newspapers that are spread out over his bed. Gordon knows that silence is acceptance. He lowers himself into a small, square space on the edge of the bed.

"You were quiet at dinner, Jeffrey. Is everything okay? Your mother is worried about you. We both are."

Jeffrey glances up. Despite the dark patches under his eyes, he still emits a zany energy. He brushes away a strand of hair."You know there has been another murder, Dad? Killed in the same way. The victim was Benjamin Conway. Bit of an oddball. Three Roman numerals engraved into the skin. The number is going up. In Rhondda this time. He is getting closer."

Gordon nods his head sagely. He wants to pick up the newspapers and burn them in the fire; but what was the point? This killer was everywhere: on the radio, on the Welsh news, on the national news; everybody was talking about him in work. If they took away one avenue then Jeffrey would merely seek out another. It was only a couple of days ago that this beast entered their world, but now he absorbed it. Jeffrey came down from his bedroom on Friday just like any other morning, but then he spotted the front page of the newspaper and he read every word of the article in a trance. He barely noticed his dad leave for work. Now Jeffrey was the first to reach for the newspaper when it dropped through the letterbox. His mother's morning routine was ruined. Gordon eyed the papers laid out on the bed with disdain. Now he knew why Jeffrey hurried back to his room after tea.

"I'm aware, son," Gordon replies, carefully choosing his words. "This man is obviously very sick. I don't know if he is evil or mad, or maybe an evil madman, but either way, he is very dangerous. I'm sure he'll be caught soon enough, though."

"You reckon?"

"Of course. These people always are."

"What about Jack the Ripper?"

Gordon hoped his son didn't notice him rolling his eyes.

No seventeen-year-old boy ever wanted to be patronised. "Those were different times, Jeffrey. We have DNA. We have instant radio communication. This animal won't be able to run forever."

"I think he is cleverer than the police, though," Jeffrey says.

"No clever man would ever commit these evil crimes, son. You know we don't like you reading about all this, Jeffrey. It just isn't healthy. And your mum felt so sorry for that poor couple. Imagine if your personal life was dragged through the gutter like that."

"There isn't much to say about *my* personal life," Jeffrey mutters.

"Anyway, let's not waste our time talking about him. Life is too precious. The Euro's start in a couple of weeks, don't they? That should be good. Shame Wales aren't in it. Been thirty years since we got to the final of anything. Our best chance was against Scotland two years ago, but the ref did us again, didn't he? Will you be supporting England?"

"Guess."

"They've got a good team this year, haven't they? That John Barnes is something else when he gets the ball at his feet..."

His son silently shrugs his shoulders. Gordon decides to try a different tact, anything to keep his mind away from this killer. "So, you break up from school soon, and then it is those dreaded A Levels next year, isn't it? Your studies going okay?"

"Yeah. Just taking a break."

Gordon nods his head. "Obviously we want you to do well, son, but we don't want it to be at the expense of you being happy. You know you don't have to go to university if you don't think it's right for you, don't you?"

Jeffrey fixes him a look. "Really?"

"Of course. We'll be proud of you whatever path you take."

"I don't really know what else there is to do in life. I think I will end up going to university, but I'll keep it in mind."

Gordon pats his son on the shoulder. He'd discussed this with Yvette. Jeffrey was becoming more and more isolated and distant, and if it had anything to do with his studies then they needed to relieve some pressure.

"Any young ladies on the go, son?"

Jeffrey's cheeks redden as he smiles bashfully. This was encouraging. "There is one I like," he says.

"That's the way, son," Gordon says. "Shall we be meeting her soon? I'm sure your mum would love to meet her."

Jeffrey bows his head. "Doubt it. We haven't really spoken yet. She is a bit older than me and to be honest I think she may be out of my league. I may be blowing everything out of proportion."

Gordon laughs. "These things are never easy. She'd be a fool not to fall for you, son. Good luck with it."

"Thanks. I might need it."

"Fancy coming down and watching some TV with us? We don't see much of you these days."

Jeffrey shuffles on the bed. "I'm just going to finish reading this article and then I'm going to do some more study."

"Fair enough. I'm not going to keep you away from your studies."

Gordon stands up and walks to the door. His little man to son chat hadn't gone particularly well, but at least he could tell Yvette that there was a girl on the scene.

"Dad?"

Gordon turns to his son.

"Thanks for asking, yeah."

"Any time, son. Anytime."

Gordon shuts the door and climbs down the stairs. He just hoped that anytime would be some time soon, before it was too late.

DAY SEVEN
7TH JUNE 2018

Back in my day these places served a single, definitive
purpose. The shelves were jam-packed with (primarily
hardback) books. Revellers rarely spoke and, if they did, they
did so in raspy whispers. The librarian was usually old and
dusty like the books and they chose to work in a library
because they didn't want to speak to other people. The
library was where you came to read free books, or where you
came to take books away so you didn't have to pay for them.

I hovered around my local library in the months before
Emma was born. I was looking for an instruction manual. I
wanted to be the best daddy in the whole wide world, I just
didn't have the foggiest idea what I was expected to do. And
how do you identify normal baby behaviour? As it turned
out, the first couple of years, despite the chronic sleep
deprivation, were pure bliss. Really, I should have searched
for books about the Terrible Twos. For some reason,
probably because I didn't pay much attention before I had
my own child, I assumed they had something to do with
number two's. I'd been dealing with them ever since I changed
Emma's first nappy, so what was the big fuss? How wrong I
was! I'd dealt with every variety of adult in work, yet I had no

idea what to do with a toddler lying down in the middle of a crowded shopping centre, refusing to move.

The world is much more complicated now and, I observe with interest, the library has moved with the times. Today it appears to serve a multitude of purposes. My eyes flicker at the posters as I enter the foyer. What is all this about? Rhythm and Rhyme. Baby Yoga. *When did babies take up yoga?* I sniff in the fragrant, musty air. Somebody is asleep on the sofa, smothered by plastic shopping bags. Old men browse the newspapers, no doubt already bored with talk of Theresa May's backstop to avoid a hard Irish border. There are rows and rows of other punters with headsets on, listening to music, applying for jobs and watching videos. The attractive librarian is happily speaking to a customer. Taking in my surroundings, my jaw drops.

The rucksack digs into my shoulders. Taking my seat at a solitary table in the corner, I'm overshadowed by the high and commanding bookshelves. I pull the books I collected out of my bag and offload them onto the table. The books slope, reminding me of steps on a staircase. Opening the book on the top of the pile, I'm not quite sure what I'm looking for, just certain that I have a sudden thirst to find out more.

I quickly realised that the crime section was one of the largest in the library. I started at the beginning and my feet shuffled to the right, and they kept on shuffling until finally I was met by a book about cats. Some of the books were about gangsters. Others were about football hooligans. Most, though, were about serial killers. My eyes widened when I realised just how many books there were. It was a simple matter of supply and demand: people wanted to read these books. I knew there was interest; I just didn't realise that the fascination was this broad and widespread. What was the appeal? Was it an escape from reality? Most likely, for the huge majority. But what about for the minority? Were there people out there who got turned on by this stuff? Did others use the material for inspiration?

The pages are faded yellow. My cheeks cool as I flick through the book. The photos of the first two victims stare back at me: John and Valerie Watts. This was where it all began, a terrible nightmare that opened one Wednesday morning, presumably like any other, on the first day of June. The black and white images remind me of passport photos. Both husband and wife are remarkably void of expression. Their eyes are wide, sullen and sad. I can't help but imagine what their faces looked like in the moment before they were both stabbed to death with a cut-throat razor.

I blink the image out of my mind. It is replaced by another. I imagine my own face in the final moment before he made my world turn black. I force my eyes to stare at the

words on the page, just to stay focussed on something -
anything - other than that image. Seconds pass. Eventually I
start absorbing the words. The dark clouds part and my
mind clears.

The media tore into these two much more brutally than
he ever did. It was a frenzy. I woke up one morning two
days after the first killing and I could just tell from the
atmosphere in the kitchen that something was wrong. My
dad was quiet and my mum glanced nervously at her beloved
newspaper. This was my cue to grab for it. My mouth
dropped when I read the first page. I devoured every single
word much more eagerly than I ever devoured my morning
toast with butter.

The paper didn't disclose the full details, but they
exposed as much as they could. The killer hadn't fled the
scene immediately. He stayed around and carved one straight
line down the chest of Valerie and then two straight lines
down the chest of John.

I run a finger over my chest now, across my pink scars,
just as Erica likes to do. An image floods my mind and I
wince. I quickly pull my hand away.

The police said that the lines were most likely Roman
numerals. The newspapers said that he was keeping count,
recording a tally of his victims on their dead bodies. Baldwin
gave a quote. He'd get slated for it over the coming days and

weeks. They said that he'd created a media storm, that he had incited fear in the public. Baldwin said that it meant he intended to kill again and again. After all, who counts up to two? It was a public relations disaster. The media jumped on this, quickly gave the killer a name.

Spartacus was born.

The names they give to killers are rarely imaginative; they are usually simplistic. The media reaches out to the mass population, to lay people with limited knowledge and understanding. Everybody could relate to the significance of the name. Unfortunately, there was an element of grandeur to it. Even more unfortunately, the names often do.

And just as quickly as the name was born, just as Baldwin predicted, more people started to die.

My eyes flick over the pages. It floods back. Details of John and Valerie's alternative lifestyle trickled through on a daily basis. For a few days, *they* were the big story, not Spartacus. We didn't even know who he was, of course, but *their* dirty laundry was there for everybody to see. I dragged my seventeen-year-old self out of bed and ran down the stairs in the mornings to pick up the newspaper before my mum or dad just so I could discover what new obscenities had been uncovered about them. *She liked to whip. He liked to watch.* My parents pleaded for me not to read it, said that no good would come of it, but I ignored them. The stories about John and Valerie were just too fantastic to ignore; they sucked me in.

They'd been to a club in Cardiff the night they were killed. The paper made it clear that it was not a normal club that their respectable readers would ever contemplate visiting. Their motives were not innocent. And they went to the club *together,* for the same purpose. It wasn't just John (as the red-blooded male) who was a deviant; they both were. They were, it was revealed, sexual predators. John and Valerie often frequented the club and, by all accounts, they often brought singles or couples back to their house. Not for coffee or a game of Cluedo. For sex. John and Valerie were perfect fodder for the papers. They became the butt of jokes in the workplace and the playground.

The police interviewed a whole range of people who had seen them at the club that night. A handful admitted they'd previously engaged in intimate relations with John and Valerie. Their faces appeared in the newspapers. Most were middle-aged and unattractive. They were all women. None of them saw John and Valerie with anybody else that night. Definitely not a man. Many vouched that they left alone. The police concluded that John and Valerie Watts must have picked Spartacus up on their way home.

I turn the pages of the book and then, suddenly, it feels like somebody has punched my chest. Hard. I wipe away a layer of cold sweat from my forehead with the back of my hand. This was the murder where it really hit home. This was the first victim I could really relate to; whose life was even remotely anything like my own.

Marie Davies.

She was the fifth victim, killed on the 16th night of June. The fourth victim, Judy Spencer, a middle-aged housewife who, by all accounts, was the victim of domestic violence, was found dead by Julie and Kate Phillips on the 8th day of the month.

Marie's pretty, plump face stares up at me, the large oval eyes burning my skin. I run the tip of my middle finger along the edge of her outline. She was only nineteen when her throat was shredded - two years older than I was - and she looked younger. The smile is wide, gap-toothed and innocent. The murders started in Cardiff and they had been getting closer and closer to home. This was the first - but not the last- in Bridgend. It was only after this murder that people in my home town truly felt that they were at risk on a night out. Cardiff was close, but still far enough. It was still happening somewhere else, in the newspapers and on the TV. They walked past *this* murder scene on a daily basis. This was when it truly got real. This was when my parents really got concerned.

Marie was on a night out with her friend in Sinatra's

nightclub. They were enjoying a drink when Marie got up and left. Her friend saw Marie leave on her own. They were sat together when Marie just stood up, gave her friend the briefest of waves and walked out without uttering a word. *Apparently*, her friend considered going after her, checking that she was alright, but then thought better of it; she assumed she was just a bit worse for wear and had popped out for some fresh air. It was only when Marie didn't return ten minutes or so later that she started panicking. She went looking for her outside the club, but she was nowhere to be seen.

The doormen confirmed they saw a girl matching Marie's description leave the club at the approximate time her friend said she just upped and left. They said she turned left out of the club; this tallied with where she was found dead the next morning. And, most importantly, the doormen confirmed that she left alone. Sure, people came and went shortly after her, but they headed in different directions. The two knucklehead bouncers were adamant that nobody followed her; the police had no reason to suspect they weren't telling the truth.

The police investigation, headed up by DCI Baldwin, concluded that, just with the first two murders, Spartacus most likely came into contact with his victim on her way home. It begged the question, though: who picked up whom?

I slam the book shut. Circle my forehead with my fingers. Open up another book. There I am. *Me.* Staring back at myself. Only, it truly does feel like a previous version of myself, from a past life. I am seventeen and clean-cut, without a glimmer of a hair on my chin. My cheeks are puffy, my skin is oily and there are black shadows under my eyes. The blond hair is cut short at the sides and is spiky on top. My heavy eyes look tired and uncertain.

I'm ravenous now, desperate to view more of my old life. It was a closed book for so many years and now - literally - I've opened the book again. I open another. There I am again. The photograph is almost a replica of the first; it is just as unflattering. I long to read what is written about me, but I dare not. Richard's whispering, disapproving voice taunts me. The horrific memories knock on my front door and somehow I need to keep them on the doorstep. It is futile. I am suddenly an addict, desperate for my next hit.

I open the final book and the title chapter is big and bold. *Jeffrey Allen - A lucky escape?*

I stare at this title until the words are a blur. I blink my eyes to re-focus. There is nothing particularly extravagant or creative about this title. It doesn't vary much from the titles of the numerous books I picked up. None of those captivated my attention. The hairs on my forearms didn't prickle like they do now. There is a solitary difference with this title. What is it? The question mark. It changes everything.

I flip to the back cover and look at the photograph of the writer in the bottom corner. I stifle a smirk. Was this the best photograph he could find? It looks like a police mug shot. The writer could be a serial killer himself. I make a mental note of the name; I'm not quite sure why.

Something flashes past my eye line on the far side of the book shelves. I glance up; nothing is there. I lower my head and start reading the pages of the book, but almost instantly I'm distracted again. I jerk my head up. Nothing, or nobody, is there. This time I keep looking, certain that as soon as I lower my gaze it will appear again. I keep looking, but nothing appears, and nothing disappears.

I tell myself that this is a slippery slope to paranoia. I remind myself what DCI Reeves said: it is probably nothing, that I should just forget about it, that I should just get on with my life. I curse myself for even being here, for letting Spartacus back into my life, for opening the door even though I know he is an uninvited guest. Richard will not be impressed.

I leave the books on the desk and rise to my feet. The light on the other side of the window is fading. The librarian announces that the library will be shutting in ten minutes. I glance around. The rows of computers are mainly vacant. Newspapers have been scattered on tables. I've been oblivious to the time passing. There are only a few people left now; they are probably homeless or don't have a home they want to go home to. I am neither of those things. I have a beautiful girlfriend waiting at home for me. It is time I head off, go home.

I don't do this. Instead, I pick up a newspaper that has been left on a table and head to the toilets. The librarian glances over her glasses at the newspaper and raises her eyes. I feel like I've been caught with my trousers down. Again. I expect her to tell me to put the paper down, to remind me again that the library is about to close. She returns to her computer screen. I walk on tiptoes, trying to be oblivious. It crosses my mind that this might not be a good idea, that it really isn't worth the effort or the guilt. Then I curse myself for being so melodramatic. Who do I think I am? I'm only popping to the toilet for a quick browse of the paper, for God's sake. What difference can ten minutes make? They are hardly going to lock me in now, are they?

I dutifully follow the signs directing me upstairs and then I climb the wide, concrete spiral staircase. Nobody is about. It is just me. Bliss. I shut the cubicle door. Pull the lock across. Take a seat. Unfold the newspaper and take a cursory look at the headings. I have a thought. A wonderful one. I dig my hand inside my rucksack, all the way to the bottom. I cup an orange, then an apple. I packed them in my bag with the best of intentions, but I know I'll throw them both out once they start moulding. That is more like it. I pull out my cigar and then light up. Inhaling, I savour the aroma. I never had any doubts that this was worth the effort.

The rest room door opens. I am no longer alone.

My mouth is full of smoke, but I'm afraid to exhale. I blow out my cheeks to the point that they're ready to pop like a couple of balloons. I lower my head between my knees and blow the smoke in the direction of the floor. Then I close my legs to act as a barrier to stop the smoke from rising. I wave my hand in the air.

"Cleaner!"

What am I expected to do in these circumstances? Am I supposed to notify the cleaner that I am in the cubicle? I stay silent, and I remain motionless. My eyes momentarily return to the newspaper, but my focus is broken. I'm aware that the library will lock the doors in just a few minutes. Unless I leave now then I may be locked in after all. I stand up to pull across the lock.

The cleaner starts humming a tune. I sit back down.

My buttocks are glued to the toilet seat. My eyes stare at the blank canvas of the toilet door. There is something about the tune that grips tightly at my throat, that strangles my windpipe. Or maybe - just maybe - it is the way he hums the tune? It is jovial and upbeat. It is passionate. Nothing untoward there. But it is in dire conflict with the tune. It becomes louder. He is walking towards me. The footsteps are slow and measured, but he is definitely getting closer. Then he stops. I crouch down and glance under the gap at the bottom of the door, like an excited kid at the swimming baths for the first time. I can see his shoes. He is stood just a few feet from the door. I flinch and silently move away.

My hands grip the side of the plastic toilet seat. I try to calm my nerves, to think rationally. But why is he stood on the other side of the door? *What is the worst that can happen?* I realise that if it is him then the worst that can happen is I am bludgeoned to death with a razor blade. Thinking rationally doesn't help. I decide not to think at all. I shut my eyes and try to focus on the words that he is humming.

Don't fear the reaper - Baby I'm your Man.

And then the words stop. I can hear his footsteps on the tiled floor. He is walking away. It feels like the vice-like grip around my neck has been released. I wait for the toilet door to open. I keep waiting. He hasn't headed for the door. He hasn't left. He is still in the room. What is he doing? I stare at the floor, at the spidery cracks in the tiles, counting down the seconds, waiting for the inevitable. My time has finally come, thirty years and seven days after it should have come.

The toilet door opens and then - seconds later - it closes.

I begin to think clearer. I *have* become paranoid. It was just the cleaner, pissed off because I was smoking in the toilets. It was against all the regulations. The fire alarm could have gone off. The guy was just trying to intimidate me. It worked. *Hell,* it worked, but not for reasons he could ever realise. I shake my head and emit a loud, excited laugh. The cleaner could smell my smoke. I push my hands down on the seat, jolted into action, suddenly focussed on what really does matter. The library is about to shut, and I need to get out of here quick.

I pull across the bolt and push open the cubicle door. I take one step forward and then stop. My eyes widen as they fix on the mirror, on the words that have been scrawled in blood.

Twenty-three days.

DAY EIGHT
8TH JUNE 1988

Kate Phillips grips her mother's hand as they walk down the library's concrete steps.

Fair play, the afternoon had passed surprisingly quickly since her mum picked her up from school. Kate wasn't going to tell her mum that, though; she knew her game. It was a strategic game of chess. Her mother's tactic was to keep her busy, keep her focussed on anything but the damn Amstrad CPC she'd bought Kate for her 9th birthday. Kate knew her mum and dad rued the day they decided to buy her that computer. She didn't feel too much guilt, though; it was their fault that they were so naive. They had these grand ideas that she'd spend hours, days, writing stories about fairies, and creating pie charts. Just who did they think she was? Just why would they possibly think she wouldn't waste endless hours in her bedroom on the computer playing *Double Dragon?* Her mum was at her wits' end. Said Kate would get square eyes if she didn't stop playing on that damn computer. But then, she also said her face would stay like that if the wind changed, and Kate knew that simply wasn't true (she'd tested the theory).

Yesterday they'd followed the twisting trail of the river.

Last time she'd been down by the river, the water had been choppy and aggressive, but this time there was so much less of it, and it seemed so much calmer and at peace with the world. They spotted a couple of dead fish floating on the surface of the water, just lying there, exposed. It seemed so degrading and yet - and *yet* - so freakishly fascinating. Today they'd located a table in the corner of the library and flicked through books. Her mum tried to get her interested in *Cinderalla,* but Kate picked up a picture book about *Jossy's Giants.* Regardless, the quiet and tranquillity of the library made a pleasant change to the non-stop action of her computer games.

The other children are all home from school by now and yet, as the shops and offices are not quite shut, the streets are quiet as they head to the bus stop. They cross the road, then turn the corner.

"Look, Mum. Look!" Kate raises her hand and points.

Her mother tugs on her hand. "Oh, yes," she says. "How odd."

Kate knew this tactic, too. Mum tried to dismiss anything that was even remotely different by saying it was odd, just like she did when those two men kissed on *Eastenders.* Seriously, Kate thinks; she is just so embarrassing sometimes. Kate plays her own chess move. She tugs at her mother's arm so they step off the bumpy, hot pavement and onto the road. Her mother is sure to tell her off for this later, Kate thinks; but later is later and this is now. Now they are crossing the road and they will have no choice but to speak to the man waiting for them on the other side. It was rude not to, and her mother was forever saying that rudeness was a disease of modern society.

The man bounces up and down on the spot in black and white striped trousers and blazer, reminding Kate of an American Football referee. He wears bulky leather boots. His frizzy green hair has the look of a mad professor, or somebody who has been electrocuted. The chalk white face highlights the blood red lips and the black circles around his eyes. His tongue hangs out of his mouth like a thirsty dog.

Mummy isn't going to like this man one bit, Kate thinks, as she picks up her pace and widens her smile.

"We come for your daughter, Chuck," he announces as they move within touching distance. Kate notices that his manic eyes dart everywhere. He bows to Kate's mum. "I'm the ghost with the most, babe!"

Kate puts her hand to her mouth. Her mother's hand feels cold against her own. "Look, Mum," Kate says. "It's Beetlejuice."

"Oh, yes," her mum says, "so it is. How very odd."

Beetlejuice jiggles a red bucket under their noses. Kate hears the jingling of coins. "Just doing my bit for charity, ma'am," he explains. "Raising money for cancer research."

Kate's mother crinkles her nose as though sniffing dog muck. "Quite," she says. "Very good."

The bucket remains dangling and Mrs Phillips has no choice but to open her handbag and dig inside her purse. She drops a few bronze and silver coins inside. Kate feels a tug at her hand. She goes to protest, but when she looks up she thinks better of it: her mum has the same face she had when gypsies settled on their local park.

"You are a queen, ma'am," the man says, bowing down again. "That twenty pence will surely go a long way to saving the lives of the sick and vulnerable."

"Quite," Mrs Phillips says. Kate can tell by the flush to her mother's cheeks that even she can tell the man isn't being straight with her.

"That Spartacus is killing so many innocent people that I think we need to save as many as we can," the man says. He fixes Mrs Phillips with a pensive look. "Wouldn't you agree?"

Kate feels her mother's eyes on her, but she looks away. They don't talk about that man in their house. Her mother turns the channel when he comes on the news. Of course, Kate knew everything there was to know about the crazy killer who was roaming the streets of South Wales. They had a game in school where one of the kids pretended to be him and chased after the other children, with a stick as a prop.

"He's killed again. Did you know?" he asks.

Kate feels the grip on her hand tighten. She is hurting her now.

"Really? You sure? I read the newspaper this morning and there was nothing about it in there. Since when? When did somebody die?"

Kate is surprised by the sharpness of her mother's tone. She can tell that, for whatever reason, her mother doesn't like this man. Maybe she thinks he is the real Beetlejuice?

The man taps the side of his nose. "Since today, madam. Another innocent victim is dead."

"No. No, I didn't know that," Mrs Phillips says. "How very awful."

Kate looks up at Beetlejuice as he leans close to her mother; close enough, she thinks, for her to feel his breath on her face. Kate tugs at her hand. She wants to leave now. There is something about this man that she doesn't like now, either. She doesn't like the way he speaks to her mum, the way he looks at her, the way he doesn't seem to mean any of what he says.

The man leans even closer now, close enough to dig his teeth into her neck, and then he whispers in her ear. Kate can see his lips moving, the spit on his tongue. Her mother's jaw drops and her hand turns icy cold, then her body goes oddly still, like she is frozen in time.

The man raises his hand in the air to bid farewell as he moves swiftly down the street, happily jingling the bucket down by his side. Takes a turn. Then he is gone.

"Come on, Kate, we need to get a hurry on before we miss that bus."

Kate is relieved to see her mum alert again, to see her back to normal. Suddenly, she is full of energy, like she has been on the Lucozade again. Kate has to skip to keep up with her. Her mum moves daintily, like she is walking on hot coals. Suddenly, she stops. She closes her eyes, just for a few seconds, before opening them again. Kate dreads to think what thoughts go through her mind. She puts her palms on Kate's shoulders and speaks very clearly.

"Kate. Wait here. Just one moment. Please, do not move."

Kate watches her mother turn back in the same direction they just came from. Kate has no idea why she is going back, but she is certain nothing good can come of it. Just what did that odd man whisper to her? It is like some magnificent invisible force is pulling her mum by the wrists. Her movements are slower now, more reluctant. She stops again. Stands still. Maybe she is having second thoughts? Then, just as Kate thinks she might turn around and come back - and she *really* hopes that she does - her mum disappears down a dark, narrow alleyway.

Seconds pass in silence. Kate taps the soles of her black school shoes against the crooked pavement. She eyes the moss that sprouts from the cracks. She begins to worry for her mother.

Her head jerks up. The silence has been broken by the horrific sound of her mother screaming.

DAY NINE
9TH JUNE 2018

Sinking my buttocks deeply into the sofa that curves in a u-shape , my shoulders slope downwards and my hands rest on the flat of my thighs. My feet are somewhere - attached to my legs, no doubt, as they usually are - and yet they're so numb and heavy that I can barely feel them.

My eyes blink open. My back straightens and I pull my shoulders almost up to my ears. What was that? Moments earlier I was oblivious to my surroundings on the boat, my home. I'm here alone because it is the middle of the day and Erica is in her workshop. Now I push my neck forward and squint, actively searching for things, chasing shadows - seeking out danger. *Stop doing this. You know it is all in your head; all in your mind.*

I close my eyes again. Force them shut. Teasing my forehead with the tips of my fingers, I sink my face into the comfort and security of my palms. I count one, two, three as I inhale through my nose; count one, two, three as I exhale out from my mouth. My body feels so heavy that I am disappearing into the floor, tumbling into the grotty, rancid canal water that lies below, sinking into the epicentre of the earth.

I spring to attention, suddenly alert. I am not imagining it this time. My mind is not playing games. This is not paranoia. I *did* hear something. I heard *somebody*. My mind plays tricks; my ears do not lie. There is somebody outside. I can hear him moving. He is circling the boat, a predator assessing the prey, waiting for the right moment to pounce, to attack.

The windows span all the way along the boat, on both sides. The glass is flimsy, easily broken. I look up. Sun roof. I look for hiding places. There are none.

Bang.

What was that? Something hit the boat, struck it with force. I pull my knees up to my chest, wrap my arms around my legs, curl up into a ball. The noise came from the far end of the boat, the other side, furthest away from me. This is the safest place. Right here. Right where I am.

I want to stand up to him, my fists raised and ready, just like Luke would. I want to hunt down the intruder, to turn the tables, to become the attacker. I can't. My body feels like it has been stuck to the seat with superglue. I am strapped down, completely and utterly defenceless.

I see it happening. See it with my own eyes. Like it is in slow motion. The door handle pushes down. The door slides open. The door slides shut. He is on my boat, in my home.

The feet move towards me. Slowly, like they are treading through water. He is getting closer, though. He will reach me, eventually.

I try to lift my legs. The resistance is much stronger now. They are tied down with rope. I no longer want to attack. I just want to escape, to run.

He moves close enough for me to see his face. He looks exactly the same. He has not changed. He still looks beautiful, like his features have been sculpted by hand. His smile is subtle, unnerving. It widens; stretches his face.

I am distracted for a moment. But then I see it. In his hand. There is something in his hand. The light rebounds from it so sharply that I cover my eyes. I glimpse over the top of my hand and I watch him raise his own hand, high above his head.

Suddenly, I *can* move. My body has never felt so free, so light, so *capable*. I jump up from the chair. My fists are like shovels. I swing with speed, with force. My fists sink into his face. I grip his skull. I have so much power that it feels like I can crush his skull until it disintegrates like dust. He squeals like a pig, but my teeth are sharp and I have never felt so fantastic.

The cabin stops moving, stops swaying from side to side. Comes into focus. My forehead is damp. I feel slender arms clinging tightly to my body. He talks to me, pleads with me.

"Stop, Marcus. Please, stop."

My eyes are open, wide like hollows. I pull away, sit up. I pull my hands behind my back and twist them together to stop me throwing wild and dangerous punches, to stop them from doing *anything*.

Erica pulls her own hands to her face. She looks tinier than ever, more fragile and delicate than I've ever seen her, so feline and childlike, lying with her back pressed against the bed sheet. I dab my forehead with my finger and realise that the dampness is a dreadful cocktail of sweat, tears and blood.

Erica's blood.

I lean down and nestle my forehead against hers. Her hands part and her arms wrap around me. I tell her that I am sorry; tell her again and again.

"It is okay," she says. Her breathing has calmed. She whispers the words. They are soothing. Her fingers caress my naked back now, run down the curve of my spine. "It is just dream. Everything is fine, Marcus. Everything is fine."

I bury my head in the warmth of her neck. My hand caresses her long, soft hair. Her body is floppy and relaxed. My own body is rigid. I cling to her tighter. I need to wash the blood from her forehead, need to clean her up, but for now she is content to just drift, to daydream, safely wrapped in my arms.

I have a nagging thought, that just keeps repeating in my mind. I try to push it away, but it pushes back, even stronger.

It would be so much better if this whole nightmare *was* just a dream.

DAY TEN
10TH JUNE 2018

Twisting his face into an array of shapes, Richard digs his hefty hand inside the dark depths of his even heftier black bag. He has placed the bag on the table that separates us, and it stretches all the way up to his chin. Pulling out a banana, all bruised, brown patches and decaying yellow, Richard crinkles his nose like he has never seen one quite like this before.

"What on earth...?" he says, returning the banana back into the bag.

My eyes are drawn alluringly to the fabulous cuckoo clock on the wall to my right. Even *I* know it is nine minutes past eleven, though since I quit my job in the city five years ago, I try my best not to take much notice of the time. The slip of paper on the table has my name and then '11am' scrawled on it in Richard's fantastically messy handwriting. I'm forever pulling these slips out of my pocket with the odd coin and tissue. Why is he only searching for this now? Surely this cannot be his first appointment of the day? I smile. I thought I was supposed to be the one that needed help. It doesn't bother me, really. I am not often in a rush to be anywhere else.

To think, though, I thought I might be late myself this morning. I just knew I needn't have worried, that however late I might be, Richard would surely be even later. Erica made an early start. Her parting kiss was a distant memory when I finally rose from my pit. It was only when I was ready to leave I realised I couldn't locate the door key. Normally this wouldn't be too much of a worry - I'd just leave it unlocked; not any more. I checked an array of pockets, a range of hiding places. Nothing. My temperature was beginning to rise, my temper starting to be tested. I was just about ready to pull my phone from my pocket, ring Richard and tell him that I wouldn't be able to make it today, when I spotted it. I blew air from my mouth and cursed myself for being such a drama queen. I picked it up from the doormat and hurriedly went on my way, just about ahead of time. I must have dropped it after I'd unlocked the door last night.

This room is like a second home, I am here so often. It must be ten years or so since the letter unexpectedly dropped through my letterbox in Clapham inviting me for an appointment with Richard McCoy. I say unexpectedly, but by that time I'd come to expect the unexpected.

I'd been receiving support for my mental health ever since the attack. Back then it wasn't fashionable to see a psychiatrist or a counsellor, especially for men. Mental health was another term for madness. It was spoken about in hushed tones, if at all. This was a million miles from the Prozac age that followed in the nineties. Initially the support I received was mandatory. I was a victim and so I needed support. Even as a naive and pretty dumb eighteen-year-old kid lost in the big city I could see that there was a fair amount of box ticking involved – the system needed to ensure that they had taken the appropriate steps to cover their own butt should I decide to harm myself or somebody else. I was high profile, wasn't I? I went along to whatever they sent me to and nodded my head and made all the right noises without really thinking too much about it.

It is difficult to say whether any of the treatment worked, because I don't know what I would have been like had I not received it. For all I know, I could be ten feet under now were it not for the drugs. None of it was visibly useful, though. I was a revolutionary, however, because I was on drugs a decade before it became fashionable. The counsellor usually prescribed me on a dose of antidepressants, sent me away, called me back and then asked whether they'd worked. I'd tell him (or her, of course) that it felt like I'd been walking through a black fog, that I barely felt alive any more. They told me that wasn't their desired effect. No shit. And so they'd take me off that medication and put me on another one that was fundamentally the same but with a different name and then we'd start the process again and have the same conversation in another four weeks. I was a test rat in a laboratory.

My file is big, but then it isn't all about size, is it? I know it is big because I saw it, back before data was transferred onto the computer. The file was A4 and breaking at the seams. I'd received the full works of support; the deluxe package. The group sessions were the worst. The crux of the idea was that I'd be able to converse with other people with similar problems I could relate to. It was just like on the TV. We sat on stained, plastic chairs in a small room with no air. Nearly everybody looked what they were: a victim. There was a specific reason I only attended one session, though. One guy told his story, just like all the others. Unlike all the others, though, his was a success story. He told us that he had been huddled on bare floorboards covered in his own faeces, high on drugs and low on life. And yet he pulled it all around and now he had a home, a job and a wife. The broadness of his smile told you everything you needed to know.

"Do you know how I did it?" he asked the group, glancing around the circle one by one. We each in turn shook our heads. This felt like a monumental moment for me. This guy had it sorted. He was a genie with a bottle. He was going to tell us the secret. He was my way out of this pit of misery. I was on my way back up.

"I found Jesus Christ Our Saviour," the man announced, beaming.

"Oh for fucks sake," I muttered.

I thought I said the words under my breath, but clearly I didn't, for the whole room turned to look at me. I swear the words came out of my mouth involuntarily, that I just couldn't keep them in.

"You got a problem with that?" the guy asked. I noticed for the first time that he was a large man, much bigger than me.

"Not at all," I replied. I really didn't. Horses for courses, that's what I say. This one just wasn't right for me. "I was just hoping," I continued, holding my hands up, "that you were going to come up with a practical solution."

"Practical?"

I never did find out whether I was the first person to be punched in a group session, but it was agreed by both myself and my counsellor that the environment was probably not the best fit for me. I suspect the whole room released a long sigh of relief when they spotted an empty seat at the meeting the following week.

I hadn't expected much the first appointment with Richard. Previous disappointments had sucked the optimism right out of me. My last counsellor had been a nice lady but she was happy enough to just let me talk and look at me sympathetically as I told her my woes. I'd go into the meeting thinking that maybe my life wasn't so bad, all things considered, but I'd leave feeling the pits. The letter didn't give much information. It didn't explain why they'd decided to change my counsellor.

I liked Richard as soon as I saw him. For one thing, he made me feel a whole lot better about my own appearance. I'm naturally drawn to ugly people for this very reason. He held my gaze as he shook my hand and I noticed that he had one bloodshot eye. Richard was as wide as he was high, but he was mainly comprised of soft cushion. Suddenly I felt tall and I felt lean and I felt beautiful. I knew that he was the right counsellor for me.

I glance over Richard's shoulder now, through the window. A sparrow sits on the branch of one of the trees, eyeing the fish in the pond. I know that the fish are safe, for I have stood by the window and looked outside on many occasions when Richard has gone searching for something or other, and I know that the pond is covered with a green net. The garden is small and shaped like a triangle, narrowing at the tip, but the lawn is flat and the grass is bright, fresh and green. I often think it would be wonderful to sit on the wooden bench in the garden in the middle of the day with a book and a cup of coffee. The magnificent pine bookcase behind me, just a few steps on the wooden floorboards away, always looks like it is only one hardback book from toppling over. The leather sofa I lay on just over a week ago is pressed tight against the wall to my left. In front of the sofa is a fluffy burgundy rug that I often long to curl up and fall asleep on.

"Ah," Richard says, puckering his rubbery red lips into an enormous smile. "That is where the little blighter got to. Now we can really get started, Marcus. Now we can *really* get this show on the road."

Glancing at the tip of the black biro he has finally located, I suspect, after all that, the pen probably won't work. I am convinced Richard puts the pens that don't work back in his bag, for hardly any of his pens actually manage to write. Richard's cheeks become unusually rounded when he smiles. Richard has an unusually rounded face, for he is usually smiling. His skin is so alarmingly smooth and free of creases that he is almost boyish, and yet I am sure the man sitting in front of me is in his fifties. His black hair is shaven close to his scalp on the sides but it is frizzy and wild on the top. I look down on him when he stands up. His perfectly round belly reminds me of a Buddha. Richard is far from being an attractive man, but his face is so amenable I often gaze at him with sheer fascination.

"So how have things been with you since our last session,

Marcus?" Richard asks. His red, watery eyes glance at the blank pad. He scribbles with the pen, then sighs when nothing comes out. Richard puts the pen down and rests both elbows on the table. He knows I've noticed that the pen doesn't work but decides to ignore this. He rubs the thick stubble on his chin with the underside of his thumbs.

"It has not been a great week," I say. "I have given into some temptations that I would normally resist-"

I am about to tell Richard more, when he interrupts me and says, "Tell me more."

We normally avoid specifics. For me, today, this is just as well. I don't particularly want to tell him that I woke in the middle of the night, my fists sprinkled with my girlfriend's blood, that a dark cloud has been following me since the first day of the month. For me, today, I want to be as general as possible and just hope he doesn't probe deeper.

Our sessions focus on three key things: thoughts, behaviours and feelings. We discuss how our thoughts and behaviours directly affect how we feel. The events of the previous week - however unexpected and interesting - can usually be broken down into these three things. There is usually no need to delve into specifics.

This week has been different, though, hasn't it? This has not been like any other week. I tell Richard that, after all these years, *he* has re-entered my life.

"And you let him in?" Richard asks, leaning forward.

This was the question I just knew Richard was going to ask. I know him just as well as he knows me. This time it was the obvious question to ask, though. I lower my eyes. I don't want to see his reaction when he realises I let him down. "I opened the door," I say.

"Why did you open the door? What was different this time? What thoughts brought about this behaviour?"

"I think I opened the door mainly out of uncontrollable curiosity. It has been so long, so many years. I think that, initially, and possibly only for a few moments, the curiosity was just too much. I opened the door just enough to look outside and see him-"

"And what did you think?"

"So many different things. I felt fear and I felt hatred. That was clear. That was expected. But there was something else..." I theatrically dangle my fingers like I'm playing an imaginary piano. "There was a sense of familiarity. Of a time that I used to know, that no longer exists."

Richard's face gives nothing away. "We are drawn to familiarity. It makes us feel safe, however dreadful it may be. We fear things we don't know, of course, even though they often excite us, too. The allure would have been strong. You know what the crucial question is, though, don't you?"

I nod my head.

Richard sits back in his chair. He folds his arms across his chest. "So, *did* you?"

I shake my head. "I only opened the door wide enough to take a good look at him. I longed to open the door wider. I had to forcibly push the damn thing shut. But I did. I didn't open the door wide enough for him to come in, for him to enter."

The effect of my words is instant. His dark skin glistens. There is a brightness to his glassy eyes. "You're not telling the truth, Marcus," he says.

"I am," I reply. "I swear to God I am."

Richard smirks. "I believe in your story, Marcus," he says. "And unlike you, I actually *believe* in God. But you are deceiving yourself when you say you haven't had a great week. Sure, it sounds like you've had an awful week. My knees are wobbly just from listening to it, and I'm supposed to be a big, strong man. But you cannot worry about things that are outside of your control. Those AA guys did have at least one thing right. You were tested. Who wouldn't be? You are human. If I stuck a needle in your arm then you would bleed, just like every human. You think. You act. You feel. But you had the courage and the sanity to amend your thoughts. And then you acted on them. You resisted the initial destructive thoughts. You beat the temptation. You closed that door. You didn't let him in. Do you not think that is good, Marcus?"

I just know, from the tingling in my cheeks, that my face has reddened. It takes a lot to make me blush, but I am blushing.

"You got me there. I accept that is good. Of course that is good."

Richard nods his head and raises his eyebrows in unison. It is rather distracting. "You know what it means?"

I shake my head and look away from his eyebrows.

"It means," he says, "that now you *know* you can beat him. You thought you could before. But your belief had not been tested. Not for a long, long time. You've developed and grown from an introverted teenager into a strong, confident man. The transformation has been dramatic. This should give you even more confidence. Before you were like an elephant. You were big and strong and respected, but not really doing a great deal. Now you are like a lion. You are King of the Jungle. How does that make you feel?"

I feel like hammering my fists against my almighty chest. I rock back and forth in the chair. "I feel good," I say.

"Do you think you could have beaten him the first time you sat opposite me in that chair, all those years ago? Ten years ago now, is it?"

"No way. He would have beaten me down and spat me out."

I don't know if Richard is aware, but we tend to have the same conversations again and again. We have for ten years now and there is a decent chance we will do so in another ten years. Sometimes I wonder whether he has the same conversations with all of his other clients, too, or if I'm the chosen one. Richard doggedly sticks to the same approach. His belief is unfaltering and borderline irrational. But unlike that guy in the group session all those years ago, I don't question it.

Richard guffaws. And then he snorts. He sniffs through his impressive nostrils. "You know what that is?" he asks.

I shrug my shoulders.

"That, my friend," he says, "is the scent of progress."

His laughter is thunderous, and it fills each corner of the room.

I thought that I was supposed to be the crazy one. I should have known that Richard would try and take all the credit. I break into a smile and give him a high-five.

DAY ELEVEN
11TH JUNE 2018

I stand still, on the spot, and it feels like the rest of the world is moving around me in fast forward. My feet remain motionless but my thoughts are racing, moving faster than any of the people that surround me. I have a decision to make. An important one. This can't be rushed.

My fingers rub against the card in my hand. I considered throwing it in the bin, hoping I wouldn't need it, but then I kept it, just in case. I eye the building, large and intimidating. I imagine DCI Reeves sat in his office, watering his plants or polishing his desk, maybe sipping his herbal tea. I picture his reaction when he sees me. He will be polite but brisk, making sure he does what is expected of him but at the same time bristling with irritation. After all, I'm a waste of his invaluable time. Picture his face when I brief him on the developments. Things have changed. I have something more substantial for him.

I think back to the library. I pressed my hand to my mouth when I saw the words on the mirror, felt bile rise up my throat. Then I pulled my hand away and grabbed my phone and took a photo. It was my gut reaction, the first thing that came to my mind. My second thought was that he'd left evidence. His blood was smothered on the mirror. Forensics would have a field day. The last thing I wanted to do was go anywhere near it, for it repulsed me - but I had to, didn't I? But as I stepped closer, I realised something: it wasn't blood, it was lipstick. What did I feel? Disappointment? Or relief? Right then, I wasn't quite sure.

I thought about wiping away the writing with some toilet paper and water, for it made me feel exposed, that a dirty secret was up on the wall for the world to see. But then, it didn't actually mean anything, did it? So, I just ran, partly to get out of there and partly because the library was about to shut. My senses were on red alert, looking around, expecting him to spring from behind a bookshelf. Nothing. And there has been nothing since. Four days.

I wonder what Reeves will say when I tell him. He'll probably get hung up on the trivial details, smirk that I sneaked into the cubicle for a cheeky read of the newspaper at closing time, roll his eyes when I show him the photo. I know what he'll think, though: somebody is messing with me. He'll reassure me that they take harassment *very* seriously. He'll take a statement. Ask some questions of the library staff. Maybe check the CCTV.

But what he *won't* accept is that it is him, that this is the work of Spartacus. He'll fire out a comprehensive list of reasons why it isn't him, deliver a longer list of alternatives. I don't want him to half-heartedly investigate a possible stalker, tick the boxes to show he's doing his job. I want him to hunt down and slay one of the most notorious serial killers of recent times.

That's what Baldwin would have done. He would have rolled his sleeves up and taken whatever means necessary - fair or foul - to catch the evil bastard.

Another memory from the library plays in my mind. It is an alternative. Another way.

I make my decision.

I turn from the building. Start walking away.

Somebody knocks into me. I'm surprised they didn't see me; I'm walking slowly in a straight line. The man raises his cap, smiles, and then continues walking.

I only see the face briefly. I turn around, and he has disappeared amidst the crowd of people. I have a nagging thought, though, one that only develops and gets stronger, that the polite, smiling man with the cap was *him*.

DAY TWELVE
12TH JUNE 2018

Richard's disapproving face sits on my right shoulder. He doesn't say anything, just widens his eyes and raises his eyebrows. I know he'd cast out a line and reel me back in like a fish if he could.

I shouldn't be here, just as I shouldn't have been snooping around in the library five days ago. These stones are best unturned. Let sleeping dogs lie. He'd come out with all the lines, for sure. But I either go through the official channels (which, of course, is what I'm *expected* to do) or I do it myself. So here I am, on the outskirts of London, passing the identical houses with freshly cut green lawns (fading yellow from the relentless sun) and then stopping to glance at the piece of scrap paper in my hand. The hairs on my arm bristle as I wipe my forehead.

Don't be that one. Please, don't be that one.

I glance again at the number on the piece of paper. It is that one. Of course it is that one.

The lawn has been dug up and replaced with tired , grey concrete slabs. An old, rusty bicycle with a punctured tyre has been discarded on the floor. I glance around for an abandoned washing machine or a stained mattress, and I'm surprised when I can't locate one.

Somebody appears through the glass panel of the front door and, although their outline grows larger, they don't appear to be in any rush to actually answer the door.

"Oh," I say, when the door is finally opened, "I was hoping to find Simon here."

An elderly lady looks me up and down and then narrows her eyes, as if to see me properly. Her face is wrinkled and rubbery, like a pair of testicles that have sat in the bath for too long. "We all have hopes, dear," she says. "But when you get to my age, you're old and wise enough to realise hardly any of them ever come true."

She stands to one side to let me enter. I'm befuddled by this. The woman hasn't even asked who I am, or what I am doing here. I'm not hot on health and safety, but even I can identify some potential risks. Before I can put my words in the right order to make my point, the woman shouts at the top of her voice. "Simon! There is a man here for you! I have no idea who he is, but he's a middle-aged white guy, if that helps?"

I tell her my name on the assumption this will help identify who I am.

"And my name is Janet," she replies, without a flicker of a smile. We remain looking at each other in the hallway until, frankly, it becomes a bit awkward. It does not appear to cross Janet's mind to give Simon the name of his unexpected visitor. I bounce on the tips of my toes. There is a light bulb moment. "Downstairs, dear. Silly me. Head straight down to the basement. I gave him advance warning that you were coming; you never know what he might be up to down there now, do you?"

I brush away some cobwebs with one hand and clasp the stair rail with the other. I can just about make out the brick wall through the darkness as I continue my descent. The wooden steps audibly creak under my weight. I am relieved when my feet touch the bottom. There is light. I look around. My mouth opens. I don't know what I expected, but it wasn't this. Even my lowest expectation wasn't of something quite this weird.

The basement spans the length and breadth of the house. It is a bat cave. Lights flicker and fade on computer screens. Disbanded books lie on the concrete floor, UFO posters cover the walls. I spot a dartboard in the far corner. Breathing in, I 'm greeted by the odour of dirty socks and two-day old pizza.

A chair swivels around. My first thought is of the Timotei advert, the one where the beautiful young woman seductively flicks her long luscious hair to appreciative gasps from viewers in their homes. This young man sat in front of me, though, has greasy, straggly hair down to his waist. He adjusts his black, horn-rimmed square glasses and looks up at me. Takes a second look. Perversely, I suddenly feel important. The man springs out of his chair and walks soundlessly towards me, holding out his hand.

"Nice to meet you," he says, grinning. "It is kind of odd, you know? It feels like I already know you and yet we haven't actually met. It is kind of like having a best friend you only know from the internet. You know?"

I don't know, and so I'm not sure what to say. Instead, I nod my head and deliver a reassuring smile. After all, I'm an uninvited guest and, more importantly, it is in my interest to be on my best behaviour. Simon looks around for a chair that is not covered in clutter. This is mission impossible. Failing to find the desired chair, he settles for the one that has the least clutter and flings a pile of books onto the floor with one wild sweep of his hand.

"Mind the mess," he says. "I'm not used to guests in my dungeon, and so I probably don't keep it as tidy as I ought to. This place is hardly a hub of social activity, if you know what I mean?"

"You don't say."

"Would you like a drink?"

Sometimes I go black. Sometimes I have sugar. Sometimes, if I'm feeling particularly rebellious, I even have chocolate sprinklings on top. "A white coffee, no sugar, would be just grand."

Simon has long legs and suitably long strides, and he reaches the stairs in no time. He is keen to play the perfect host, I think. Stopping at the bottom of the stairs, he stretches his narrow body so that the blue veins in his neck are visible.

"Mum!" he shouts. "Can you please make a white coffee? Oh, and bring me an energy drink, please."

His mother groans from somewhere upstairs, somewhere in the house.

"Listen, I'm sorry to hear what happened to your mum, yeah?"

"That's okay," I reply. "And thank you."

"My dad is no longer with us, either," he says. "The circumstances surrounding that weren't good, either."

"Right."

"So...?"

"So...?"

He shifts on his seat. "It is obviously a privilege to have you visit my humble abode," he says, looking around at the dark, dismal surroundings and allowing himself a smile. I'm momentarily impressed by his self mockery. "This isn't purely a social visit, is it? Why are you here? What has happened...?"

I've asked myself these very questions over the last few days - repeatedly - and yet I still don't have a credible answer. But the simple answer is that I need help. I doubt that he can give any, but I'm running out of options. At the very least this guy should be *interested* in what I have to say.

"I would like your opinion on something."

"My proverbial door is always open."

"You're a writer, right?"

"I write books, yes. It still doesn't sound quite right to me when I say that I'm a writer, but I'll accept the compliment, for sure."

"You write books about serial killers?"

"I'm a true crime writer, incorporating serial killers."

"And you know who I am, yes?"

"Better than you can imagine. You're Marcus Clancy; formerly Jeffrey Allen. "

"Right. Well. The other day I was in the library, browsing through books about Spartacus. I was amazed how many books there are. This guy kills people. What can possibly be the fascination? *Anyway.* One book caught my attention. I looked at the back cover and it was your ugly mug. You're something of an expert, right?"

Simon theatrically fans his face. The guy (I think) has a sense of humour. Clearly, though, he is not used to this level of flattery. "Put it this way, if I ever appeared on

Mastermind, then serial killers would be my specialist subject. I don't know much about anything else really. Spartacus is easily my *favourite* serial killer. He's the one that really gets my blood racing."

I bow my head. "Thought so."

I remind myself that I know something about him, something about his theories on what happened, that he won't be aware of. I do this to give me some inner-strength. It somehow feels like it gives me the upper hand.

"I'm hoping you might be able to help with my current predicament."

I sense Simon leaning forward. We are linked in a conspiracy. I can smell his aftershave. It is surprisingly (and welcomingly) overpowering, like he has sprayed on too much to drown out all the other stale odours in his den. It must have taken copious sprays. Reminds me that Baldwin always smelt good. Simon whispers, "Is he back?"

I look up and notice that his eyes, under his glasses, are like saucers: large and round and expectant. I'm shocked by this question. "Why would you think that?"

Simon chuckles. His teeth are unexpectedly small, orderly and white. My first impression was of a crooked, yellow teeth kind of guy. He runs his hands through his long hair. "Oh, come on, Marcus. Why else would you be here...? You've been completely off the grid for thirty years. You've done everything you physically could do to remove yourself from your past life. And then one day - *today* - you appear in my den asking for a white coffee. Where on earth *is* that drink by the way? I'm prone to an afternoon dip if I don't get my energy drink." Simon gets up on his feet and stares at the ceiling, like a man might look to the heavens, but then he shakes his head and sits down again. I presume that, now he is on something of a roll, he has concluded that this is far more important. "Listen. My point is that you moved away, you changed your identity, you did everything you possibly could to get away from him, and now suddenly here you are, asking questions. Look at it from my perspective. Put yourself in my size tens for a moment. What *else* could possibly drive you to make that radical, crazy step...?"

I seize the opportunity. I don't want his professional opinion as an academic; I want his personal opinion, off the record. Some colour has risen to his chalky complexion. His emotions are running high; he is a kid visiting Disneyland, or an Apple store, for the first time. There is a decent chance he has lowered his guard. "So, you think he is still out there?"

Simon shrugs his narrow shoulders. "Why wouldn't he be? I see no reason why Spartacus shouldn't be a fit, healthy and functioning member of society. Sure, he could be in prison, but I think he is too clever to get caught. By all accounts, from the very little we know, and, to be blunt, most of that information has come from *you,* he was just a teenager when he went on his killing spree. Spartacus was probably eighteen or nineteen back in June 1988. The statements from Julie and Kate Phillips back this up, even though he *was* dressed as a bio-exorcist when they encountered him. And so, thirty years later, he is still only a guy in his late forties, the same as you."

"Middle-aged?" I say, smiling.

Again, Simon chuckles. "Hey, you said it, not me. What you *haven't* told me," he continues, rubbing his thighs with his hands, "is what exactly has happened that brings you here."

I held back with Reeves, of course. He wasn't taking me seriously, and so I didn't want him to know everything. This guy is different. I tell Simon about the lift, and about the library. This time, however, I tell him what he said about the thirty days. He listens intently, his eyes growing larger, like I'm shining a torch in his face.

Simon's mother, Janet, appears with the coffee. She sweeps her hand over a side table, not caring that papers fly everywhere. Simon gives her a vexed look. I thank her profusely, more than a little embarrassed by the situation. She nods her head at me, acknowledging my existence, face still frozen like she has been injecting Botox, and then disappears back upstairs without uttering a single word.

"Sorry about that," Simon says, though it isn't clear what exactly he's apologising for. "So, have you been to the police?"

I tell him about my meeting with Reeves. My words fade away before I get to the end. Simon glances around the room. He releases a dismissive grunt. It reminds me of one of the exercises I use in my workshops. I can tell he is waiting for me to get to the end, counting down the seconds, so I decide to get there quick.

"Have you told Baldwin?" he asks.

I pull my head back. Of course, he knows all about DCI Baldwin. His books are filled with candid observations and descriptions of the detective. Other writers failed to resist the temptation to depict him as a caricature, as the pantomime villain. Simon delved deeper than this. He considered the full circumstances at the time, the motives for what he did, for how he behaved.

"Why would I go to him?" I ask. "You know what happened last time. And he didn't solve it then, so what good would he be now?"

Simon blows out hot air. I sense disappointment. He thought I was serious; now he suspects I am hiding from the truth. I wonder just how much he does know. I wonder whether he knows everything. This terrifies me.

"Nobody could have solved it last time," he says. These

words are a relief. He has decided to not tell it how it is, decided not to get to the crux of the matter. "But you know he put his life and soul into catching him. He turned stones than should have been left untouched, but that was only because he was prepared to do anything to catch the monster. You know that." Simon glances away. I sense he is priming himself to say something. The dread returns; it wraps around my throat and strangles me. "And if you really *are* serious, then you'd forget what happened last time and speak to him anyway."

This is a test. The guy is challenging my masculinity, sizing up my balls. Right now they feel like I've been playing football in skimpy shorts in the freezing cold. I prickle with a mixture of simmering anger and respect. At least, I think, he is prepared to speak his mind. Truth be told, I'm not sure whether I can face DCI Baldwin yet, for reasons even this guy doesn't realise. Are my balls really big enough? For a brief moment, it crosses my mind that I'd come face to face with Spartacus before I'd dare face DCI Baldwin. This is ridiculous, though. DCI Baldwin (hopefully) wouldn't be carrying a cut-throat razor.

I do my best to deflect the challenge, to bat it away. "Do you think it is him?" I ask.

Simon tangles his hands together and cracks his knuckles. "Who knows?"

"But what is your professional opinion? Or even your personal one? Does this sound like something he'd do?"

"*That* - right there - is partly what fascinates me about Spartacus, more than any other killer I've studied. Sure, there are others who killed more, who were infinitely more gruesome, but then none of them made less sense, were more of a paradox. Serial killers usually fall into two categories. The disorganised killer is often a social outcast, driven by compulsion and need. They're usually of below average intelligence. They often fit the stereotypical weirdo or oddball tag. Organised killers, on the other hand, can be intelligent, respected members of society, the last person you'd expect to be a killer. Now, I've no doubt that Spartacus is an organised killer..."

"What's your point...?"

Simon stares dreamily into space, presumably creating an image in his mind, probably contemplating the wonderful complexity of Spartacus.

"Even organised killers have patterns. The supposedly complex ones are still driven by some underlying urge or motive. Their killings follow some sort of routine. Their motive may not be outwardly clear, but you can work it out, with research and a little head scratching. Spartacus, though; now he *is* different. The victims follow no pattern. There are couples, young girls, older women, a young guy. The locations are sporadic. It is almost like he has gone out of his way to avoid any pattern. The only thing that is consistent is how he cuts the victim, down the chest, in Roman numerals, to indicate what number victim they are. Unfortunately, you know about this, of course, even though you survived."

I nod my head. Feeling his eyes on my chest, like he is undressing me, I wonder about *his* urges. I need to move the conversation forward quickly before he asks me for a picture. "So, you're a leading expert on the subject. You *must* have an opinion. Why do you think Spartacus kills? Killing is *quite* a big deal. It isn't like deciding to collect Panini stickers for the World Cup. He *must* have a reason. Folk get angry that their football team is losing, and so they wash their car. Men find out that their girlfriend is sleeping with their brother, and so they beat their brother to a pulp and then drink themselves to oblivion. They don't go on a killing rampage. There must be something that drove Spartacus to do what he did..."

Simon shrugs his shoulders. I feel like killing him, right there and then, with my bare hands. Talking of motive, I have real motive, for sure - the lanky shit really *pissed* me off. But I am a guest. Simon regrets his shrug, I can tell, for he quickly continues to - or at least *tries* to - give some sort of explanation. "We know less about Spartacus than any other killer, with the exception - possibly - of Jack the Ripper. But

Jack had it easy. He was in the right place at the right time. There was no DNA, no cameras, an abundance of dimly lit alleyways, and most of London at the time had a drinking problem. But I digress. Most of what we know about Spartacus is merely speculation, based on circumstantial evidence, law of averages and, probably most significantly, common sense, or lack of it. I suspect the Roman numerals tell us more about his motives than anything..."

I have an urge to rub my hand over my chest, along the outline of my scars, my dark secret. It itches. I resist the temptation to scratch. "What are the Roman numerals about?" I ask. "Surely it is for show? He only killed six people. It can't be that difficult to keep count, can it?"

Simon smirks. I wish he wouldn't. His eyes penetrate into the hollows of my own eyes. I wonder what he sees. "Have you ever been a bit of a stud, Marcus?" he asks. "Slept around a bit?"

"What the fuck is *wrong* with you?"

Simon holds his hands up in protest. "Let me explain. I think, for Spartacus, it might merely be notches on his bed post. The ultimate sign of disrespect. His way of saying that I've killed somebody - but you know what - it didn't really mean anything. Just another number. He is trivialising the murders. Just a bit of fun..."

"Just a bit of *fun*? He killed innocent people, most with

their whole lives ahead of them. How can it just be *fun*?"

"I know. I know. Don't shoot the messenger. It is just my theory. But that is what - for me - makes Spartacus more terrifying than any killer. If what drives him is excitement - if it really is just a big game - then just how dangerous does *that* make him...?"

I want to wipe the excited smile from his face. I shake my head to show him that I'm not convinced. Really, though, I've never been so convinced by anything my whole life. If Simon were to tell me right now that the world was flat, that if I kept walking and walking then eventually I'd drop over the edge and into an abyss, then I'd make damn sure I walked on the spot, or maybe in a circle. Now, I doubt I really knew Spartacus at all. I thought I was morbidly obsessed at the time of the killings, but this is *real* obsession. My fingers twitch. I have no idea what is going to happen to me. I do know, however, that it is going to be much worse than what happened last time, and I never even thought that was possible.

"So why did he suddenly stop killing?"

"Possibly because he got bored. The eighth ride of the roller coaster will never be as exciting as the first. Maybe he'd completed the challenge? No longer gave him the buzz he sought? On the other hand, maybe you were the game changer? It is quite possible - and perfectly logical - that nearly getting caught made him rethink this whole adventure of his."

I look away. I'm getting answers, much more than I've had before, and so I'm keen to keep asking questions. "If it is him, then what has he been doing all this time? How could he disappear off the face of the earth and then suddenly reappear thirty years later?"

"He's probably capable of doing whatever he wants to do. The most logical answer is that he's been doing whatever he chose to do. That could be something, or it could be nothing. I very much doubt that he is driven in any way by what others expect of him. He might fit perfectly into society, but probably only to deflect suspicion. And so, he could have been doing absolutely anything..."

"That's kind of general," I reply, trying to keep my voice level. "If he is back, then why? And why now? It has been thirty years, for God's sake!"

"We don't know he's back, though, do we? As far as we're aware, even if it is him, he hasn't killed anybody, has he? Yet. He's only been playing with you. And he's already had ample opportunity to kill you. You'd be dead now if he wanted you dead, we both know that." His eyes flicker. He is contemplating whether to add any more. "Unless..."

"Unless?"

"Unless he is bored of the way he killed people before. It

just isn't exciting enough. Unless he wants to do things differently. Make the game more interesting: add new dimensions. Now, the dates he made contact are interesting, aren't they? There actually *is* a pattern there. If I were a betting man - and I'm not - then I would wager that he wants to do things differently, really savour the experience and take his time. It sounds like he has already set a date..."

30th June.

I sense Spartacus is totally in control of everything that happens from here. I am a cartoon character and he is the cartoonist. Maybe he has already sketched how it will play out? Maybe he could use an eraser and start again? Maybe he is waiting to see what move I make next before deciding?

"How can I beat him?"

Simon looks at me like I'm joking. "However clever you think you are, he is much, much cleverer. You can't do it yourself. You need help. And you need to decide your game plan. Are you going to run? Are you going to hide? Or are you going to set a trap...?"

Simon has toppled me from my chair and now he is kicking me when I'm down. I decide to take flight of our little meeting. There is no good news. I can't take any more. Spartacus had better get to me quick before I jump from London Bridge.

I shake Simon's reluctant hand and thank him for his

time, tell him to thank his mother for her kind hospitality. Clearly, he is distraught that I'm leaving. I'm one of his projects, and ideally he'd like to stick me in a jar so he can prod and experiment on me.

Simon starts talking again just as I reach the stairs. "There is one thing that has troubled me more than any other," he says. I stop to wait for him to continue. He takes his time. The guy starts picking his nails. I feel like I'm sat in the cinema waiting for the credits to finish just in case there might be an extra scene. "I still don't know why he didn't manage to finish you off the first time..."

I walk up the stairs, much colder and narrower than on the way down. I need to get out of here quick.

DAY THIRTEEN
13TH JUNE 2018

This isn't the sort of establishment I usually frequent. It isn't the sort of place I usually spend my money.

It is unexpectedly busy, mainly with lone wolves perched on high stools, gazing out of the window and, presumably, people-watching. Don't people work anymore? There are forecasts of doom and gloom ahead, but two years after the Brexit vote more and more people are in work, so how come so many are idling with me in this coffee shop in the middle of the day?

I'm reminded of when Emma was a toddler; we were social butterflies on the cafe scene back then. Not fancy places like this, more out of principle than the expense, but anywhere that sold a cheap tea and an orange or blackcurrant. Mainly on the weekends, when I gave Jenny some much-deserved time to herself. It wasn't that I craved lukewarm tea from a polystyrene cup, it was just that Emma was so much better behaved when we were in public that I sometimes couldn't wait to get out of the house, break up the day. We'd sit on opposite sides of the table and just talk.

"What do you call a spider with six legs?" Emma asked, when she was probably about five.

"I don't know. What *do* you call a spider with six legs?"

"A six-legged spider."

"Makes sense."

Jokes (or at least that's what I thought this was) were wonderful, but I had a responsibility to enquire about her education and understanding of the world (didn't I?).

"So, do you know who Jesus is?"

I recall that Emma crinkled her nose and looked to the ceiling. "Yes, I do. Jesus died."

"That's right-"

"But I don't think he really died..."

"No? What really happened to Jesus?"

"I think he's in prison..."

Another time, Emma excitedly told me about a man who was bringing animals into the school for the children to observe. "Do you think he'll bring a tiger, Dad?"

"Too scary. I don't think he'll be allowed to bring any animal that might eat the children," I said, logically.

"How about a giraffe?"

"Too big. He won't be able to fit one in his van."

"Well, I know he won't bring any dinosaurs, because the dinosaurs are all dead."

I nodded my head, impressed.

"Plus, they're way too big and scary."

By then, I'd already stopped reading those books on parenting from the library. I realised you didn't need any instruction manuals. You just had to talk and, most importantly, listen.

Waiting in turn now like a good little boy at the school canteen, I then order two coffees. The young girl behind the counter asks for my name. Oh, I think, *this* is nice.

"It is Marcus," I reply. "And thank you for asking. People just don't *talk* enough these days, don't you think? Everyone is always so busy, busy, busy. So, what is *your* name?"

The young girl looks at me blankly. Her face gives away little, but if anything, she shows a torrid mix of concern and disgust. I glance down at my fly to make sure nothing is hanging out. At least she isn't laughing. Still looking at me, the girl writes my name on a cardboard cup. It crosses my mind that I should apologise for my outrageous mistake, that maybe I should leave a tip for any offence I might have caused, but thankfully, it is just a fleeting thought.

I pay the money, wait for the coffee and leave the shop as quickly as I can, with a whole lot less coinage jingling in my pocket than when I walked *into* the shop.

I walk at pace, for it is crucial I reach my destination before the coffees go cold. I'm aware that there is a trend for cold coffees, but I'm old-fashioned (and maybe just *old*); surely the whole point of a coffee is that it's a hot beverage? The plastic lids are wet from the overflowing drink; the warm fluid trickles down the sides of the cups. My pace is a careful balancing act, for there is no point getting to my destination quickly if there is no coffee left in the cups. Nobody is around as I enter the underpass. I have a familiar thought, deja vu: I realise that *anybody* could be lurking on the other side, ready to pounce, possibly to kill. Both my hands are full. What am I going to do - throw the coffee into his face? I dismiss the whole scenario as fantasy. Anybody else but him could be waiting on the other side, or maybe following close behind me. That just wouldn't be his style at all. It is far too simple, no fun at all. And from what Simon said, Spartacus wants to play games.

I glance around the dimly lit car park. The pillars are wide and high and, again, a fantastic hiding place. Maybe I do just have a stalker, a nutcase who is playing with my mind? Thinking back to my little chat with Simon, Jack the Ripper would have a fantastic time in this place. The relief that nobody appears to be lurking is replaced with disappointment that I seem to be on my own. This is supposed to be a coffee date for two, not one; after all, that is why I hold a coffee in both hands. I curse my stupidity. My compulsive ideas are not always thought through properly. Erica loves my spontaneity, whether it comes to something or not; sometimes, though, I let it spill into the rest of my life. Why *would* he be here? He doesn't work twenty-four hours a day, does he? I have no idea what hours he works. I don't know him at all. It is just that I only ever envisage him here, that is all.

Ah well. In the grand scheme of things, it is no big deal. It is not the end of the world. Not yet. I consider that I will just have to find a bench and drink *both* coffees. Why not? That might be sweet. Or maybe I could still rescue one of the coffees, give it to some lost soul walking the streets with nowhere to go? After all, that could be me one day. It has already been me on a previous day.

Then I spot him, heading down the slope and into the car park, coming from the direction of the supermarket.

"Ken," I say, holding out one of the cups.

I have an active imagination and (until recently, when I've increasingly come to believe that a notorious serial killer is planning to murder me) it is unrealistically positive, bordering on the fantastical. In my idle daydream, as I walked from the coffee shop and through the underpass, I imagined Ken graciously thanking me for the wonderfully thoughtful gift with warm, open arms, excitedly telling me that the only thing missing in his life was a (now lukewarm, despite my best efforts) cup of coffee. In reality, Ken stares at me with narrow, accusing eyes. I try to read the blankness of his hollows, the horizontal lines in his cheeks. I sense he is irritated that I have dared to disturb him from his job.

"What is it?" Ken mumbles, his eyes moving from me to the coffee and then back to me again.

I consider telling him what coffee is, maybe some trivia about its origins but, as is often the case, decide against it. "I was just passing and I thought you might fancy a cup of coffee, Ken. Don't worry; I have a couple of sugars in my pocket because I don't know how you take it."

Still, the coffee remains in my hand. I take a sip from my own cup, possibly from nerves, potentially to show that it is not poisoned. Appreciatively, I nod my head, despite thinking that it could really do with thirty seconds in the microwave. My mind is so scrambled that I'm not sure what I'm thinking. I'm a nervous student on one of my workshops.

"You were just passing with two cups of coffee?"

I realise that this is a reasonable question. It does feel, however, that I'm unnecessarily justifying dipping my hands into my pockets and purchasing him a coffee. The money is not the issue here; I have more money than I know what to do with, though I don't tell anybody that. It is the principle. It is not like I'm trying to sell him life insurance. "Sometimes one just isn't enough, you know? So, I bought a second, just in case. Today, though, one is definitely enough and so, as I just happened to be passing, this one is for you..."

Ken growls. "You have more money than sense," he says. His face flickers with a smile. "Ta. Kind of you. I've just come from my break, though. I'll have to drink it quick, before they think I'm taking the piss."

Ken takes a sip of coffee and then nods his head. He taps his toes on the tarmac. I don't think he is used to standing around chewing the fat. Bending over, he picks up a packet of crisps and a coke can from the floor and pulls out a white polythene bag from his pocket. I'm just glad that he is wearing gloves.

"Don't they give you equipment to pick up the litter, Ken? At your age, you'll get a bad back."

He glances at me as if to say that I'm no spring chicken, either, you cheeky git. "They don't, because it isn't my job to pick up the mess people leave. I do it because I like to keep the place looking nice. This gaff is my second home, isn't it, and I clean up my home, don't I? My job is to collect the trolleys, but this is my place, and I like it to look nice."

I nod my head. I get that. It is surprising, though, because Ken doesn't look too clean and tidy himself. He is lucky, because he still has thick dark hair, yet he appears to do nothing to look after it, for it is full of tufts that flow in no particular direction. There is a dark patch on his forehead the shape of Australia. His cheeks are lighter than the rest of his face. The guy would benefit from a good hose down. I decide, for good reason, not to pursue this line of conversation.

Our inactive and stunted conversation becomes even more inactive and stunted by the unexpected appearance of an old woman on a mobility scooter. I have no idea what the speed limit is, but whatever it is, she appears to be exceeding it. Her purple hair is in rollers. Her face lights up when she sees Ken. Already, I like the woman.

"Kenneth!" she shouts. "Working hard, I see." She glances down at the coffee and then winks. "I can't stop. I have a date. And I see you have company. I'm quite sure I can't compete with this handsome young man, even if you are straight. But I will see you tomorrow and we will have a proper chat. You hear?"

"I hear," Ken says. His wave is to her retreating back.

Clearly, Ken is part of this woman's life. He is possibly not as isolated as I imagined. I warm to him.

"So, Ken," I begin, clearing my throat, "I was just wondering whether you've had any more trouble off those lads from the other day? No more grief, I hope?"

The spark disappears from Ken's eyes. He takes another gulp of his drink. He looks away. I follow his gaze, almost expecting something to be there. "Not those boys, no. And thank you for that, by the way."

I look closely at him for more clues. His face remains a mask. "There are others?"

He nods his head. "There are always others." He turns to me now, his eyes almost pleading. Even the whites are grey and cloudy. "All I want to do is put the trolleys away and keep the place looking nice." He looks up to the heavens, even though we are under cover. "Is that too much to ask?"

I assure him that it isn't. It isn't right. "Any trouble in particular?"

"Trouble is always there, on and off. I can go for days without any bother, and then the next day it can feel like all I'm doing is brushing them off. Can't actually say I've had any for days. But somehow it feels worse than ever..."

"What do you mean?"

Ken crushes the empty cup in his hand and puts it in his polythene bag. "Think I'm going mad. Feels like somebody is watching me. Must be paranoid. Who would waste their time watching me? Dull as dishwater I am."

I assure him that he isn't paranoid, then I assure him that nobody is watching him. I expect him to query that he must be one or the other, but he doesn't. Keen to move things along, I pull my card from my pocket. It is faded and creased and just a little pathetic. Patrick Bateman would *not* be impressed. Ken stares at the words. Can he read?

"You want me to go on one of your workshops?" he asks. "What the fuck for? You trying to better me? I'm happy doing what I'm doing."

"No, no," I say, talking hurriedly. "The card has my telephone number on it. You give me a call if you get any more trouble..."

Ken fixes me a stare. It is much more intimidating than any given to me in the boardroom. "Why?"

This - again - is a reasonable question. Again, I don't really have a reasonable answer. "Why not?"

Ken pauses and then nods his head. Uncertain. I shake his hand and then go on my way. Maybe I am content that I have done my good deed for the day. This is what Mum would have done.

Ken calls after me. "Oh. And thank you..."

I tell him that it really is no problem at all, none whatsoever.

DAY FOURTEEN
14TH JUNE 2018

They say once is unlucky, twice is careless.

I won't be tricked a second time. Something reassures me
- maybe it is a voice, only this time it is the virtuous one, the
one that is on my side - that it is alright, that although it feels
*fa*r from alright, it i*s*, because none of this is real. Is Richard
speaking to me? Whatever, it is a protective shield, and
because I am protected, I know that however bad the shit
goes down, I'll be alright. This time I know I'm dreaming.
None of this is real. It is just a...

He is on the boat again. My boat. *Our* boat. Me. Erica.
Him. His movements are slow. He doesn't want to move
quickly - that would be too simple. Simon said he craves
excitement, didn't he? *Simon says*. Spartacus wants to torture
me. He wants to kill me slowly, to leisurely suck the life out
of me merely for his own sadistic thrill.

I want to spring out of bed, to stand up and fight him
but, just like the last time, I can't. My ankles are tied together
with shroud-laid rope. I try to kick, but somebody is sitting
on my knees, applying their full bodyweight. I am a bird that

has fallen from his perch and landed on the bottom of the cage. My body is laden with an almighty weight. I am too heavy, but the excess weight has not translated into strength, for not only am I too heavy, but I am too weak, too.

But it is fine, because I won't be tricked again. I have a protective shield, and none of this is real. It is all just a dream.

He moves closer. He moves agonizingly slowly, but he *does* move, nevertheless. He will get to me in the end, whether it is today or tomorrow or just some day in the distant future, he will get to me.

His outline is getting larger. Stops walking. Stands over me. He is taller, more formidable, than even I remember. He raises his hands. Above his head. He is holding something.

He lowers his hands and, just as he is about to plunge the razor into me, just as he is about to kill me, the rope is released, and I am freed. I sit up, like a mummy rising from a tomb, and lunge madly with my fists. My punches go nowhere near him, for he casually takes a step back, just watches me.

After all, this is not real. This is all just a dream. I *have* been tricked twice but, I try to reassure myself, not *really*.

Smiling from the uppermost corner of his mouth, his look is one of pity. That look is familiar. I cannot hurt him, for he is not really there. Lowers his arms. Even though he is not real, I *still* expect him to plunge the razor into my chest. I feel nothing. He doesn't want to kill me. Not yet. Not this painlessly. Killing me in my bed, in my sleep, would be no fun now, would it? Instead, he plunges the razor into the mattress, just inches from my body, most likely tearing the bed sheet.

His outline becomes smaller. And then, he is gone. Back the way he came.

I don't know how much time passes before I wake, but when I do, it feels like hands are strangling my windpipe, for I can barely breathe. My whole body is drenched in sweat, stinging my half-opened eyes, causing me to blink. Shapes and colours make up the room, and they move around, just won't stay still, not for a single fucking moment.

I turn to Erica. She is there, lying in the bed next to me, cheek resting against the plump, fluffy pillow. My wet, sticky hand grazes the curve of her back. Her body peacefully rises and falls. She is asleep. Completely unaware. Thank God. I haven't hurt her this time, not spilt blood. Planting a kiss on her forehead, she responds with a purr, a helicopter taking off. Turning away, I lie on my back. My head sinks into the comfort of the pillow as I stare up to the ceiling. The warmth from the cabin begins to dry my damp, salty skin, and yet still, there is a refreshing breeze blowing through the door.

There is a vibration: a muted, stifled buzz. What was that? Where did it come from? I sit up. It came from the edge of the bed, by my feet. It sounded like a mobile phone. Pushing my hand underneath my pillow, I take hold of my phone. I move more carefully now. My hand slides under Erica's pillow. She stirs, but remains asleep. My hand grazes her phone.

I scramble to the bottom of the bed on my hands and knees, just like I did when I was a kid, racing against my older brother in his bed (he always won). Erica's purr grows louder. Usually, this would excite me. Now, it frightens me. I slow down my movements, make them more deliberate and composed, as the flat of my hands explore the bed sheets.

There *is* something there. At the bottom of the bed. I pick it up. It *is* a phone. But not mine. Not Erica's. I click on the phone; the screen lights up.

You have a nice home, Jeffrey. I do so enjoy popping by for a visit. Let us keep in touch on this phone from now on. It has been too long. Sorry to have disturbed you tonight. We're coming up to the halfway point of the month. Enjoy the rest of your night.

DAY FIFTEEN
15TH JUNE 2018

This is what normal life is supposed to be like, I think. This is the sort of place decent, honest, salt-of-the-earth people go to for recreation. It is a good, clean, honest family venue, the sort of establishment that society expects you to go to.

I can't remember the last time I was in a place like this, and it feels like these decent, honest, salt-of-the-earth-people are looking at me, that they are privy to my secrets, they know I don't belong here, that they have a charlatan in their midst.

The video games have developed beyond all recognition since my days. We'd cross the bridge into town in our school uniforms and then play Space Invaders and Pac Man in tiny, darkened rooms, buttons greasy from the chips we'd hurriedly eaten on the pavements outside. We huddled around the machines in packs of three or four, twenty pence coins (dinner money) disappearing at an alarming rate within the slots. For many of us, on the weekends it was either here, the snooker halls or our bedrooms. Steve Davis could either have become World Snooker Champion, or just really fantastic at Donkey Kong. I, on the other hand, remain shit at snooker, but I always saved Pauline.

Now everything is fresh, bright, wholesome and expensive. The flashing lights and occasional, exuberant noises, though, are a familiar reminder of a misspent youth. The arcade is just a side attraction, something to keep you occupied, keep you slotting those pound coins, help pay the rent. The real, committed hardcore gamers have red eyes and white skin because they live in their bedrooms. This is for amateurs, weekenders. You are not supposed to come here just to play video games; but please feel free to spend as much money on them as you can whilst you are here. Luckily, money doesn't serve much purpose for me.

Jenny sips weak coffee from a cardboard cup. Pulling a face, she pushes the cup away, apparently surprised that the coffee is lukewarm, even though I bought it for her over twenty minutes ago. The young guy behind the bar in a black waistcoat and white shirt *didn't* ask for my name, thank God. Jenny leans forward, her elbows digging into the plastic table, her chin cupped in her hands. Holding my gaze, she inquisitively raises her eyebrows. Straight lines appear on her forehead. I remember the photograph that was pride and place in our living room in Clapham for so many years when she was Mrs Jenny Clancy; we were a magazine depiction of the perfect, married couple. Looking at her now, I think that she really hasn't changed much, even though so many years have passed and nearly everything else *has* changed.

Usually, I'm barely even aware of my phone. Sometimes I leave it in the boat when I'm out all day. Now, though, I'm a teenager, fraught with worry that I may – God forbid - have misplaced it. Only now, since last night, there are two phones. My usual phone, which is blue, is in my left pocket. My new phone, the important one, is red, and this is in my right pocket. Suddenly, I am a married man with a mistress.

I glance around, aware of the look Jenny has given me and knowing exactly what it means. We were married for so long. Really, we should *still* be married, we both know that. The barman in the black waistcoat busies himself by slowly and meticulously updating the blackboard behind the bar with white chalk. An old lady with a Tesco bag hanging from the handles of her mobility scooter zooms from one game to another. I'm reminded of Ken and his lady friend, wonder whether he is working today, curious if he's had any more trouble from unidentified sources. I smile at a young mother, standing over a young toddler at her feet. She smiles back and I notice the wetness of her lips, the possible undertone of the look.

"Daddy, I scored a 92!"

There is a tinge of guilt as I feel the weight of my daughter on my thigh. I don't even think I would have a blue phone were it not for Emma. The rest of the room disappears as I remember the first time I set eyes on her, twelve years ago. Emma was a pink, bloody bundle with a dome-shaped head like a member of the Ku Klux Klan, and yet I stared at her, amazed that this beautiful little girl could possibly have anything to do with me. Now I'm amazed she is so tall, that she is so delightful, that she possibly has anything to do with me. I often don't absorb the words she says because my mind is fascinated by her very being. I recall what she tells me, but I am unsure what it really means.

"Is that good?"

Emma's face opens into mock frustration. She turns to her mum, who shakes her head, sharing her agony. Emma slaps her palm against her forehead. There is plenty to slap, to be honest, for her long, blonde hair is clawed back into a ponytail. Jenny chuckles, just as she used to when she was my wife, when we were happy.

"Well, it might not be a great score for say Liz Johnson..."

"Who?"

Emma turns back to her mum for support. Jenny shakes her head again, although it is clear to both of us she doesn't have a clue who Liz Johnson is either.

"Just one of the best female bowlers ever, that's all!"

"So not as good as the men, then...?"

Emma playfully punches my shoulder. Her playful

punches are much harder than I remember. I'm sure she must be the tallest girl in her class. "You've just explained that 92 is a good score - for *you* - and so now I'm *extremely* impressed and *massively* proud. Maybe we can forget school and those awful exams and just focus on a career in bowls instead? At the *very* least, it justifies the £4.90 I spent for you to play..."

Emma makes a sign with her fingers which, I hope, indicated I was a cheapskate, although, to be fair, it does look very much like the letter 'L'. Jenny waves a hand in front of my eyes. I am in a trance, again, gazing open-mouthed at our daughter.

"Daddy, what did the floor say to the door?"

She still tells me a joke, every time we meet. It is kind of a thing we have going.

"I don't know. What did the floor say to the door?"

"I can see your knob."

Wow, I think, as Emma puts her hand to her mouth, these jokes certainly have progressed with the passing years.

"So how is that boyfriend of yours?" I ask, grinning. "Jack, is it? You need to tell me if he is not treating you right, and I'll have that quiet fatherly word in his ear. I've always wanted to do that. Just like in the movies. Just give me the sign, Emma."

Emma slaps my chest. My right leg has gone numb. She

really is getting big. Every time I mention this to Jenny - express my amazement that our daughter has grown - she reassures me that this is what children do, that it is perfectly normal for them to grow. "Jack isn't my *boyfriend*. I'm much too young to settle down with a boy, Dad, and have far too much life to enjoy first. And besides, Jack is the biggest boy in our class. He probably wouldn't be scared by your quiet word in his ear. He is nearly as tall as you are, and much younger and fitter, of course."

I ask myself if this girl really is still only twelve, or if I've absent-mindedly missed a few years. Jenny laughs. I join in. Emma jumps to her feet. "You gave me enough money for a second game," she informs me. I think that I should have checked how much a game was before freely giving away my money. Of course, I'm not really a cheapskate, I just don't give a damn about money, and I play up to it. She skips off.

Jenny puts her face back into the clutches of her hands. I have delayed her for long enough. I can't put her off any longer. "You didn't message or phone her. She was missing her daddy. You've always been her favourite; we both know that."

Jenny always says this, and it is always in jest. I don't protest, because I know she'll only reply with a list of reasons why I'm Emma's favourite.

It wasn't supposed to end like this, of course. I wasn't

supposed to be the dad who met his daughter for a few hours at the bowling complex, who bought her presents and treated her to fizzy drinks and popcorn before she returned to her real life with her mother. I detested those fathers. Being a daddy was about getting up in the middle of the night to comfort my girl when she was ill or upset. It was not about presents and trips out. All that shit was just compensation for abandoning the kid, merely a token gesture to say sorry. I'm aware that I'm a contradiction, that I'm a hypocrite. It grates me, but not enough to hide my true feelings. Not this time. I actually wanted to be that glossy magazine image of a perfect family, settling down together on the sofa to watch television. I loved my wife and beautiful daughter more than anything else in the world, to the point I didn't even contemplate any other life. Of course, I *still* love them. If I could turn back time and change events then I'd still be living that life. However, this is not a productive thought process; Richard would remind me to have the courage to accept the things I cannot change. I am not religious, but I agree with Richard on this point: the serenity prayer has always been – I don't know – *logical* to me.

"It was only a few days," I say. I know this isn't good enough, and I know it isn't normal, either. "I'm sorry. You know I've missed her, too. There has been a hell of a lot going on, that's all. June so far has been utter madness."

Jenny reaches across the table and squeezes my hand. She knows I'm not telling her everything. She knows why.

"June?"

I look away, so she continues talking. "I know you're distracted. You're going to strain that neck of yours the way you've been looking around everywhere, at everything but at me. This place really *isn't* that interesting, you know, and especially not for you. What is it? I just know it *can't* be work, not any more. Pretty sure you're not contemplating Robbie Williams' performance at the opening ceremony last night, either. Or how well Meghan seems to be getting along with the Queen. Wasn't like that with Diana now, was it? So, how is Erica? I really can't believe how gorgeous that girl is. You truly are a very lucky man, Marcus. I just wish she liked me a bit more..."

The curl on Jenny's lips indicates mischief. I'm not going to open that Pandora's box today. I say nothing and then turn away, again.

"There isn't trouble in Paradise, is there?" she asks, barely able to conceal her excitement at some possible gossip.

"No," I say. "It isn't that. We're better than we've ever been." I stop there. I don't want to go into specifics about my wonderful relationship with Erica. I am not deliberately cruel. Jenny is still single, or at least she was the last time I asked. I know that I shouldn't really feel guilty, that it was her that fucked everything up, that it was her who threw everything away; and for what? Some crazy little *fling*.

I still don't understand it. I have looked at it from every angle and discussed it relentlessly with Richard, but it still makes no sense. I forced myself not to be obsessive, not to be possessive. Jealousy was part of the problem when I was a teenager, comparing myself adversely to others. Sure, I wanted to protect Jenny like she was a precious jewel, but my conscience told me that was not the right thing to do. Over time, it became natural to be trusting. It became logical to be trusting. We had a beautiful life. Why would Jenny possibly risk everything that we had? It made no sense.

"What is it then?" Jenny asks. My face probably gives it away, for she quickly glances around. She knows my mind has drifted, that she has lost me to a dark place.

I did not even pick up on any signs. I was the idiot, delusional husband. Jenny had her own life outside of me and Emma, and so in my mind I had no reason to question where she was and who she was with. It was almost exactly five years ago. The three of us at Tooting Bec park. Jenny had packed a picnic and I laid a blanket on the bumpy, hard ground. Jenny wore red shorts to her knees and a green tee-shirt that exposed her sinewy arms. Saturday morning sunlight pushed through the gaps in the trees. My memory is of Emma laughing; she's always had a delightful, contagious cackle. A bee hovered threateningly around our food. Emma was not scared. She was not up on her feet, running away. Far from it. She found my inept efforts to catch the bee hilarious. Emma rolled around on the floor with her legs up in the air, her feet kicking like she was riding a bike.

Looking back, I'm convinced it was the pure perfection of the moment that pushed Jenny to the edge. She looked around at the beautiful scene, and was overcome with guilt. She couldn't live the lie. I recall wondering - with mere idle curiosity - what she was up to when she leaned forward at the waist and knelt down. Her knees were red from rubbing against the sharp grass. It took me a few moments to realise she was getting to her feet. She didn't say anything as she walked away, her arms held tight to her chest. I reached for Emma's hand and we struggled to catch up. Leaving all of our belongings behind, we caught up with Jenny just outside the entrance to the lido.

"What's the matter?" I asked, genuinely concerned.

Jenny kept trying to turn away, to turn so her back was to me. It felt like a game. We both kept spinning around in a circle. I held her around the waist, and it was only when she stopped moving that I realised her face was blotchy and wet.

"What is it?"

"I can't do this," she said. Her eyes stared at me so intently it felt like she could see through me and read my thoughts.

I kissed the tip of her nose. "We don't have to. We can just go home. We don't have to have a picnic today."

I don't know why I said that. Surely, I knew that she wasn't talking about the picnic? Why would she be so upset about a damn picnic? I think I must have known, even at that point, that I was trying to hide away from reality.

"Not this," she said, holding open her hands to our idyllic surroundings. "*This*," she continued. Her hands pointed at me now. "I love you, Marcus. You need to believe me. I love you with all my life. But I have been seeing somebody else, and I can't keep doing this to you."

I still remember exactly how I felt at that moment. I felt like pleading with her that she *could* do this to me, that I would sacrifice anything so long as I could spend my every moment with her and Emma. Instead, I walked away without uttering a word. I don't know whether Jenny tried to chase after me; I do know she never caught up.

It was only late that night that Jenny found me. I sat in the conservatory, drinking sparkling white wine, morphing uncharacteristically into the angry drunk, just waiting for her. I heard her putting Emma to bed, reading her a bedtime story. It was always *me* who read Emma a bedtime story. Daddy. I'm not sure how long Jenny sat opposite me without saying anything. I just sensed her there, huddled in a quiet ball, her knees pressed against her chest.

"Who is he?"

Her voice was meek and broken. "Does it matter who he is?" she replied. I know that she didn't mean to be cruel, to be heartless, that it was a genuine question. I sensed that she regretted the words as soon as they escaped her lips, that she would reel them back in if she could. But it *did* matter. I wanted to know what man could cast a spell so powerful on the woman I loved that she would be prepared to give up this wonderful life.

"I think I deserve to at least know who he is, don't you?"

She frantically nodded her head, trying to backtrack. "He is a doctor."

That was all she said about him at the time, but it was enough. He was my intellectual superior; he was the greater man. I tended not to fear men because of their physical strength; I was intimidated by intellect. I always feared I'd be embarrassed, exposed as a fraud. Again, it was what Richard would call distorted thinking. What mattered was that Jenny was having an affair, not who she was having an affair with.

Jenny told me more over time, over the next few days and weeks, as I began to see things clearer. We didn't discuss me moving out - it was just assumed that I would, even though she was the cheat, the fraud. I did more than move out - I quit my job, too. I moved into an apartment first before deciding that, now I was on a roll, I may as well completely transform my life. Transform was one word for it - completely fuck it up might have been a more apt description. On a whim, I purchased a long boat and made that my home. And so, for the short term at least, not only did I not have a job, but I didn't have a home that stayed in the same place for long, either.

That was five years ago, though, and of course, things have moved on since then. Jenny has already said sorry a million and one times. There is really no need to bring it all up again, not at a bowling complex in the middle of the day, not when there are so many other things I should really be worried about.

Jenny turns back to me. She knows that this isn't the catalyst, that this isn't the reason I am so distant, that there must be something else troubling me. "Marcus," she says, "whatever it is, it sounds serious."

I say nothing. My silence speaks volumes. They say that a picture can paint a thousand words. My face probably reveals a lifetime of woe.

"Has he come back?"

This is what I wanted. I knew that, if I didn't say anything, she would work it out. Jenny knows me better than any living person.

"In a way. But I'm doing my best not to let him in. I'm

working on it with Richard. It isn't as bad as it sounds; nothing ever is. There will always be challenges, you know that. Richard assures me that it isn't a sign of a relapse, that it is just a glitch. You know the method Richard uses with me."

Jenny nods her head. The way she holds my gaze unsettles me. She isn't convinced. "You know I think Richard is fantastic. I know how much he has done to help you keep on the straight and narrow, to live a relatively normal existence. But even Richard is human. He can't be right about absolutely everything, can he? I just think that sometimes you should keep an open mind. Maybe sometimes you shouldn't take everything he says as gospel."

"That I should think for myself?"

The way she arches her body back aptly indicates that I've put her on the back foot. I didn't mean to do that. Or did I? "Don't be a prick about it," she says, smiling. "I know you're perfectly capable of thinking for yourself, Marcus. You know as well as I do what an awkward, pretentious little shit you can be. I just mean exactly what I said. Don't assume that Richard is right about absolutely everything..."

I grimace. I just don't want to admit she is right. Richard is the one lifeline I hold on to for dear life. If I doubt Richard then I doubt everything, and where does that leave me? I nod my head to show I've taken what she said on board. There is no commitment to do anything about it, though. My wandering eyes locate Emma, right in the middle of the multitude of bowling lanes. Emma hasn't changed much; she has just grown up. She has always been a fantastic bundle of energy. Emma stands with her hands on her hips as she follows the ball's slow but definite descent down the aisle. My baby girl is frozen stiff waiting to see what happens, like she is playing musical statues. Even I feel some angst from the comfort of my chair as the ball trickles closer to the skittles, or whatever it is they call them these days. I sigh with relief as the ball clatters against the skittles and each and every one of them disappears. Emma bends at the knees and jumps, pumping her fist in the air.

Jenny catches me watching Emma, and she smiles. "Sometimes it takes it out of you without you even realising, you know?" she says. "You look exhausted, sweetheart. You need a break from it all. Take a holiday. You could even head back to..."

I give her a startled look. I know where she means. We just don't speak about it, even though it is always there, consuming us both.

"Maybe you're right," I say. I decide against listing the endless list of reasons why she might be wrong, too.

Glancing at Jenny, I notice her wide eyes. Wasn't she the one who suggested it? Clearly, she wasn't expecting me to agree with her. She is shocked I didn't put up a fight, show resistance. Jenny knows how long it has been since I've been there. She knows that normally it just isn't an option. She knows that it is the absolute last resort. Similarly, she must realise now just how bad things are, that they must be much worse than even she feared.

Looking up, my eyes automatically wander. My ability to focus has abandoned me. Distraction. It is a fundamental technique I use with Richard. Only, now I suspect my use is unhealthy. I use it as a method to avoid the awful reality of life.

I blink, startled. Was that...? Here? No, it *couldn't* be. Not with my family around. My little girl. How would he know? I rise to my feet, but my hands remain fixed to the table. I close my eyes for a moment, regain my chain of thoughts.

Jenny tugs at my tee-shirt. "Darling, I think you definitely need that break. Don't you?"

I return to my seat. In the background, I hear the clatter of skittles and the familiar sound of Emma celebrating another strike.

DAY SIXTEEN
16TH JUNE 1988

Her eyes fix on nothing in particular, just stare absent-mindedly at the beer-stained carpet, marvel at the multitude of rips and tears on the flimsy fabric. A pair of black shoes appear in her line of sight. Her eyes rise to the legs. They are lean and long. The jeans are blue and fashionable. Shifting over to allow the strong frame to sit down next to her, blood rises to her cheeks, to her chest.

"Hello, Princess," he says. "What's your name?"

Marie Davies turns to the man and notices that he is young, dark and attractive. She hasn't seen him before. She would have remembered. She wonders what he wants with her, whether his intentions are innocent. She doesn't say anything. She doesn't need to. He isn't speaking to her. Marie glances to her right, just about catches her friend, Donna, pouting her painted lips and giggling like she is high on drugs. She looks at the wide shoulders that separate her from her friend. Her first impression was misjudged. He was like all the others. Just who did these young men aspire to be? Who did they look up to? A splash of beer runs from his chest to his soft, round belly. There is another - as yet unidentified - stain just below the crotch of his jeans. Marie observes that the guy is not the catch she thought he might be. Quite a relief, seeing as he hadn't actually noticed her. And yet she can't quite brush away the undercurrent of jealousy. Not for *this* man. Just for the attention, to feel wanted, to not feel invisible. Marie knows this is the cue that she'll be ignored for the next twenty minutes or so, maybe for the rest of the night, whichever happens to come first.

It has been like this all night. The sofa has been a conveyor belt for randy young men with just one thing on their mind. One leaves and another takes his place. And, to think, Marie didn't even want to come out. She'd already slid Dirty Dancing into the VHS, her hands had already dipped in the bowl of popcorn, when Donna called and said that she was having boyfriend troubles. Marie had already told her that the problem was her boyfriend was a dirty rat, but she never listened. Donna was adamant that the only solution to the problem was a girls' night out. The main problem with a girls' night out was that, inevitably, men got involved. Marie actually felt sorry for her friend at the time. She pictured her friend red-faced and tearful, huddled up on the sofa. That seemed ridiculous now, four hours or so later. *Marie* felt ridiculous now.

Marie allowed herself another glance around the club.

She'd been allowing herself these quick glances – had been quite generous, in fact - periodically throughout the night. Was she a glutton for punishment? It wasn't even in this place that they met. Why did she have to be *quite* so pathetic?

She met him a couple of weeks ago. The drinks had been flowing, as usual, and she'd left all her inhibitions at the bar. Marie was a happy, sexy drunk that night, which was not quite so usual. She'd been showing off her moves on the dance floor, handbag between her and Donna on the sticky, beer-drenched floor. Donna was oblivious to anything she did; she busily checked her reflection in the full-length mirror that spread the width of the dance floor. Marie looked up, and there he was, leaning against the pillar like it was holding him up. She smiled. The poor boy looked so shocked that his elbow slipped from the wall and he nearly toppled to the floor. Marie laughed, and his cheeks reddened and then he smiled back.

Marie still wasn't sure where she got her confidence from that night, despite the copious drink that naturally helped her along. Her dad told her often enough she needed to lose the layers of flesh that coated her body because, he slurred, boys these days just don't like fat girls. Marie's natural reaction when she felt eyes on her was to check that the guy wasn't looking at her skinny friend. But she felt none of this with this guy. She knew he was looking at her, and she knew he liked what he saw. Marie held out her outstretched arm. She laughed when the guy glanced left and right to check that she was holding the arm out for *him*. Marie didn't long for a strong, perfect guy to protect her; she wanted a guy with all the insecurities she possessed, who understood and loved her despite her flaws. It felt fantastic that *she* was the one in control. The boy put down his pint with a splash and followed her hand.

Hungry Eyes came on just as he placed his foot on the dance floor. She remembered the video that was waiting for her in the VHS when she finally got home. Marie looked up at the ceiling. There *was* a God. She held the boy close. His body felt large and warm and cuddly. His hands rested on her hips. His forehead nestled against her own. She tugged at his shirt and felt the hardness in his trousers press against her belly. Marie smiled.

The boy pulled away. She watched as he scurried away, his head bowed. Marie wanted to pull him back. He kept on walking. She looked up at Donna. She hadn't even noticed the boy. It was like he never happened, like he never existed.

Even though it was only a few weeks ago, it felt like a distant memory, a figment of her imagination. Marie wanted to see the boy again for a whole range of reasons. One was that she wanted to say sorry. She had no idea how she'd upset him, but she wanted him to know she hadn't meant to.

Another reason was that, even though they hadn't even exchanged a single word, she really liked him. But he wasn't here. She'd probably never see him again, would she?

She's had enough now. She stands up. Somebody instantly takes her place on the sofa, no doubt ready to try their luck with her friend. Marie makes sure Donna catches her eye , sees her hand held in the air in a parting gesture.

Marie heads for the exit. Reaches the corridor at the top of the wide stairs. Something tugs at her hand. She turns around, ready to give Donna some choice words. But it isn't her. It is a guy.

"I've been watching you, and I've been building up the courage to come and talk to you, and now you're leaving?"

He speaks in hushed, fluid tones, long fingers caressing her arm. His eyes are a fantastic grey, his face almost feminine in its beauty and yet, glancing down, Marie senses undeniable power in the wiry frame. His hands move from her arm to her waist, to where the boy had touched her weeks before.

Marie gives an open-mouthed nod. She *was* leaving.

"Listen," the boy says. "Let me join you? I'll just go and tell my friends I'm going and I'll meet you. I'll tell them I'm ill or something. If they see me going with you they'll want to come or they'll try to stop me going. It will be our little secret. Meet me over at the church in ten minutes? "

Stretching out his arm, he points in the direction of the church. Marie follows his hand and, mouth still open, she speaks no words.

This is ridiculous, she thinks, walking down the wide stairs with the thick, surprisingly luxurious carpet, saying goodnight to the doormen. She didn't know this boy. She didn't know his name. And she was a good girl. But then, she thought, *maybe* that was the whole point? The last thing anybody would expect her to do would be to meet this stranger. And the church? Surely his intentions were far from innocent. Maybe that was why it excited her, why the pink buds of her nipples rubbed against the fabric of her bra as she edged closer to the grounds?

Although it had been another stifling hot June day, a refreshing breeze chills her skin. Marie folds her arms across her chest as she stands against the black metal gate and waits for him. Minutes pass. She begins to feel ridiculous, just like she did in the club, nearly all night. A group of drink-fuelled boys pass and one of them shouts that she isn't going to get any business stood there, sweetheart. Marie stares at the long, straight street, longing him to appear, even if it is just to quash this feeling of stupidity. However, he is nowhere to be seen.

Long, expert fingers caress her hips.

Marie jerks around. The darkness of the night accentuate

the whiteness of his teeth.

"How did you get there?" she asks.

His hands had slid through the gaps in the churchyard gate.

"I took a different route and jumped over the wall."

The boy guides Marie to a gravestone. Her skin tingles as his hand strokes the inside of her thigh, high up her skirt. She thinks it is peculiar that he wears velvet gloves, like a magician, but the thought quickly passes as Marie arches back against the gravestone and parts her legs. He moves his hands away from her thighs and instead caresses her throat. He is a *goddamn* tease. She reaches out to stroke him, to caress the length between his legs, but he moves away.

The pain in her chest is so immediate and so horrific that Marie jerks up. Staring deep into his beautiful, grey eyes, she sees, quite clearly, that they're smiling. Marie smothers her chest with her hands.

It is *him.*

Marie clenches her body, shuts her eyelids, and waits to die.

DAY SEVENTEEN
17TH JUNE 2018

My hand slips inside my right pocket, and my fingers trace the outline of the ticket, making sure that it is still there; I am an obsessive, checking and re-checking that I have locked my car or turned the oven off. And yet, even though I'm desperate to know that the ticket is still there, I'm still not sure whether buying it was a monumental mistake, whether maybe I should just rip it from my pocket, tear it in two and throw it in the nearest trash can.

This trip goes fundamentally against Richard's advice. And I always listen to Richard. I'm opening the door just a few inches more, allowing leeway for somebody to enter inside. I need to keep him on the doorstep. I know that. And yet, still I continue walking. I'm not listening to Richard. I will need to tell him. I always tell him everything.

The Great Western Hotel looms like a dark shadow over the entrance to the train station. Inside, I pass McDonalds and Burger King, and I eye Searcys Champagne Bar. Placing my bag down on the floor next to my feet, I gaze up at the departures monitor. It has been a long time since I studied this monitor, searching for this destination. There it is. It stands out, like it is in neon lights, there just for me. I pick up my bag, suddenly laden with dumbbells, and head to my platform.

Taking my seat, I pull my head back against the cushion and close my eyes. I can hear movements around me. I blink my eyes open; our table of four is fully occupied. No more room. I sense that the girl sat opposite me is young and beautiful, with luscious golden hair that flows over her chest, but she could also be middle-aged with sharp bristles coating her chin; right now, everybody around me is faceless and unimportant.

My angst begins to fade as the train leaves the station. It feels like not only is the train leaving behind the continuous commotion of the city, but it is leaving behind my current woes. I know a range of new worries lie waiting for me, but I'm not there yet. I look out of the window. The terraced houses are replaced by detached ones and they soon become less and less regular, until all I can see are yellow and green fields. I think about lying on my back in one of the fields, with my arms and legs in the shape of a star. The thought is soothing. I begin to think that I made the right decision, that I can cope with whatever awaits me, that it cannot be any more frightening than what I left behind.

I know I should have told Erica that I was going away. I was just terrified I'd have to tell her why, that I'd have to tell her everything. It was ridiculous. We've been together three years now; we shouldn't have secrets. Yet, I have so many.

I was just about getting things back on track when she entered my life. I'd abandoned my dire and depressing bachelor pad, quit my job in the city and moved onto the boat. Some people said I'd self-destructed, but only those who didn't really know me. It took some time to adapt to a slower pace of life, but it was happening, one languid step at a time.

I'd jumped on the Northern Line one mid-morning Sunday. I chose which direction to take by the toss of a coin. If the coin landed on heads then I travelled north and if the coin landed on tails then I travelled south. It landed on tails. Initially, I was disappointed. What the hell was there south? But I quickly kicked that reaction into touch. That was the whole point, wasn't it? The not knowing, the just finding out. I jumped off the train at a stop I hadn't been to before. That was the whole point, too. I was doing whatever I could to shed layers of my previous self. Trying my best not to give a damn what others thought of me. I didn't realise at the time just how liberating it would be.

Colliers Wood was probably like every other town in London on a Sunday morning. Everybody was walking their dogs, rubbing their bleary eyes from the night before. I stopped at a cafe and looked out of the window as I sipped a cup of tea. I idled with no real intent in the retail park. I wandered along the canal, always on the lookout for a new place to park my boat. I crossed the gigantic roundabout and found myself in the market.

It was busy with people of all creeds and generations, all mingling happily together, all looking to fill a free morning away from the sofa. An enticing aroma of food filled the air. I browsed the covers of paperbacks in the bookshop. I wondered whether an ornament of an elephant would look good above the sink on the boat, then realised I'd need to get a new sink first before anything looked good above it. And then I wandered out into the main yard; it was there that I first laid eyes on Erica.

Perched on a stool, naked legs pressed high to her chest, her dark angled hair flowed effortlessly over her thighs. She looked so at ease, perched on a stool in the middle of a market, that I just stared at her, fascinated. She looked back at me, her perfectly oval eyes seemingly evaluating me.

"See something you like?"

My eyes followed her tongue as she spoke. "I was only looking," I mumbled. "I'm sorry."

"No need to apologise," she said, unrolling her body from the stool. "That's what I am here for. I want you to look, to like what you see, and then sweet talk you into taking things further. Which one takes your fancy?"

I'm sure I stood with my hands on my hips and my

mouth open for quite a few seconds. She must have noticed, for she pulled back her head and started laughing. "I'm Erica," she said, holding out her hand. Her wrists were covered in bracelets, and she had a ring on every finger.

"Marcus."

"Now, Marcus," she said, twisting her body at her hips and opening out her hands, "can I interest you in any of my creations?"

I hadn't even noticed the paintings at her feet. It didn't cross my mind that she was sat on the stool for any other purpose than to entertain me. I gazed at the paintings and smiled. I didn't know whether they were any good or not – not *really* – but I was fascinated by the array of colours and the personality that shone through. And there was such variety, from landscapes to portraits to abstract. I told her that I was intrigued by the painting of a mature lady with her grey hair in rollers, lips curling at the corners; a slightly more energised Mona Lisa.

"That is my good friend, Moira," Erica said. "Can you see that her face is void of make-up? That the fine lines by her eyes are very clear?"

I pushed my neck forward and nodded my head.

"Moira, bless her, wanted me to paint her as she really is, with no pretence or cover. That is how she views her true self."

"But didn't she want to keep the painting?"

I regretted asking the question, for it crossed my mind that maybe Moira - *bless* her - didn't like the painting. Erica smiled, displaying childlike, slanted teeth.

"Moira said that she sees the face in the mirror every morning, and that is enough for any one person. She wanted somebody else to enjoy my creation. Or, at least, that is what she told me."

And so I purchased a painting of an unattractive, elderly lady I'd never met before, went home and hung it on the wall in my boat, even though there was scarcely room to swat a fly.

I returned to the market every Sunday that summer. I no longer spun a coin. Fate had chosen the direction for me. Within no time at all I'd acquired three paintings. I had to slide one under my bed. Erica was wise to my game. She knew she was the attraction, not her paintings. We went for coffee one week; the next we walked along the canal.

"I want to paint you," Erica said. It wasn't a question, just a statement.

I visited her house on a scorching Saturday afternoon. Erica lived on a long street of terraced houses just a stone's throw away from the market. She opened the door wearing an apron, hair tied back, paintbrush already in her hand. Mouth free of lipstick, eyes absent of liner, she looked devastatingly sexy.

"So, do you feel yourself?" Erica asked.

I considered a smart remark, but instead decided to be honest. I told her I wasn't really sure who my true self was, but I felt most comfortable when I lazed around in my shorts and sandals on my deckchair with a glass in my hand.

So that was how she painted me.

Or at least, that is how she *started* painting me. After about half an hour, Erica put down her paintbrush and sat on the edge of my deckchair. She parted my feet just a few inches to make some space.

"Marcus, is this truly how you look when you are most at ease?"

"I think so," I said. "Yes."

She let that reply linger in the air for a while before saying, "So what would you wear if there was nobody in the world to judge you? That is what you seek, isn't it? Complete freedom from the chains of society? So what would you wear if you were on a deserted island? If it is this then that is fine. But just be honest, okay?"

Erica returned to her canvas and continued painting. It might have been a few minutes before I unbuttoned my shorts. It might have been a few more minutes before I removed my boxer shorts, before I lay on the chair naked. I looked up at Erica. She said nothing, but the subtle smile said much more than words ever could.

At first I was self-conscious when her eyes scanned my body, for they gave away nothing. Was I horrific? Vulgar? This quickly passed. She wanted to paint the true me, and here I was. The scar on my chest didn't matter. It was *me*. The blood flowing to my cock didn't matter, either. That was how I *felt*.

I kept glancing up at Erica. She continued peeking at me and then looking back at her canvas. Continued painting. I wondered what the painting looked like, whether I looked good; but then I decided that didn't really matter, either. It was *me*.

Eventually, Erica stopped painting. She washed her brushes in water. Did so methodically. She walked over to the edge of the deckchair, her hips shimmering, as they always did. Her eyes never left mine.

"So, are you going to ask me to put your cock in my mouth, or should I just go right ahead and put it in there anyway?"

I just groaned from my throat and the next thing I knew her long beautiful hair was splayed over my thighs and my belly.

That was the beginning of our intimate relationship. It started passionately, and the pace had never subsided.

I push my buttocks further down the chair now to stop

my erection digging into the table. I look up and wonder whether it is just coincidence the woman opposite glances at me and flashes a smile.

I know the journey like the back of my hand, even though I rarely take it. The train takes twenty-five minutes from Paddington to reach Reading before continuing onwards to Swindon and then Bristol Parkway. The next stop, and the first in Wales, is Newport. Then, just over two hours since departing Paddington Station, the train arrives into Cardiff Central.

This is where nearly all of the other passengers on our journey disembark. Cardiff is where Spartacus started his journey, on the first day of June. The train station hasn't changed much since then. The city has. It has become bigger and stronger, whilst the towns that surround it have shrunk, weakened and faded, older, more depleted. Cardiff was a different city when Spartacus began his journey of terror thirty years ago. Empty spaces have been replaced by tall, modern office buildings, each competing to be taller, and more modern, than the last. Cardiff has become the preferred option for hen weekends, for sporting events. It has become trendy and cosmopolitan. I wonder whether Spartacus - if he really is still out there - approves of the progress.

I become aware of the rest of the table now. The fog has

cleared, maybe only temporarily. Their bodies have awoken from their slumber. They each in turn stand up and collect their luggage. I notice that the girl opposite me *is* young and beautiful, and her blonde hair flows like a waterfall over the curve of her back. She notices my eyes scanning her body, and she smiles. The other eyes quickly glance at me, perhaps wondering why I remain sitting, perhaps noticing the erection that I can't quite hide. Weren't we all travelling to Cardiff? What *is* there beyond Cardiff?

The train disembarks. Nobody embarks. We were huddled together like cattle on the way to market. Now it feels like I have the whole carriage to myself. My hand dips into my pocket again, tracing the train ticket. It moves to the other item in my pocket that has become a part of me over the last few days. The new phone. The red one. *His* phone. He hasn't contacted me since that first night on the boat, when he gave the phone to me. I consider taking the phone out of my pocket and leaving it on the seat, leaving it on the train. How would he contact me then? What is the worst that can happen? How can it be worse than this? This is a very real thought, a very real option. I think better of it. I know that somehow he will know, that he is challenging me to do this, that he is inviting me to do so. It is the easy choice and, therefore, it is the wrong one. I decide to keep the phone in my pocket.

It is twenty-two minutes till my stop. I raise my head above the tops of the seats. There really aren't many going with me. My nerves, which had subsided and become almost complacent, rise again. I imagine a sudden, sharp rise on a Richter scale. What if he was on this train with me? What would I do then? I consider going to the toilet, heading to the bar, just doing *something* to help the minutes pass that little bit quicker. I stay sat. The minutes pass slowly.

The train reaches the next stop. I observe, with interest, that Bridgend train station has changed not one bit.

******

Maybe he isn't in?

I'm hit by a sudden surge of panic. I haven't even considered that he might possibly not be in. I just *assumed* he would be, you know, because he is old and all that, and therefore his life is much simpler and less fulfilling; but of *course,* he has a life, too, just like me, just like you. What am I going to do now? *Here?* I realise that there are still things I want to do, places I want to go to, that it wouldn't be a wasted trip, that I could still make the most of it, but it would feel like I was going through the motions, doing everything but the one thing I absolutely *want* to do...

The front door of this quaint house with a pretty garden

front and back and a view from the bedroom of the Bristol Channel, suddenly pushes open. The door seems reluctant, like it is fighting against some fantastic wind, like Storm Hector has got back on his feet and come back for some more. But Hector loses the fight, and the front door pushes open.

We stand just feet apart from each other, the first time in years. I suddenly feel tall. A giant. Our roles have reversed. He can't quite see me. He knows I am there. He shelters his eyes from the sun with the back of his hand, lowers his head and then his glasses slide down his nose, allowing him to look over the top of them. He squints. The process takes time - time I wish would just vanish. It makes everything even more awkward than it already is, and I find myself glancing around at the garden, marvelling at how green and luscious the lawn looks, how vibrant the red roses are.

"Son."

I'm not sure how to react. It is almost like a question. He knows it is me, of course he does; he just can't quite believe it. I don't know if he is happy or if he is angry. He has a right to be both, and more. I don't want there to be this distance between us, even if now it is only a few yards. The crinkles in the face suggest pain. That is the last thing I want. Maybe I should just turn around and jump on the first train back to Paddington? I detest the idea of putting him through any more pain. But I stand still, like a wax model, lifelike but unable to move, to function.

"*Son*," he repeats. You could slot pennies in the dimples in his cheeks. He opens out his arms. His bones feel delicate and brittle. He smells of soap and powder. Yet his grip, as he clings to my body, is amazingly strong.

Eventually, he pulls away. He looks up at me, takes me all in. "I cannot believe it," he says. "This truly is a wonderful day. I got out of bed this morning and something felt different. I had no idea what it was, because I wasn't planning to do anything different from normal. I was going to walk down to the shop to get the paper, stop off and read the paper in the cafe. I couldn't work out why today was so special, but it just felt different. In a good way."

"Well, now you know why, Dad."

He hurriedly tells me to stop standing on the doorstep like some sort of intruder, that it is just as much *my* home as it is his. I don't quite understand his eagerness to get me inside, for he has been stood outside with open eyes and hands, repeatedly expressing his amazement and disbelief that I am here.

I step inside and it does feel like my home, much more than the boat parked up in London, even though I haven't lived here for nearly thirty years, even though I haven't stepped foot in the house for all of that time.

I recall when I last walked out of the house. It was Saturday morning. Mum and Dad were in the kitchen, eating their breakfast and drinking their tea and browsing the newspapers. I know this because I stood outside the door, listening in. I heard the occasional rustling of paper, the tapping of spoons against bowls, even gentle slurping from cups. They didn't speak, but that was normal. They didn't *need* to. I literally stood on the tips of my toes as I silently opened and then closed the door. I didn't say goodbye. I repeat; I didn't say goodbye to the two people who had delivered me into the world and brought me up, even though I was disappearing from their lives forever. I couldn't. They wouldn't have let me go. Physically, my dad was the stronger of the two, but I know my mum would have put up the bigger fight.

My dad is first through the door and - naturally - he does not understand the significance of me closing the door behind me. It is the same door. Blue, plain, sturdy and wooden. So much has changed, but that door has remained exactly the same.

The delicious scent of fresh flowers is still here, too. Mum always ensured fragrant flowers filled a vase in the kitchen; my dad had continued the tradition. The house is fresh and airy, the sun blares through the open curtains. It feels slightly cranky and delicate in places, just like Dad, but really it is in amazing condition all things considered, just like Dad.

"Cup of tea?"

"That will be nice," I reply. "And thanks, Dad."

He turns around and then, without warning, he gives me another hug. His face is wet. He is blubbering. "I started to doubt that this day would come, son. And you know me, I have always had faith."

"I know, Dad," I say. "I truly am sorry."

"It's not your fault," he says. Surely, though, we both must know that it really *is*?

We've maintained regular contact on the phone. At first I'd call Mum and she'd briefly pass the phone to Dad and we'd share a few words before he passed the phone back again. There have been occasional meets, at mutual venues, first with both of them, then, of course, just with Dad. I've occasionally been back to Bridgend since Mum passed, when I just couldn't resist the urge any longer, but I didn't tell him I was here.

I sit in the living room, my body sunk into the sofa. There is a picture of the four of us in the centre of the mantelpiece, beaming to the camera, outside the penguin pool at Penscynor Wildlife Park. Mum. Dad. Me. Luke. That place *has* changed. It remains abandoned and overgrown, now just a childhood memory for many middle-aged folk, just like me. I remember that trip. Life seemed so simple. Dad had more hair and more padding to his face, but still he is instantly recognisable. Mum is just as I remember. Her face is alight with happiness. How is it possible? How did I let it happen? How did I *make* it happen?

Truth be told, the house never felt the same after Luke passed away. It became just that: a house, not a home. Nothing felt the same after Luke left. We papered over the cracks, but it was just a matter of time until something terrible happened.

I isolated myself as much as I could. I was game for anything that didn't involve other people. I devoured paperbacks. I ran along the grassy cliffs that lead to the beach, and I savoured the sensation of drowning out the outside world by swimming laps at the local pool.

I tended to live in my own bubble, like I wore a headset that played music at full blast. That was probably why I didn't notice the three boys from the conker trees until it was too late to run.

It was early evening and it must have been winter because the windows of the changing room were pitch black. I'd swum more laps than ever before, relentlessly kept going and going. I was just drying myself, wondering whether I had enough coins in my pocket to buy a chicken soup from the machine. I didn't even look up: I just saw three large shadows on the tiled floor and I knew I was in trouble. I instinctively glanced over my shoulder. My heart sunk to the pit of my stomach.

"There is no big brother to help you this time," one of them said, laughing. They picked me up and dragged me to the showers, one holding my feet, another gripping their hands around my shoulders. I kicked and scratched and screamed, but then I went completely limp, utterly silent. They pulled my bathers down so that I lay naked on the floor, the hot water from the shower burning my skin. I closed my eyes and counted. Waited for them to finish, to leave me alone. I reached the number sixty-three before they stopped firing punches and kicks down against my bruised face and body.

That was when things *really* changed, when it truly hit home that, without my brother by my side, I was weak, horrid, loathsome. I couldn't bear to look myself in the mirror anymore, so why would anybody else want to look at me, let alone spend time with me? It was years before I started making friends again. And then I discovered something that numbed my pain, that boosted my confidence, helped me hide from the torrid reality: booze.

Dad enters the room with two cups. Mine is milk and no sugar. Sometimes I take my coffee black, just to vary things up, but never my tea. Dad didn't need to ask. Never before has a simple cup of tea been so welcome, so inviting. I blow a circle around the rim of the cup. We drink in silence, just like Mum and Dad did. Dad takes away the empty cups and washes them at the sink. I hear him dutifully putting the cups on the plastic drainer. He comes back full of energy, his hands upturned.

"Want to see your bedroom?"

I am up on my feet and following him up the stairs. I remember the creeks, how I worried that I would be heard when I took the stairs that last time. I don't even question why he is keen to show me my bedroom.

"I haven't changed a thing," my dad says, glancing around the four corners, his cheeks a beautiful shade of crimson.

I break into a smile, but for all the wrong reasons. I just cannot - absolutely cannot – fail to think of the *Hot Tub Time Machine* film. It feels so wrong to think of this in the circumstances. But I'm instantly transferred to 1988. A poster of Ruud Gullit, in his short-sleeved tangerine shirt, is flimsily pinned to the wall with blue tac. A bright-eyed Paul Gascoigne in a Newcastle shirt looks over at me from the cover of a pile of *Shoot* magazines. A red plastic chair is pushed under the wooden desk where I used to complete my homework. It looks like any other teenage bedroom from the time. But then I glance at the window, the one that overlooks the Bristol Channel. I know that on the other side of the window, to the right, is a black drain pipe that is nailed to the wall, and that if you are careful and do not pull back too harshly on the pipe then you can use it to navigate all the way down to the ground, to the big world outside.

"We should have seen the signs," my dad says. He looks down at my shoes. He shakes his head. From this angle I can see that his wispy grey hair is plastered down over his scalp. There are a few red pimples coating his crown. "You started spending more and more time in this room. We just thought it was a normal part of being a teenager, of growing up and finding your feet. You know? But looking back, we should have known. You were fascinated by *him* before it even happened, weren't you? These very walls were filled with newspaper clippings. That wasn't normal. It was like it was meant to happen, like it was a story that was just unfolding..."

I feel like punching my fist against the wall. No, that is not right. I feel like punching my fist against my own forehead. I detest myself that this man could possibly feel guilt for what happened, and not only that; he said *we*.

"You did try, Dad," I say. "Remember when you came to my room for a fatherly chat? You were sent by Mum, for sure. You did everything you could. There was no way you could have avoided what happened. Everyone was obsessed,

Dad. He was a national obsession during that month of June."

My dad shimmies his shoulders, reluctantly accepts that there is *some* truth in this. But we both know he is right. Children pretended to be him in the playground. Workers gossiped in the break room. He quickly became a myth, a fantastic legend, growing ever more amazing with each passing day. People excitedly talked about him, fascinated by what he'd do next, who'd be his next victim. He enlightened people's morbid curiosity. But it was much more for me. I felt like I knew him. He felt like a dark, disturbed friend. I sprung down the stairs in the morning to pick up the newspaper before my parents took it away from me. I returned to my bedroom and absorbed every word that was written about him. I remember my dad's horrified face when he came to see me in my room and the newspapers were scattered over my bed. He did try, though. He even tried to talk about *her*.

But how can you fix a problem when you don't even know what the problem is?

Mum had some idea. I'm sure even Dad didn't know about the chat I had with Mum.

They fretted that I was spending too much time in my room, that I was lonely and isolated. Sure, I'd been lonely and isolated for years. By that time, though, the real problem, and the problem that led to my eventual downfall, was that I wasn't actually festering in the room when they thought I was. Sure, sometimes I told them when I went out. Other times I waited until they were asleep before climbing down the drain pipe. Sometimes I met up with a few friends, other times I just went out on my own. Somehow it was often more exhilarating that way; nobody I knew was there to laugh at me when I got drunk, nobody could report back what a fool I made of myself. Of course, I was painfully shy, and the booze boosted my confidence. And, just like Holden Caulfield, who became something of an inspiration, I was free to roam. I was underage, too, but only just, and besides, they were much more lenient with the licensing rules back then. Truth be told, my adventures didn't last long, and there were only a few occasions when I actually got up to anything of note.

"I know you were at your mum's funeral," my dad says.

I jerk my head up, shaken from my thoughts. He knew? I don't know whether I should lie, whether I should lie to my own dad. What difference would one more lie make? But not this. I can't lie about *this*.

"I saw you," my dad says.

"I wanted to speak to you," I say. "I so wanted to speak to you, to be there for you, to comfort you. You need to believe me. But how could I speak to you? How could I after everything I did to you? And to Mum?"

My dad shakes his head. I notice that he has shrunken, that he appears to be shrinking in front of my eyes, disappearing into the floor. "I was just so pleased that you came. I knew you would. I looked out for you. I saw you behind the wall, trying to fade into the background. You looked so smart and handsome in your black suit. I wanted you to come out and speak to me, too, because I was so proud of you. I wanted to show off my son. You were the only thing I really had left. I know your mum would have been so pleased, too, and so proud, just like me."

"That means so much, Dad."

"She got help, you know," my dad continues, absorbed in his thoughts now. "She was referred to some psychiatrist in Cardiff. It was about five years or so after you left. The appointment kind of came out of the blue, to be honest. I thought he might make a difference. She came back so much brighter after the first time she met him. Your mum gushed that he was a handsome young doctor with all these fantastic ideas and he was confident he could make her better. Give the black dog his marching orders, was what he said. But it just wasn't to be. The initial exuberance quickly faded. Your mother continued to get much worse. Not even this fantastic psychiatrist could help her. She must have seen him for about a year before it happened..."

I blank my mind of terrible thoughts, and think back to the photograph on the mantelpiece in the lounge. There were four of us. Luke was healthy then, but within a couple of years the illness ate away at him until there was nothing left. Life was taken away from him. He had no choice. How can a mother cope with the death of her own little boy? Mum only just survived his death. She spent years in pain and anguish and she was only just recovering, becoming something that resembled her old self, when I left. Through my *own* choice.

How can Dad say it wasn't my fault?

"I'm so sorry, Dad," I say. "For everything."

******

Just like the wildlife park, the club has been shut, and the building left rotting, for years.

Morning has turned to afternoon; a breeze gathers up dust and cigarette ashes from the cracks in the pavement. I look up at the wood that has been nailed into gaps in the windows. Running my fingertips over the wall, the dire paint comes away like chalk, dusty on my fingers. A crack, like a sliver of lightning, zigzags threateningly from top to bottom of the wall. The sign has faded and wilted so much over the years that it no longer tells you the name of the club. My heart sinks.

I'm far too close. Richard would lecture me, tell me that I'm opening the door far too wide, that I've virtually invited him inside, let him roam freely inside my home. He would tell me that I have a choice, and I'm taking the wrong one.

I don't seem to be listening any more - not to the voices in my head that I should be listening to, anyway. I glance to my left, then to my right. There are only a few people walking on the street, mainly moving slowly, weighed down by plastic bags. They're oblivious to my existence. There is a path to the side of the building, a narrow dark alleyway. I step around dried sick and sprinklings of dog muck. The wall looks unsteady, like it could easily collapse under my weight. I take my chances. Pressing my hands down against the top layer of bricks, the rough corners dig into my palms like jagged glass. Lifting my body and then raising my leg, I take a deep breath. I've no idea what or who I am lowering myself down onto on the other side. Thankfully, my feet touch down onto a flat surface.

It is just like a tiny abandoned garden that could belong in any terraced house. The back door was only used as an emergency exit, where the burly bouncers with fat bellies threw people out and applied whatever punishment they thought was applicable in the circumstances. Different rules in those days. The wooden door looks flimsy, like it has been rotting from the elements. I raise my knee and then kick the door. My foot goes straight through. Hopping on one foot, I pull the door. It comes away in my hand. I glance around, twisting my head as far as it will go without causing serious damage. It must be out of habit, for there is no way anybody can see me, no way anybody could be watching.

Only a few slivers of light enter through the cracks in the walls and the windows. I find my way through touch. My hands brush against the walls. I step on something soft. I stumble and fall. The side of my face is flat against the floor. I lie like that for a few moments, surprisingly at peace in the solitude of this darkened corridor. Something brushes against my skin. I flinch and pull away. Jumping to my feet, suddenly no longer at peace, I realise that I'm not alone. Rats scamper around on the floor next to my feet. I hurry to the front of the building, using some sort of sixth sense or, more likely, just moving forwards.

The entrance is much wider and, thankfully, much lighter. I remember queuing up outside, our bodies in a straight line, pressed against the wall of the building, heat blowing from the extractor. The bouncers, dressed as penguins, sometimes asked for ID, sometimes not; it depended whether they were bored, depended if they wanted to impress some young lady. You knew you were inside when you smelt the stench of feet on the thick, musty carpet. The chandelier hanging from the ceiling was surprisingly impressive, amazingly out of place. I always took a quick, discreet glance at myself in the long mirror at the opening to the club. It depended just how many drinks I'd had whether I smiled or snarled at my own reflection; when I was completely sober, I tended to wince. There was always an air of anticipation and hopeful expectation, though. *This could be the night.*

I came here a few times, looking for her, looking for the girl I told my dad about. I only found her once again, but it wasn't in this place. After that I knew I'd never find her again.

My expectation is even greater today, in the middle of the afternoon, in the club that has been shut for years. I have no idea what I am going to find.

It is like discovering a ship that has been abandoned and untouched at the bottom of the ocean. Everything is still how it was. Everything is still in place. The tears in the blue sofas allow chunks of foam, like ice cubes, to gather in small piles. Metal rails surround the wooden dance floor. It looks small and sad now it is empty of hot, sweaty, gyrating bodies and handbags on the floor. The long mahogany bar curves around two corners.

I am instantly taken back to that night.

Back to 30th June 1988.

I see him now. I know he isn't there, that it isn't possible, that he is just a figment of my imagination, but it feels like I could reach out and touch him. He rests against the bar, his open denim jacket exposing a crisp white tee-shirt underneath. He casually thrusts out his crotch, like he just doesn't care. His hair is cut short at the sides and is swept across like a giant wave on the top. It is amazing because, even though clearly he is beautiful, he is so calm and placid that he does not draw attention to himself.

Nobody notices me, either, but that is not necessarily deliberate. I sit on a hard wooden chair, hidden away from the raucous crowd by a pillar. My legs are parted, my hands pressed against my thighs. I pick up my pint and pull my head back but I'm in such a rush that I miss half my mouth. The lager fizzles down my chin, staining my tee-shirt. I put the glass back with a thud. I open my hands and start swearing. Looking up, he has his head jerked in my direction, his demeanour ice cool. A bead of sweat trickles down my neck. I know what I must look like. I know what he must think of me. He smiles from the corner of his mouth. It appears genuine. It appears friendly. My eyes remain fixed as he walks towards me.

"Tough night?" he says.

It feels like I have nails in my throat. The voice that speaks does not belong to me. "You could say that," I say, returning his smile. I dab at my tee-shirt with my hands. "I know I've already had enough to drink, but there is no need to throw it away now, is there?"

He shakes his head and laughs. I feel genuinely funny.

"Where have your mates gone?" he asks, looking around at the empty space surrounding me.

I'm aware I must look sheepish. "Think I'm last man standing," I say. "They're probably tucked up in bed now."

He holds up a triumphant hand and I slap it. "Nice one," he says. He takes a quick glance around. "Listen, I'm in pretty much the same boat as you. If you fancy keeping the party going then I'm meeting my housemates back at ours for a few more drinks. Hopefully they'll have got a few girls interested, but who knows? I could call it a party, but that would be stretching the truth somewhat. We'll just be hanging out really, see what happens..."

We both know that he doesn't have to sell it too much; I am unlikely to have many - or any - better offers. I know he has used the possibility of girls being there as a lure. Clearly I look like an adolescent at risk of incurring a repetitive strain injury on my wrist.

I decide to play it cool. "I'm just heading for a piss. Who knows, depending how I feel when I'm in there then I might make it a crap. I'll meet you outside in five minutes. If you're not there then I know you've gone on without me. No great shakes, yeah?"

He shakes my hand and indicates that he likes my style. I watch the back of his head as he walks away.

I squeeze my eyes tight and I'm brought back to the present. I push my hand against the greasy wall to stop the room spinning. The moment has gone. I turn around and leave the building through the dark, grim back door that I came through.

I can't face going through the front door and retracing the steps that unfolded that night.

I leave the same way I came in.

DAY EIGHTEEN
18TH JUNE 2018

My father said that I looked smart that day, said that he was proud of me. He wasn't just being kind, either; he wasn't just being fatherly. He meant it. But then, my dad was just naturally kind.

I wanted to laugh at the words. I wanted to scorn them. *How wrong could he be?*

I look over at the wall I hid behind. The beautiful, tall green trees left a permanent shadow on the wall; it was always in the shade. On this side, the wall only came to about waist level, but on the other side it reached the chest, just right to look over without being seen. There was the occasional passing car or pedestrian to worry about, but not many, for anybody who was anybody in the village was on the other side of the wall, heads bowed, hands clasped behind their backs, paying respects to the wonderful woman as her coffin was lowered into the ground. They stood tall and proud and wanted to be seen to be there. I was a cowering, squinting nobody, looking in from the outside; I was worse than a peeping Tom.

How on earth could I have looked smart? More to the

point, how the *fuck* could my dad have been proud?

I only realised just how much she meant to me when I moved away, when I left her. The first few months in London were the hardest. Summer had turned to autumn and then the crisp leaves coating the pavements turned to mush. I shared a house with housemates that were neither mates nor in the house very often, and I spent most evenings lying on my single bed in a tiny darkened box room, TV silently flashing in the background, opened cans of lager on my dressing table. Always, the first person I thought of speaking to was my mum.

One night I left my room with pound coins jingling in my joggers. It was a dry night, but steam blew from my mouth. Huddled inside the red phone box, my mum picked up the phone after a single ring.

"Mum," I said, "I haven't spoken to anybody for two whole days..."

She soothed me as I broke down in tears, told me that everything was okay, that she was always there with me. Instantly I felt stronger. I told her about my days, reassured her that I was determined to get a job, that everything would fit into place once I got some work. My mum told me that I was the bravest person she knew, to do what I'd done, that she was so proud of me.

Somebody banged on the window of the phone box, told

me to hurry up. They bounced up and down on the spot in the cold, face hidden in a cloud of steam. I didn't care. I was speaking to my mum.

I ended the call and promised I'd call again the next day. My mum told me she loved me. I held the door open for the guy that had been knocking on the window, but he just gave me a look. It was the look that did it for me. I went to pass him the phone but instead I cracked it hard over the side of his head. I caught his cheekbone with my elbow as he dropped to the floor. His moans rattled my ears as I walked back to my empty house.

That was the second time in my short life I realised just what I was capable of.

I'm in my dad's shoes now, viewing events from where he stood. Any eyes that were not on the beautiful mahogany coffin were on him, watching his every move, subconsciously judging how he coped or, maybe, how he didn't. The eyes and the looks would have been full of sympathy; surely that just made it all the more unbearable? My eyes scan the marble tombstone. It is in miraculously good condition. Only, it *isn't* miraculous. A miracle is void of explanation. There is a perfectly good explanation. My dad has a little bottle of polish and a cloth and he cleans the marble every time he comes here. It is a habit, a routine. But a good one. I read the words. I always read them again and again, like I can't quite believe them, like I expect them to disappear the next time I visit. And every time I have come back to Bridgend - even when I haven't had the courage to go and visit my dad - I have always come here. My dad knows that, for he seemingly knows everything. Of course, my mum was the beloved and devoted wife of my dad. But she was also the proud mother of her two loving sons, Jeffrey and Luke.

Luke.

My eyes scan to the adjacent tombstone, with the identical polished marble, and it is like somebody has tugged hard at my tongue, pulled it from my throat. This tombstone has been here even longer than my mother's.

I didn't want to laugh at my father's words to be cruel. It was just because of the ridiculous - *outrageous* - irony of the comments. I remember events from that day as though they were yesterday. The images in my mind are so vivid and colourful. Even though I was hiding behind the wall like a coward, part of me felt like it had escaped the rest of my body and was there next to my dad, holding his hand. He is such a slight and diminutive figure, and his outsized grey suit swamped his body, and yet he held himself with such dignity and respect on that day, he looked ten feet tall. I didn't need my dad to tell me that he spotted me. He caught my eye and held the look for just a moment, and then, subtly so that none of the congregation noticed, his face broke into a smile.

My dad was proud of me? It *was* ridiculous.

I bend down and kiss the smooth, rounded corners of both of the marble tombstones. I tell Luke that I miss him. I tell Mum that I am sorry. I'm sure I hear her tell me, clear as day, that she knows.

******

Sunday morning fades away and Sunday afternoon raises its lazy head. The population of South Wales has eaten lunch and is now most likely relaxing in front of the box.

It has been a surreal twenty-four hours. I slept last night in my old house, in my old room. I had almost literally turned back the hand of time. This morning I drank tea in the kitchen with Dad, just like he used to do with Mum. I gave him a warm hug and promised to keep in regular contact. I told him that I was off to see Mum, and he said she'd be so pleased to see me again.

I should really have caught the late morning train from Bridgend after visiting Mum at the cemetery. I wanted to. I just knew I couldn't leave without doing one last thing. Instead, I'll now have to catch an early evening train from Cardiff Central.

The strong fragrant air freshener in the taxi stings my cheeks. The roads are quiet as we head out of Bridgend on the A48. We turn off. Now the narrow and winding roads are occupied only by villagers walking their dogs who, in turn, stop and wave (the villagers, not the dogs). We are in the shadow of the glorious, overhanging trees, and so the light is limited. Many of the brick houses have thatched roofs. I cannot help but think of Hansel and Gretel, then the house made of straw in The Little Pigs. I do miss reading Emma her bedtime story.

I pull out my blue phone and type a message.

Going much better than I feared, Jenny.

I keep the phone in my hands, wait for the inevitable vibration.

I'm so glad. You're so brave.

The cab slows down and stops outside the house number he dialled into his satellite navigation. I ask the driver if he can await; I assure him that I won't be long. He looks at me uncertainly, and so I pay him for the journey here and ensure he catches the wad of notes in my wallet. Money is no object. It never is. He waits.

The door is again opened by an elderly lady. This one, though, is quite different from Simon's mum. She is even older, for starters - she must be nearly eighty. This lady actually smiles when she opens the door. She is dressed smartly, in an auburn blouse and a black skirt. I look down on her, because there is no option; she is absolutely tiny.

"I was wondering whether DCI Baldwin is in?"

Again, I feel like a child asking if my friend can come out to play. The woman smiles. "He is Mr Baldwin these days, dear. And could I please ask who you are? Mr Baldwin has upset quite a few people over the years, and so I need to be sure you mean no harm."

I have no doubt that Mr Baldwin has upset a whole range of people over the years. If he ever got shot then there would be an endless list of possible suspects. I wonder what this meek, old lady would do if a foe ever did come knocking on the door, though. She is not exactly the most intimidating bouncer in the world.

"My name is Marcus Clancy," I say. "Mr Baldwin was the lead detective in a case that goes back a number of years. I was the victim."

The smile vanishes from her face. I'm quite sure that the colour does, too. She knows who I am. Her face freezes. But then it is as if she presses the 'on' button. The smile returns, bigger and more colourful than before. She stands to the side to let me in, actually gives me enough room to enter her home.

"He is out the back, dear, in the garden." She leads me through the living room. The carpet and the curtains are in dire need of updating, but the house is immaculate, and it smells wonderful. "Could I get you a cup of tea?" she asks. "And some biscuits? I am sure you two men have quite a lot to catch up on. You were but a boy the last time you met."

I assure her that I am absolutely fine, thank you. She leads me outside. I have no idea what I will find. She is right. So many years have passed. DCI Baldwin was on a destructive downward spiral even then. Part of me is relieved that he isn't dead. Another part of me, of course, is disappointed that he is alive.

The garden is peaceful, though. And beautiful. The colourful flowers look like they have been lovingly nurtured with kind, caring green fingers. The shiny lawn slopes gently downwards. I head in the direction of a large metal cage at the bottom of the garden.

There he is. Inside the cage. I notice that he is surrounded by budgerigars, all blues, greys and greens. His concentration is such that he doesn't even notice me. I awkwardly stand with my hands nestled in my pockets, an intruder. I wonder how I can gain his attention without being overtly rude or startling him.

"DCI Baldwin?"

I know that he is just Mr Baldwin these days, just as Mrs Baldwin dutifully informed me. It somehow feels disrespectful to call him that, though, like calling an old teacher by their first name. He slowly turns to me, like a sloth. He holds my eyes for a few seconds, his face neutral. And then, he smiles.

"Marcus," he says. "It has been so long. You look well. And very, very, different from the last time I saw you."

He looks different, too. Naturally; after all, a lifetime has passed since we last met. He is an old man now. There are more grey hairs sprouting from his nostrils than from the crown of his head, and his face is lined like dried cowpat. But - to me, at least, then just a boy - DCI Baldwin was an old man even back in the eighties. His face looked grey and shallow and exhausted, just one sleepless night from running out of gas. Now, despite the inevitable passing of time, he somehow looks healthier, like he is further away from the grave. His cheeks have a surprisingly rosy tinge, like he spends a great amount of time outdoors. He stands straight and there does not appear to be much baggage circling his midriff. To put it bluntly, I expected much, much worse.

DCI Baldwin opens the cage door and steps out. This is a relief. There are tens of budgies in the cage and I don't fancy any of them plopping on my head.

I'm guided to a wooden bench. I blink my eyes. *Brut*. He smells exactly the same. Sitting down, he stares at me with apparent wonderment for a few moments, like he can't quite believe it is me sat there. I don't sense any negativity towards me. Time really must be a great healer.

"I heard that you have done rather well for yourself, young man," he says. "Which is amazing really, all things considered. No offence, like. You were a prime candidate to end up at the bottom of the River Taff, weren't you? You proved me - for one - wrong, and I do like being proved wrong. Good on you, I say. Don't think me a stalker or anything, but I did keep an eye on your progress. Couldn't help it."

I laugh. "Depends what your idea of doing well is, Mr Baldwin," I say. "I earned some decent money working in the city, for sure. And the money enabled me to live a good life. But I can't say it provided all the answers. I've taken a step back now, and I must say, my life is better for it."

I don't really want to talk about my life to date. I turn to DCI - *Mr* - Baldwin. "You're looking well."

His face breaks into a broad smile. I can't remember the old DCI Baldwin *ever* smiling. "I bet you're surprised I'm even alive, aren't you? You and me both, son!" His laugh is deep and raucous. "I had to quit the drink to save my sanity and I had to give up the fags to save my lungs. I've been clean of both for over twenty years now. If I hadn't, then I'm sure the only way you'd be communicating with me would be through a medium."

He doesn't ask what the hell I'm doing there. He must be

thinking it, though. Ideally, I'd like to avoid that awkward moment, so I take the initiative.

"I'm really sorry to come to your house and disturb your retirement, Mr Baldwin..."

"I'm hardly rushed off my feet now, am I? What is it you want? You want my opinion on Ant running off with his wife's friend?"

"*What?*"

"You know. Ant from Ant and Dec. The one with the big forehead. Got done for drink-driving. That one..."

"*Oh,*" I say, breaking into a smile. "Surprisingly not. But now you mention it, I *do* want your opinion on something..."

He presses his hands down on his knees. I suspect it has been some time since anybody asked his opinion on anything important. "Whether England will win tonight? I hope not..."

I laugh. Pause. Take a deep breath.

"Do you think he could still be out there...?"

He gazes at me again. His blue, sparkling eyes are truly intense, totally intimidating. I long to look away, but that would feel disrespectful. I look right back at him.

"Why are you asking...?"

He doesn't ask who I'm talking about. I like that: there is no bullshit, no pointless foreplay leading to the main event.

"Somebody has been playing with my mind, bringing up

the past. It came out of the blue. Only been the last couple of weeks. Since the beginning of the month, to be exact. Now it is either *him*, or somebody who wants me to believe they are him. You knew the case better than anyone. You knew *him* better than anyone. If anyone could tell me if there is even the remotest possibility that he is still out there, then it is you..."

DCI Baldwin looks away, stares into space. "I don't deny that I know him better than most, but that doesn't mean much. The bastard consumed my life for over five years. I was obsessed. Every time I felt like I was getting close, that I was within touching distance, I realised that I was nowhere, that he was just pulling me close so he could laugh in my face. The longer I was on the case the more I realised that I knew shit. I wasn't one of his victims, but I may as well have been. He killed me just like the others, only he tortured me. The guy is an enigma. I haven't a clue who he is..."

The words trail off. Plump, wet tears trickle down his cheek. I feel torrid for bringing up the subject, for being here, in his home, disturbing his retirement, bringing up memories of a life long gone. This old man doesn't need this, doesn't need *me*. He looks at me now and, though his eyes are red, salty slits, I'm scared. "We both know I don't know him better than anybody," he says.

I look away.

"You were the only clue I ever had to solving the whole thing," he says. "That's why I tried to suck everything I could out of you. I was doing my job, damn it."

"I know that," I say. Looking down, I notice his hands are cracked and threaded with blue veins. The fingers tremble.

"So what do you think?" he asks. "Do *you* think he is still out there?"

I've been asking myself this question repeatedly over the last few weeks. It is only now I feel certain of the answer. "I do," I say. "I think all of this is him. I can feel him. Watching me. Laughing at me. I just don't know what he wants."

"He wants revenge," Baldwin says. "And he wants it in kind."

He speaks the words so matter-of-factly that I flinch.

"So you already know the answer to your question," DCI Baldwin says. "I'm no longer a detective, but I suspect that isn't the real reason you're here?"

I turn to him now. Make sure my eyes stay fixed on his. "I just wanted to say thank you," I say.

His eyes flicker over my face, but his mouth remains closed. Moments pass with us sat in silence. Then DCI Baldwin nods his head and smiles.

******

I put my key in the lock to the door to my home. I haven't checked the time, but a full, white moon tells me it is late. I take a deep breath. It is odd - it is *bizarre* - but I haven't lived in the house back in Bridgend for thirty years and I've not visited in all of that time, and yet it still feels like my real home, not the home in Clapham, and *definitely* not this makeshift, temporary one that isn't even designed to remain in one place. It can be moved at any time. The fucking thing *floats!*

There is a reason for the deep breath, of course. I am taking a moment. It reminds me of when Emma was a baby. I'd stand over her cot in the morning and just watch the gentle rising and falling of her body. I savoured the few, peaceful moments before she woke. Emma was, and still is, a beautiful, tiny bundle of joy and happiness and yet - and yet she was a *baby* - and so she was also a beautiful, tiny bundle of manic, zany energy.

Now, these are my final quiet moments before the storm erupts.

I push open the door, and the storm erupts even faster than I expected. Footsteps charge down the narrow passageway, a Labrador protecting his home from an intruder. The footsteps are fast and frantic and they're coming straight for me. My face begins breaking into a friendly smile, but before it can do so, my face is struck. On the cheek. Hard.

"Where the *fuck* have you been?"

My natural reaction, the response that is spontaneous to Marcus Clancy and not to Jeffrey Allen, is to say something sarcastic. *Nice to see you, too.* But even Marcus Clancy is not that shallow, not that pathetic. Not *quite.* Erica has done nothing with her hair; it flows freely to the nape of her back. Her scent feels natural, like she has just jumped out of bed without spraying any perfume. I notice that her face is free of make-up. The light sprinkling of freckles are visible on her nose and cheeks. Paradoxically, considering she'd just slapped me, my first thought is that she looks impossibly sexy. My second thought is that I want to tear those flimsy clothes from her body. My third thought is that I want to be inside her, right now; I want to hear her moan and writhe as she rides me.

The rapid thoughts are thrown into disarray as she continues her onslaught.

"You are gone for days without even a phone call. Just what sort of a prick are you? I've been calling you, texting you. Do I mean that little that you can't even bother to reply? To me? Where the *fuck* have you been, you dumb little shit?"

My eyes lower to the spittle on her lips; her sharp incisors glisten. I watch, wide-eyed, as she opens her hand, my eyes focussing on the long, pointed nails that protrude over the tips of her fingers. I know Erica. She is preparing to scrape those fingernails down the side of my face, use them as weapons. She wants blood. I grab both her wrists and I push her away. I just need to keep those hands away from me. I feel her tension ease away, feel her strength fade. Staring into her beautiful, angry eyes for signs, I need to know that her attack is over. I release my grip from her wrists. There is a moment of silence, of inactivity, where we both look at each other, two boxers considering their opponent's next move. Erica pummels her fists into my chest. She is like a drummer. This is harmless. I let her hit me, use my chest as a punch bag. She just needs to let her anger out. She needs to wear herself out. The erection in my pants grows.

"I'm sorry, I'm sorry," I say. "I love you so much. You *know* I love you so much."

Erica arches her neck to the side. I know that look: are you *fucking* with me? Are you *really* fucking with me, you little son-of-a-bitch? After days and days away, I tell her I love her? But it is how I feel. It is probably how a husband feels after hitting his wife, but that doesn't make it any better, does it?

"My brain was fucked, Erica. I needed time away. Like, *really* needed it. I didn't tell you because I didn't want you to stop me going. I knew you'd worry. I really am sorry."

"Where did you go?"

I look away. I can't bear to look at her. Jenny knows where I went. I *do* love her. Erica.

"I can't say. It was nowhere. Just *somewhere*. I just needed to be somewhere else. Somewhere other than here."

She has a million and one angry questions to ask me. Her mouth opens and she begins to speak but I think she realises my answer is likely so pathetic that it is beyond taking it any further. Just isn't worth going there.

"Why? What is wrong with you? Are you sick?"

I think about this. I feel sick, and maybe I am sick. It feels like a disease has infected my body over the last few weeks, since the beginning of the month – this awful, decrepit month of June - has spread over every fibre of my being. But I can't use that as the reason. It isn't the reason, not really.

"My mind hasn't been in the right place, darling," I say. "My brain has been messed up. I needed to get away before it got really bad, before I got into major trouble."

A few cute lines appear on her forehead. She crinkles her nose. Erica knows I struggle. I think it was part of the appeal when she first met me, like a bird with an injured wing she wanted to heal. She knows I have a history that is always there, lurking like a monster at the bottom of the bed. I've told her I have a past, that I used to be a different person.

She just doesn't realise I meant literally a different person. Does she *need* to?

"Why couldn't you tell me this before you went?"

"Because I didn't want you to stop me going."

"You think that little of me?"

No, no, no. That isn't it at all. "It is because I think that *much* of you. I know you love me, although I have no idea why you fucking do. I know you would have tried to stop me because you didn't want me to get hurt."

"Did you tell *her* where you were going? Was it *her* you went with?"

I press my forehead gently against hers, tell her that of course I didn't. She doesn't move away. I lower my hands. Erica rubs her thumb along the length of my middle finger. I kiss the tip of her nose. "You need to think enough of me to know that I wouldn't stop you from doing anything you believe you need to," she says. I pull my face back and nod my head. My lips caress her own. She tastes salty. I dread to think how I taste. Raw sewerage probably has nothing on me right now. Still, Erica allows her tongue to slip inside my mouth. I wonder whether she can feel me pressing against the smoothness of her inner thigh. Erica pulls way. Maybe she does feel it?

"Don't ever fuck off like that again," she says. "Or I swear, it'll be me who leaves you. You can go back to her, to your perfect little wife."

I make a million and one promises to her. Sensing the tension fade away, like the air has been released from the balloon, I tell her that I'm going to take a shower. Erica doesn't argue. She can smell me. I need to wash the dirt from my body. I need to wash away the guilty thoughts, the lies.

Deliberately, the shower is cold, that kind of shower I'd take to soothe my sunburned body after a day by the pool. Lowering my head, the jet sprays bullets against my neck. The boat is shaking. Looking down, I realise it is not the boat; it is me. I am shaking. I stare at my upturned hands like they are tea leaves, offering all the answers. My palms are white and crinkled. I find no answers.

I hear something outside the bathroom. I *think* I hear something outside. Was it the door? Is he on the boat? *Again?* I turn off the shower. I stand in the tiny cubicle-naked, wet and shivering. I listen for noises, for signs, for anything. Erica is pottering around. She is washing the dishes. He'd get to her before he'd get to me.

My nerves are shot to pieces. He is getting to me. I haven't heard from him for days, for all the time I was in Wales. The phone was in my pocket all the time. At first it felt like it was alive. I was sure I felt it vibrate with every movement I made. I compulsively pulled the phone out of my pocket and checked it. The red phone. Nothing. As the seconds and minutes and days passed I became used to it. It became a weight, a shape, just a harmless part of me. I very nearly - *nearly* - forgot that it was there.

I know damn well what I need to do. I need to do what Richard told me to do. I always listen to Richard. I need to make the right choice. I need to choose to ignore him.

It is all in my mind. He is not outside. If he was, I'd confront him, stop him from getting close to Erica. I pull the shower curtain open. Step out of the shower. Dry myself down in the towel. My mind drifts. I suddenly feel stronger than I have for weeks, for *years*. I am empowered. I have a choice. I can make the right choice. I am strong enough. I am brave enough. Things are going to be alright.

My phone vibrates.

The red phone. His phone. Whoever *he* is. I stare at it. I somehow wish that I can make it vanish, make it disintegrate into dust. It stays there, lying on the floor on the rug, next to my discarded trousers, seemingly growing in size. I want to pick the thing up and throw it against the wall, smash it into tiny pieces. I pick up the phone. I click on a button. The screen lights up.

I do hope you enjoyed your little trip away, Jeffrey. I expect you got used to the break I gave you. Holiday is over! I've kindly sent you a video so you don't get any post holiday blues.

I stare at the screen. I read the words again. And then

again. There is no video. What is he talking about? He is just playing games. The phone vibrates in my hand.

This time there is a video. I don't want to open it. I long to put the phone in my pocket and take it straight to DCI Reeves. This is real evidence. This is something for his stats. Whatever the video is, the mere fact that I have one on my phone would make him salivate with anticipation.

I click the button to open the video. I watch with an open mouth. I arch my neck and adjust my position to make sure I believe what I am seeing. I close my eyes and squeeze the handset. I drop it to the floor. It is the only thing I can do to stop myself from crushing it.

I have just watched a video of my dad, sat alone in our kitchen, cup of tea by his side, palms of his hands rubbing his face.

I am quite sure that he is quietly sobbing.

DAY NINETEEN
19TH JUNE 2018

This is a bad sign. This is the second time I've been here in less than a week, and the first time wasn't exactly a jovial experience, either. Then I'd been in and out and on my way to the supermarket car park to gift Ken his unexpected treat. Now I perch on the edge of a high stool, absent-mindedly gazing at the endless flow of pedestrian traffic through the window. Of course, England is a happier place this week. They won. Harry is the new hero of the nation. Unfortunately, I'm not one of the happy people. Last time I was here it had been two cardboard cups to take away; now it is one white china mug please for Billy No Mates in the corner.

Years and years of a relentless working environment made me adept at making decisions. There was no time for dithering. There was no room for niceties. Sometimes I got it right. Sometimes I got it wrong. Most of the time I really didn't give a fuck. Nothing puts things into perspective more than getting slashed seven times with a cut-throat razor. Most of the time I was just glad to be alive. The rest of the time I was glad I was not sitting alone in an empty house, like when I first moved to London.

Now the odds are serious, and I'm clueless what to do. I spend my working days (when I bother to work, that is) telling others how to speak and how to behave. Usually I playfully mock and undermine the students. Now I'm a duck, keeping calm on the surface but madly kicking my legs under the water. I don't want to over-think, but then I do want to put my thoughts into some sort of order. Right now they are rebounding off each other like bumper cars at a makeshift fair.

Last time he only impacted me. I was an adolescent, with no wife or girlfriend, no children. The aftermath, of course, was a different matter. But – physically at least - he only hurt me. That was enough, really. The rest unravelled by itself. So many more could get hurt this time. Now, of course, I can't even be sure who I am dealing with. DCI Reeves was pretty certain it wasn't him. If it wasn't him then what sort of a sick bastard would play copycat? What was their motive? Where did they want it to end? Why should he stop at me? I can cope with him hurting me, but not my dad. And why would he stop at Dad? Why not move on to Erica? Maybe move onto Jenny? And then finish with...

I glance inside my cup. I'm irritated that there is just froth at the bottom. I squeeze the mug tight and almost dare it to crack, for a fragment of china to dig into my hand and draw blood. There must be a pained, or psychotic, look to my face, for a middle-aged man with lank hair on the pavement outside (the sort of guy that must gets looks wherever he goes) pulls his head back and stares at me as he passes.

There is a queue at the till. Even though my fingers are already tingling and a woodpecker has been chipping away at my forehead for the last half an hour, I want a coffee. *Nobody* seems to be in any hurry, and yet *everybody* seems to annoy me. The customers disperse until I'm face to face with the girl who served me last week. She has a fresh complexion, with full rosy cheeks. I can imagine her sat cross-legged on a bail of straw in a barn. She is pointlessly pretty, though, because her permanently vacant face makes her sexless. I am irritable. There is no doubt about that. I want to ask the girl whether she's had a personality transplant. I doubt this passes as standard coffee shop etiquette, but I don't care. Last time the girl's expression was mute. This time it is worse. Is something written on my forehead? Does white powder coat my nostrils? She winces when she sees me. I talk at pace and smile frantically, order my coffee and tell her I want this one to take away. She asks for my name - again - and I give it this time without engaging in any further discussion, then I move away from her and loiter by the newspapers.

Pacing in a circle, tapping my toes on the wooden floor as I do so, I sniff, then wipe the tip of my nose with the back of my hand. I pick up a napkin and dab at my sticky forehead. I keep glancing at the girl, longing her to hurry the fuck up but then, at the same time, trying to remain inconspicuous. My mind is so frazzled I can barely even pronounce the word, let alone spell it. Then - eventually - the girl looks up and shouts at the top of her voice.

"Jeffrey Allen!"

I throw the napkin on the floor. I blink out the sweat that has trickled into my eyes. I pull my hands out from my pockets.

"What the *fuck* did you just say?" I ask.

She glances at me with disgust, before looking over both shoulders for support. Two guys in matching aprons and tattooed arms slowly turn to me.

"I called your name," the girl says, her voice monotone.

"What name?"

The two guys smirk. The realisation hits that they are dealing with a nutcase. "Your name," the girl says. "Whatever name you gave me." She takes a cursory glance at the cardboard cup. "Jeffrey Allen."

"That isn't my name."

She glances at the developing queue. There are more than six eyes on me now. Coins tap against the side of the counter. I turn around, and the whole coffee shop is looking at me: staring and evaluating.

"Listen," the girl says, colour rising to her cheeks. "I really don't care what your name is. Do you want this coffee, or not?"

I grab at the coffee and it spills over the edge. I turn on my heel and leave the shop as quickly as I can.

This makes no sense. I am going mad. It is only when I am down the street and around the corner that I realise what happened.

He is on my mind all the time. I must have given my old name.

DAY TWENTY
20TH JUNE 2018

I have morphed into a caricature of the sort of person I despise, that I secretly (never openly) make fun of. I'm aware I possess eccentricities that make others raise their eyebrows, so surely I'm entitled to mock others under my breath?

Normally I prefer to take my time when I'm out and about. My lifestyle affords me to do this, to make this choice. Not today. Today I'm Usain Bolt on Red Bull. If I had wings then I'm sure I'd fly. My body is high up in the sky somewhere; my mind is down by my feet, sinking into the ground, disintegrating into the depths of nothingness.

My baggy, grey joggers are in danger of being trodden on by my light running trainers. My fists are in a ball; my arms pump with purpose. My upturned scalp is drenched with hot, itchy sweat. The volume on my iPod is turned to the max; I mouth the words of the beat.

I like to move it move it, I like to move it move it, I like to move it!

The orange sun is just beginning to rise, no doubt signalling the beginning of another sweltering day. Airports are packed with commuters setting off on package holidays to Spain, yet they're leaving more than enough sun behind.

The sun is so close it feels like I can reach out and catch it. Flies rise from the pungent canal water; even they don't fancy their chances in that shit. A man walking his dog moves to the side as we cross paths on the grass that is turning more yellow and flaky by the day.

I like to move it move it, I like to move it move it, I like to move it!

The man winces, just like they did in the coffee shop, only yesterday. He tugs harder on the lead, fearful this crazy, manic man might attack him. Winking as I pass doesn't appease his fears. I feel like telling him not to worry, that it isn't me he needs to fear, it is the serial killer out on the loose, hunting us down. I turn around, but the back of his head becomes smaller and smaller.

I keep walking, yet I still keep glancing over my shoulder. It is an urge, a compulsion, some kind of nervous twitch. I remember I did the same during my Welsh O Level in school. The desks were set in straight lines in the gymnasium. Rows and rows of desks. I had the feeling that the boy sat behind me was doing something behind my back, something with his hands. I had no idea what, but whatever it was put me in great danger. I kept turning around, but he had his head down, scribbling away, just like everybody else in the hall; everybody else in the hall but me. I knew that I had to concentrate to pass the exam; but, how *could* I? I was in terrible danger, but I had no idea what of.

Nothing happened in that gym hall, of course, apart from me failing the exam.

I keep swinging my arms, long and high until they're almost punches. I raise my knees high to my waist. The perceptions through my senses are dull and foggy; the images in my mind are bright, clear and clinical. My world feels like it has been turned upside down. I picture the girl in the coffee shop, though I'd like to blank her out. Her lips curled and her eyes widened, didn't they? The girl knew something, didn't she? But how? It isn't possible. My mind has to be playing tricks. Her image is replaced by the girls from school. We were just children. I was shy, overweight and awkward and I didn't have many friends, at least, not after my brother left me I didn't. *Luke, why did you leave me?* I repulsed girls. I was neither attractive enough nor cool enough for them to want to be associated with me. Quite the reverse: they didn't want to be tarnished by association. This was over thirty years ago, of course. What can it matter now? But I still long to push the images out of my mind: the girls are glancing and whispering and pointing. I felt exposed. I felt like a freak.

Of course, one girl was different. One girl seemed more like me, seemed to understand me. And yet, I ruined that, too, didn't I?

My pace quickens until I'm almost jogging. The sound of

the girls laughing quietens, becomes more distant, and it is replaced by the words of Baldwin, in the interview room, speaking in my ear.

I know you're not telling me everything. I know you have a secret.

I press my body against the brick wall and bend at the waist, hands grazing my knees. The world becomes clear again as I look down at the dry pebbles and the wet worms slithering on the floor. My hands move to my waist and my eyes rise to the curve of the tunnel, to the cobwebs and the pigeons that lurk like shadows, like danger. A car rumbles and splutters over the bridge. The back of my head knocks against the wall. It feels damp. I press the palm of my hand to my mouth to smother my gasps.

And then, I wait.

I wait and wait until I wonder what it is I'm waiting for, but then I catch the leather of his shoe as he comes around the corner, as he enters the tunnel. Does he have any idea what or who is waiting for him?

My hands circle his throat, the tips of my thumbs press into his Adams Apple. The whites of his eyes widen as the black fades away.

"*You*," I say.

****

Blaming everything on paranoia has given me some comfort.

After all, if I'm merely paranoid, then all of the perceived atrocities of the world exist only in my mind. I am only a risk to myself. Heal my mind and the world around me heals itself. Now, the only reassurance is that I wasn't going mad.

I'd prefer madness.

A table separates us, just like in Richard's office. I estimate that I could reach his throat if I leaned forward and pressed my belly against the curved edge of the table. On the other hand, my chair is the closest to the exit. I'd be the favourite in a chase. I need to keep my options open: fight or flight.

His face was one of sheer terror when I pinned him in the tunnel. I recognised that look. From my dreams. My nightmares. My dreams are nearly always nightmares. I recognised the look as that of my own when *he* was about to slash me with the razor. The look sucked the life out of me.

I watch him now as he eyes his cup of tea like it is a precious jewel. I make sure he knows I'm watching him. He appears fascinated by the rim of the cup. My eyes burn into him. One of his cheeks flushes pink, like a birthmark.

"You were at the bowling complex," I tell him. "I saw you. I thought I imagined it, but I didn't, did I? You were following me, just like you were following me today. I was there with my daughter. My little girl. Just what sort of a sick fucker are you?"

There's something I'm hanging onto, something that is giving me hope. An absolute game changer. I tell myself that, however messed up this is, it could all still be alright. It all clings on what he tells me next. I'm urging him to say the words, to spit them out, but then I'm pushing them back into his mouth, fearing what he'll say.

I hope it *is* him who's been playing these games. I can cope if it is. I can beat this guy physically and - possibly - mentally. I don't fear him. And, it would quash my greatest fear.

Spartacus isn't out there after all.

"Yes," he says. "I was there at the bowling."

My heart races. Open up my hands. Ask him to continue. He keeps avoiding eye contact. Remains silent.

"Tell me why I shouldn't just go to the police."

He looks up. *His* eyes burn into me now, making *my* cheeks flush. "You tell me. I don't know why you don't go to the police. That's something I've wanted to ask *you*."

I go to explain, go to justify the reasons, but then I stop. Why am I explaining anything to *him?* I'm not giving him the upper hand, letting him back me into a corner. "Why have you done this?" I ask. "What have I done to you, Simon?"

"What exactly is it you think I've done?"

"Everything."

I hope that it *is* everything.

"I haven't done anything."

I slam my fist on the table. His precious tea spills over the rim of the cup. "Bullshit! You've already said you followed me at the bowling. And I've just caught you following me down by the canal. Didn't you realise I knew you were there all along? Why do you think I picked up my pace? You think you're the one playing games? Don't sit there and tell me you haven't done anything, okay?"

Leaning back, Simon holds up his hands. "Okay, I've been following you. But I haven't done anything..."

"Not done anything? So why were you following me then?"

"Because I want to catch him. And you're the key to finding him."

My heart sinks. My shoulders hunch forward. I've heard those words before. From Baldwin. Repeatedly. It didn't end well.

Now I want to slam my fist into the side of his face. Not because he wants to catch him. I want to pummel his face because he is convinced Spartacus really *is* doing this. It crushes any last hopes I have that it isn't him.

"I know what you think about me," Simon says. "You think I'm some loser kid who lives in his basement with his mum, don't you?"

"But you do. That isn't opinion. It is merely fact."

Simon jerks his head. He needs to approach this from a different angle, doesn't he? One that actually makes sense. "Yes, I still live with my mum. Yes, I spend a lot of time in the basement. I know better than anybody that this is classic serial killer fodder. I know it would be easier for you if I was the psycho, that you hope I am the psycho..."

Damn. He knows what I'm thinking. He is right. Never before have I wanted somebody to be a psychopath so much. "Sometimes if it looks like shit and smells like shit then it probably *is* shit," I reply, but even as the words come out of my mouth I know I'm punching from the ropes.

"That there might be the problem," Simon says. The sparkle in his eyes - hidden somewhere behind his glasses - has returned. "You've reverted to stereotype because it is the easiest thing to do, because you don't want to face up to reality. Let us start with the basement, shall we? That is my workplace, my sanctuary, my little piece of the world that is separate from everything and everybody. It is just like an office or a shed. I work long hours..."

"Sounds delightful."

"I write a lot of books..."

"About serial killers."

"About serial killers," he says. "Somebody has to, because there is a demand for it, there is a thirst for it from millions of people who live perfectly normal lives. I just happen to be better than most other people at it, that's all. I'll come back to that. You know that house, though, Marcus? That house is mine. I paid for it with *my* money, primarily from the sales of books that I wrote. About serial killers. So really - no, fuck it, there is no *really* about it - my mum lives with *me*. I moved her in to live with me. She isn't getting any younger and, if she didn't live with me, then she'd either live on her own or in a nursing home. I just want you to reconsider those preconceptions before you reach your conclusions about this situation. I look after my mum just as much as she looks after me..."

I consider this. It is only his living arrangements. It does change the preconception I had about him. But then - really - who *gives* a fuck? Goddamn, plenty of men live with their mums these days, it is just the way of the world. The real issue at hand is whether or not he is behind these games, isn't it? And none of this changes any of that. My hope that he is the psychopath I want him to be, though, does feel like it is draining away.

"She used to own her own home," Simon continues. "She used to live with my dad until my dad died."

He told me when we first met that his dad died. He appeared keen to tell me about it but I didn't really want to know, did I? Strange, but his mum didn't seem like the type to ever be affectionate with a man. I *do* know how the reproductive process works. I now Richard would scorn me for my irrational thinking. I feel bad for Simon, of course I do, especially after what happened to Mum. But again, I'm struggling to locate the point. This isn't a counselling session. I usually sit on the other side of that particular desk. "I'm sorry to hear about your dad but, without meaning to sound harsh, dad's *do* die. What does that have to do with you becoming a psycho stalker?"

He leans forward, his elbows digging into the table. "Dads do die. Sure. But most dads aren't killed," Simon states. "Most dads aren't killed by a serial killer."

The penny suddenly drops. Things, or at least some things, are beginning to make more sense. "Oh," I say. There is silence for a few moments. I search for the next appropriate question. "So how old were you when your dad died?"

"Fifteen," Simon says. "They say adolescence is a difficult time for the best of us. There was so much more division when you were kids, don't you think? There was a hierarchy in the school and a nerdy kid like me was most definitely on the lower end of the spectrum. I know these years were difficult for you, too. Well, try being fifteen when you get a knock on the door in the early hours of the morning and it is the police, and they tell you that your dad has been brutally murdered. Suddenly, examinations and acne become rather trivial, if you know what I mean?"

I'm definitely feeling bad for this guy now, and I'm aware this is his intention. I bow my head. I don't want to fall into his net. I try to work out just what it is Simon is saying to me. I was left for dead by a serial killer. His dad was killed by a serial killer. He thinks Spartacus is still out there. What is the logical conclusion?

"Did Spartacus kill your dad?"

His eyes open wide. Then he laughs. "No," he says. "Sorry, I've just realised why you came to that conclusion. I'm sorry, I didn't mean to mislead you."

"So why are you telling me all this then? Are you trying to explain why you've become a nut job? Trying to justify it to me? Make me understand?"

Simon's repulsed face makes me wince. I somehow know I am up against the clock. Spartacus set that clock. I don't have time for niceties.

"I'm not a nut job. That is what I've been trying to tell you," Simon says. "I became obsessed with the man - if you can call him *that* - who killed my father. I wanted to know every tiny detail about him. This was only a means to an end, though. Ultimately, I wanted to find him and I wanted to kill him. I was driven by this single, crystal clear goal. He dominated my every thought. This obsession with one man expanded. I became fascinated by other serial killers.

Admittedly, it is a morbid, troubled fascination. But the key point is this: it isn't because I admire the killers. I hate them with every fibre in my body because of what one of them did to my dad. Don't you see?"

I think I already know the answer to the question I'm about to ask but regardless, I have to ask it anyway. "So why exactly have you been following me, Simon?"

He takes a slow, deliberate sip of his tea before answering. "Spartacus fascinates me more than any of the other serial killers, partly because he is the one that was never caught, but also because to him it is just a big game. We have no idea who he is. He has become a myth. But he is still out there. And the only way we are ever going to find him is to make your move before he makes his move on you..."

DAY TWENTY-ONE
21ST JUNE 2018

Clasping his large hands together, Richard leans forward in his chair. Pausing for a moment, he takes a deep breath before posing his question, as he always does. I watch, open-mouthed, admiring his poise. "So, Marcus, how have you been since our last meeting?"

Just where do I start? So much has happened. There has been so much temptation and, on the whole, I've resisted most of it. There have been moments when I could have self-destructed, but I didn't. Just. Yesterday was the closest I came to breaking. I thought I had my man, thought I had him caught, but it was a false trail. Realising it wasn't him was a heavy blow. But then I talked to Simon, and that gave me some hope again. It drained me physically and emotionally, but it *did* give me some hope.

Regardless, I decide to muster all the energy I can to take a rambling approach to answering his question.

"It's been my most challenging period since I've been coming to see you, Richard," I say. The raising of both eyebrows indicates he knows there is a 'but' coming. "But," I say, and he smiles, "I've risen to the challenge. My nerves have been ripped to shreds and, on occasions, I've been paranoid to the point I've doubted myself and everyone around me, but I've still come out the other side fighting. I'm still here, aren't I, sat opposite you, telling you this? That surely has to count for something, doesn't it? I'll be honest, the fact I'm still here kind of proves to me just how strong I actually am..."

Richard smiles. It truly is a wonderful sight to behold. He leans back in his chair and then decides against this and leans forward again. "That is fantastic, Marcus. I am proud of you. I'm fully aware that this has been a traumatic time. That was clear as day the last time I saw you. You were putting on a brave face, but there were cracks under that mask, let me tell you. You can only keep a mask on for so long before the cracks appear. But this time your emotions are heightened. They are at stretching point. Your positive energy, though, is genuine. It is not a mask. And that, my friend, is music to my ears."

He puts a hand to his ear. Sometimes I wonder what the point of certain body language is; I know, for example, where his ear is. I wait for Richard to take all the glory for *my* progress, to tell me how much I have improved since I first sat in front of *him,* how *his* techniques must be working. I'm already grinning, waiting for the inevitable. Bizarrely, this is the calmest I've felt since I sat in that board room, acting the brute, interrogating the poor girl who bravely stood up and delivered a presentation to her colleagues. It was all part of the workshop, of course: there to challenge and test. Part of me thrived in those sessions, though: loved playing the role.

"I think now is the time we should try a different approach, Marcus..."

I double-take. My rapid thoughts rebound in so many directions that I think somehow they've tangled together, taken the wrong direction.

"What did you just say?"

His broad, white smile vanishes. Suddenly, his face is an ordinance survey map of lines and creases. I've always admired my counsellor's youthful glow, his baby-face, but now Richard appears different: he looks every single day of his age. "I think we should try a different approach to the one that we have been employing," he says.

I sit back in my chair, creating further space between us, a divide. "Why? You just said you're proud of me. Said it is music to your ears. Listen, if the music is too loud then I'll turn the volume down. This is the approach you've been drumming into me for years, over and over. It is working, so why change now? Why change something that is working? How does that make any sense?"

I grip the underside of the swivel chair; I want to keep my trembling hands out of sight. Richard glances around the room. I try to catch his eyes, to see what they're telling me, what secrets they expose, but they just won't stay still, not for a millisecond. He clears his throat. "From what you have said, this is a massively tricky period for you. *He* has returned. The seed has been planted. Your circumstances have moved onto a totally new playing field. I don't think you can keep ignoring him, and if you do, then you're a sitting target, there to be shot. I don't think he is going to go away. Not yet, anyway. This time he isn't going to go away just because you are ignoring him. He is going to keep on knocking on that door until it drives you insane. This time, the noise *will* be too much for you to cope with. You are nothing without your sanity, Marcus, nothing..."

The room is shrinking. Reminds me of when the walls start coming together in the trash compactor in *Star Wars*. I want to - I *need* to - get out of here before the walls crush me, turn my skull and bones to dust. Somebody is squeezing my temple so hard it feels like it will explode.

"You always said that if I ignored him then he would go away. I believed you. It is what I've always believed. Were you lying?"

Richard puts up his hands. "No, no, no...no. I think you're taking things out of context here, Marcus. That was the right approach at the right time. And it worked, didn't it?"

"Damn right it worked," I say. My voice is high and it is loud. "It has kept me alive all these years. That's my *fucking* point. It worked. So why the hell are we changing it?"

Richard manages to hold my look now. With any other patient he'd ask them to tone it down, to curb their language, to keep things professional. His eyes are watery and bloodshot, his eyelids heavy and droopy. I feel his pain, but don't care because my own is so much more intense. He doesn't want to tell me this, does he? The poor sod feels compelled to do so, I can see that. "It worked for all the different situations you were in. This is different. Each problem does not have the same solution. Sometimes you need to adapt, even if that takes you way out of your comfort zone. Sometimes you have to adapt *especially* when it takes you out of your comfort zone..."

"So you say we have to do it differently, I get that at a push. Just *what* are we going to do, though? What do you suggest now?"

"You know about the fight or flight theory...?"

The palm of my hand slams down against the flat of my forehead. I physically want to push these thoughts from my mind. I remove my hand and catch Richard flinching. Both my hands disappear underneath the table. Both hands resume gripping the side of the chair, holding on for dear life, just to keep them under control. "Of course I know about the fight or flight theory," I say. "You think I'm dumb? You know me, Richard. You know how long I have been coming to these sessions. You know everything I've been through, and for how long. I'm not new to any of this. I'm not in kindergarten. Please don't patronise me."

Again, Richard holds his cumbersome hands up in protest. He does know what I'm like, and whilst he expects me to challenge and to question, I'm beginning to push the boundaries of his patience now. He is a paid professional first, my friend second. There has to be a limit to what he'll accept from me. I've been many things in this room, but I've never openly been rude. We're both in totally new territory here. I'm struggling with this new side to Richard and I can see that he sure as hell is struggling to cope with me.

"Sorry, Marcus," he says."You know I didn't mean to offend you. I was just trying to explain the basic principle I'm adopting. I wanted to make it as clear as day, because I know right now it isn't clear at all. All I'm saying is that if you continue to ignore him then he'll continue to grow stronger. You need to stop that before he completely overpowers you. Again..."

"How? Just how the fuck do I do that?"

Richard remains nearly motionless as he continues talking, hands clasped tightly together, only his mouth moving, like a ventriloquist's dummy . "You need to face him. You need to stand up to him. In essence, Marcus, you need to *fight* him..."

I stand up and flip over the chair in one fell swoop. Turn my back to Richard, my mentor. I don't hear him protest. Hold on to the magnificent bookshelf for support on the way out. I open the door but don't shut it. I feel the receptionist's eyes on me, curious and concerned, as I walk past her, but I don't turn to look at her and I don't acknowledge her existence. The whole building is claustrophobic, sucking the breath from my body. I need to get out.

I stand in the car park, bent over with my hands on my knees, just like I did in the tunnel when I waited for Simon. People walk past me. I can tell that they are stopping, wondering whether to ask whether I'm alright or, alternatively, if I'm having a breakdown. Possibly, they weigh up how much time they have available to deal with me, whether they'll make their next appointment in time. It is possible that some *do* stop; I don't know. I stand up straight. Look around. The sky is gloriously blue, the pavements dry as a bone, just as they have been for the whole of June.

And I am alone.

I can deal with this. I can cope. I am strong. I have coped with everything so far, and I will deal with everything moving forward. With or without Richard. *Fuck* Richard.

Scumbag. Traitor. Judas.

And then, just as the clouds in my mind begin to clear, as a rainbow forms, as my thoughts start to make sense, my phone rings.

The red phone.

****

I pull the phone from my pocket and then just stare at it, letting it ring.

Is my mind playing tricks on me? Again? Maybe I *am* paranoid? I pine for insanity. No. It is the red phone. It is the phone *he* gave me. There is a number. I could just put the phone back in my pocket, let it ring. I could turn the phone off. I could throw the phone on the floor and stamp on it until it crumbles into tiny, broken pieces. I have choices. He can only speak to me if I decide to speak to him. I am in control. Richard's words taunt me. He whispers them in my ear. *You can't keep ignoring him. He is only growing stronger.*

I press a button, pull the phone to my ear.

I don't say anything. I am in control here. I *am* in control here. Could just be a wrong number. Some old dear or a prank caller. I wait for whoever is on the other end of the line to speak. I keep waiting. They don't say anything. Somebody breathes into the receiver. It is gentle and rhythmic, rather than heavy and deliberate. I need to know who it is. I need to reassure myself that it is not *him*.

"Hello?" I say, breaking the silence.

The silence returns. It is just somebody playing games,. It is just a prank caller. I'm ready to put the phone down.

He speaks.

"Hello, Jeffrey," he says. "Or should I call you Marcus now? No, I think I'll stick with Jeffrey. Seems so much more suitable for the real you. It has been a long time and, I must say, it has been absolutely glorious to catch up with you over the last few weeks..."

It is the voice in my head, the voice I've been hearing more and more frequently recently. It is the uninvited voice that has got into my head and stayed there. I tell myself that it might not be him. It could be somebody imitating him. After all, whoever it is wants me to believe they are Spartacus.

"What do you want?"

"Want? Why do you think I *want* anything, Jeffrey? Haven't we had a splendid time recently? Have I not added some fun to that dreadfully dull and predictable life of yours? You should be *thanking* me. Okay, but you've got me. The days are passing till the end of the month and I think it is time I progress things to the next level, don't you? Before I lose interest..."

"I *want* you to lose interest."

"But if I lose interest, Jeffrey, then you know I'll just kill you right now..."

I look around. Is he watching me? A stretch of lawn runs along the edge of the pavement, and every twelve feet or so there is a tree with a wide trunk. On the other side of the road is a row of terraced houses. He could be anywhere. The quiet laughter builds and builds until I pull the phone away from my ear. He can see me looking around.

"What do you want me to do?"

"Now you're getting the idea, Jeffrey. I need to make sure you are committed, that's all. The first thing I want you to do is to tell me what the time is. I do have such tedious problems with my watch. Frightful thing. It has this terrible tendency to speed up, completely unannounced, with no prior warning..."

I look at my watch. "10:50," I say.

"Fantastic. That is the time I have, too, give or take a minute or two. Listen to these instructions very carefully, Jeffrey, because it could be the difference between life and death, for you or somebody else. I give you until 12:00 today to tell that lovely DCI Reeves what you failed to tell DCI Baldwin in that interview room all those years ago. That little something that was really rather important when you think about it-"

"Or else...?"

"Tick-tock, Jeffrey. Tick-tock..."

And then the phone goes dead.

****

Pacing the car park, the soles of my feet burn against the hard, hot concrete. I check my watch. 10:55. The minutes are passing, and I'm doing nothing.

Tick-tock.

I have to make a decision. Now. I can't tell Reeves. I just can't. But he said it was life or death. It was worth dying for. I am prepared to give up my life. That is my choice.

I sink my face into my hands. My eyes close and my mind opens. I know it is not as simple as that. He knows I'd make that choice. He is not talking about my life. He is not talking about my death. He mentioned others. Who is he talking about?

I pull the other phone from my pocket. The blue one. I stab at the buttons with the tips of my fingers.

"Hello?"

"Dad."

"Hello, son. It is wonderful to hear from you. I have been thinking-"

"Dad," I interrupt, trying to keep my voice calm; failing

to keep my voice calm. "Please, please, stay indoors until I say everything is safe. Lock yourself in. Don't let anybody in your house. Get a weapon. Be alert..."

"What is the matter?"

"Dad. Please. Just trust me."

"Okay, son."

I hang up the phone. Every second counts. I check my watch. 10:57. I can't stop the passing seconds. I phone my wife - my *ex-wife* - and then I phone my girlfriend. I give them the same hurried, frantic message: stay indoors, keep safe. They ask questions, of course they do, but then they assure me they will do what I tell them. They know. I check my phone. 11:01.

I think about my dad. I think about Emma. I imagine them dead. I imagine my own daughter dead. Killed.

I phone Reeves. I've made my decision. The phone rings. And the phone keeps ringing. I look at my watch. 11:03.

I wipe my forehead with my sleeve. And then I make my next decision.

If Reeves is not answering his phone, then I am going to have to go to Reeves.

****

It is about a mile to the tube station.

The road is full of cars, buses and scooters. The pavement is full of pedestrians with bags and buggies, dawdling and taking up too much space. They're suddenly intent on taking in the beauty of the world. I stretch out my legs. I run fast, ignoring the sharp, stabbing pain in my chest. I dodge in and out of the people in my way, pushing anybody else to the side. I can barely speak to utter an apology. The red circle of the train station is like the bright beam emitting from a lighthouse. It is tiny, so far away. My eyes don't move away from it for a single second. The circle grows bigger, the colour becomes more vivid.

Glancing at the ticket office, at the ticket machines, I run straight past them. I get the energy - the *strength* - from somewhere, and I have no idea where - to increase my speed. I lunge over the ticket barriers like an Olympic hurdler.

I'm met by shouts of protest from the attendants, but I keep running, only faster. Looking over my shoulder, all I see is a flash of orange. An attendant chases after me with heavy steps and a jiggling midriff. Making progress down the steep stairs, pushing people out of the way, I expect somebody to act the hero - to grab me, to rugby tackle me - but they are too slow, too perplexed, to do anything.

I turn the corner at the bottom of the stairs. The train is waiting for me, like a getaway car. The doors are sliding closer together. I have been here before, on the first day of the month. Closing my eyes, I push with my back leg and then jump, like Lynn the Leap.

I am on the train. The doors meet in the middle just as my back foot touches down.

Turning to the window, I watch the attendant through the grubby glass, his eyes a watery blue, his face a swollen red. His clenched fist bangs against the window, just inches from my face. I wave to him as the train moves away. I spin on the spot and look around. Normally nobody ever dares to look at anybody on these damn germ buckets. Now everybody is looking up from their newspapers, from their phones, from the back of their hands. Looking at *me*.

"Just a slight misunderstanding with the ticket," I gasp.

They look back at their newspapers, at their phones, at the back of their hands, at anything and anybody else, except me.

I'm powerless to do anything about the speed of the train. *Grant me the serenity to accept the things I cannot change...*

Still, I urge the train to go faster. I count down the stops, one by one. I regain my breath, knowing that shortly I'll need it more than I ever have. I stare at my phone, willing the seconds to slow down, the minutes to stop completely. 11:50.

The doors of the train fly open and I'm straight out before anybody else has a chance to move, has a chance to think.

The courage to change the things I can.

I run up the stairs and there is no ticket barrier. I blink away the brightness of the world outside. The pavements are full. I glance over my shoulder before stepping off the kerb, ignoring the horns as I run along the inside of the cars.

There it is. The building is up ahead of me. I can see it. I glance at my phone. 11:58.

The realisation hits. It is over. I won't be able to make it in time. I still need to get to the building and get past security and climb the stairs to his office.

I stop running. I stop moving. I bend over at the waist and gasp for air, just as I did in the tunnel. I pull the blue phone out of my pocket. I press redial. I call Reeves. I'm met by the familiar sound of the phone ringing. Just ringing.

I look at my watch. 11:59. I only have one choice left now. I no longer have a decision to make. Again, it has been made for me. I push my hand back inside my pocket. I pull out my red phone. I dial another number, the only number I have on the phone.

"Ah, Jeffrey," he says. "It is so nice of you to make contact again. How can I be of assistance?"

"I need to sort something out with you. *Anything*. I need to plead with you for mercy," I say.

He pauses. "I really would like to help you, Jeffrey, but

we had a deal, remember?"

"Break the deal."

"Unfortunately, you are already too late, my dear old friend."

My words are broken. "But it is not even 12:00 yet," I say. "You said 12:00."

His high-pitched laugh gains momentum, like a runaway train. "You only hear the things you want to hear, Jeffrey. You forgot the intricate details of our arrangement. I said 12:00. You inconveniently forget that I said I have the same time as you, give or take a minute. Well, I have taken a minute, Jeffrey. My sincere apologies about that. If only I had decided to give a minute instead then maybe things could have been rather different. Please don't trouble yourself with telling Reeves now. You need to save all of your energy. He'll find out for himself in due course. You go home and get some rest, Jeffrey..."

The phone goes dead for the second time in just over an hour, give or take a minute.

DAY TWENTY-TWO
22ND JUNE 2018

My arms are in a straight line, my open hands by my side, down by my hips. Normally I'm a side sleeper, with my knees raised high, resembling a step. Now, though, I lie on my back, my upturned head sinking into the depths of my pillow. The sticky bed sheet feels like it will need to be prised from my perspiring body.

It was dark when I went to sleep, which is the norm, even for me. Many hours and countless dreams passed before the sunlight crept through the flimsy fabric of the curtain. Opening my eyes briefly, I absorbed the delicious curve of Erica's backside as she sleepily pulled herself from the bed, commenced the arduous routine of preparing for another working day. Normally, my eyes follow the fluid movements of her naked body as she dresses. Usually, I tell myself I must be the luckiest man alive to be the only one to see her naked that day. Often, my hands drift to my stiffened cock, my movements light, my breathing heavy. This morning, however, I closed my eyes and blacked out the world around me. I sensed her muffled movements as she dressed, and I tasted the sweetness of her kiss as she left, but beyond that I was oblivious to everything outside the world that existed only in my mind.

I think back to that Friday afternoon. The 1st day of June. Spring had blossomed and we had the whole summer to look forward to. I didn't realise it then, but this was perfection. I should have savoured the moment. Ironically, hardly anybody is ever lucky enough to be told that this will be their last day. If they were, then surely they'd embrace life for everything that it offered? I didn't realise it then, and I didn't fully believe it over the days that followed, but now I am certain: the life I lived then ended that Friday afternoon.

My phone rings.

I jerk up in one movement like I've been stabbed through the thigh with a needle. I scramble around amongst the mess on the floor, searching for my phone. Only now, I have two phones, don't I? My jeans lie in a heap. Searching inside the pockets, I pull out the red phone, the only one that matters. I stare at it. I keep staring to make sure my eyes aren't playing tricks. No. It isn't ringing. My hand disappears inside the other pocket. I pull out my other phone. The phone I've had for years, the one I bought. My blue phone. This phone is ringing. I slump back on the bed, with none of the energy or urgency I mustered to sit up. Any calls to my blue phone relate to the life I lived prior to that Friday afternoon on the 1st June. That life is not important. Not really. It is not a matter of life and death.

The ringing is drowned by my duvet until, finally, it stops. Take a deep breath. I start counting, praying for silence, only when I reach the number three, the phone rings again. Stops, then starts again. My mind is aroused by mild curiosity. Somebody in the world really wants to speak to me. And not *him*. I suffocate my thoughts by pulling my pillow over my face. I know I am leaving a wet trail from my mouth. My breath is rancid.

Throwing the pillow through the air, I thrust open my eyes. It feels like I'm being sucked through a vacuum, as the realisation hits me.

My old life *does* matter. He has got to somebody from my old life, hasn't he?

My feet stomp down on the floorboard so heavily that I nearly sink into the murky depths of the canal water that lie underneath. I press the redial button. Close my eyes. Hope for the best.

There is a knock on the door. The knock is heavy, and it is urgent. They want to be let in, no questions asked.

He has come for me. He has finally come to finish the job once and for all.

You need to stand up to him. In essence, you need to fight him.

I untangle my jeans and pull them up over my legs, pushing my arms inside my grubby, dishevelled tee-shirt. I tiptoe over to the door, hoping not to make any noise, perhaps to take him unaware. Who knows? I forget the phone that is ringing in my hand. I think about picking up a weapon from the cutlery drawer but I decide against it. My fate is inevitable. Prolonging it will just add to the pain. If I am to fight then I am to fight like a man, with my bare hands. Not like the first time. The only time. I push out my chest, pull open the door.

DCI Reeves stands on my doorstep, his hands nestled inside his navy suit trousers, feet slanted in different directions like a penguin. Gum rotates around his mouth. I am aware he isn't alone. He has brought backup: faceless suits with plenty of attitude. Pulling up the cuff on his shirt, DCI Reeves glances at his watch. The movement is so quick, so urgent, there is no way in this world he actually checked the time. The blazing sun reflects against the silver strap, forces me to shield my bleary eyes with my hand.

"Not waking you up are we, Marcus?" he asks, looking up and down at my dishevelled attire and then sniffing. "Late night, was it?"

"I couldn't sleep," I reply. I had no idea my throat was so dry until I tried to speak; had I been using my tongue as sandpaper? Suddenly, I'm Vito Corleone. I struggle to stop my eyelids from drooping. Just how long have I been sleeping? It feels like I've been living in a cave for the last ten years. What day is it?

"Something playing on your mind, is it?"

"Nothing major. You know I've been worried recently. I came to see you, remember?"

DCI Reeves removes the gum from his mouth with his two middle fingers. He eyes it suspiciously like something he's just dislodged from his nose. This seems like an odd act for somebody who, outwardly, appears so pristine, so clean, so sterile. Reeves flicks the gum onto the floor. I thought you could get fined for littering? Where is a policeman when you need one? Clearly, he has more pressing things on his mind.

"I remember. That's what I'm here about, Marcus. There have been some developments on that score. Myself and my fellow officers would like you to come down to the station for a little informal chat, if that is okay with you...?"

*****

The room is shaped like a shoebox and is just as bland as cardboard. The lack of windows leaves the air stale like a teenager's bedroom. I switch from buttock to buttock on the hard chair. Just a table between us, just as there was the last time we met. Was that really just a few weeks ago? He is not alone this time. Next to him is a stiff in a suit, so mechanical

I wonder whether batteries are included. The stiff has laid a pad on the table and he is armed with a pen, ready to get going. Reeves stretches out his arms and rolls up his sleeves, warming up. Even his committed moisturising routine can't hide the astonishing panda eyes. Looks like he had a tough night, too. He is a little jittery. It can't be the coffee. I'm still convinced he is more of a green tea kind of guy.

"This is just a little informal chat," he says, grinning wolfishly. "And so, we're not recording the conversation. My colleague here will take some notes if he thinks you provide any information that may be of use to us."

"So I'm free to leave at any time?"

"Yes," he says. "This interview is completely voluntary."

"So it is an interview now? I thought it was a chat? So on what basis am I here? Am I a suspect?"

Reeves glances at his colleague. It is evident they'd discussed beforehand that I'd be an awkward bastard. Probably told him about the crossing of the legs incident. I recall Jenny assuring me how difficult I can be when we were at the bowling complex. Richard's words keep replaying in my mind: I need to fight.

"No, Marcus. I assure you that you're not a suspect. We're investigating a serious crime. You're here as a secondary witness. We've identified you as somebody who might potentially possess information relating to the crime."

I could be in serious shit here. I just need to make sure Reeves doesn't pick up that I'm aware of this. I need to utilise all the know-how from my workshops, finally put it to good use.

"So," I say, leaning back in my chair, "you've finally decided to take me seriously, then?"

Reeves gives me the briefest smile. Perfect dimples form on both cheeks. He'd make January on any calendar. He really is a handsome bastard. I despise him.

"Oh, we're taking you *very* seriously now, Marcus," he says. The whites of his teeth almost blind me. Where are my sunglasses when I need them?

"You are?"

"Oh, yes..."

"That's good then. Glad the tax I pay hasn't completely gone to waste."

"What aren't you telling us, Marcus?"

I've heard those words before, too; only he didn't call me Marcus, not back then. "I thought you weren't suspecting me of anything? Should I call my lawyer?"

This counter appears to work. Reeves leans back and assures me that I am not a suspect. He apologises for ever giving me the impression that I was. The minor victory is enough incentive for me to continue with my approach.

"What makes you think I'm not telling you everything?"

"So you're not?"

"Listen. I was the one who came to you. Remember? Why would I come to you if I had something to hide? You don't piss on a wall and then go and tell a copper. I came to you because I was worried. You didn't appear to share my concern. I told you everything. Now, I'm having a kip today and you come knocking on my door with your sidekicks. Right now, it seems you need me more than I need you. What has changed? It seems, from where I'm sat, that you're the one who isn't telling *me* everything..."

Reeves' eyes don't move away from me as he pulls open his drawer, ready to throw the first metaphorical punch. There was me thinking he only had a piece of paper and a pen in his armoury. He lays something down on the table and then pushes it forward so that it sits underneath my nose.

"I'd like you to take a look at the photograph please, Marcus, and then tell me whether you recognise the man."

So, it is a *man*. I don't want to look at the photograph. Reeves is hardly showing me his holiday snaps. Rubbing my swollen eyes, I look to the ceiling, seeking solace. I remember the fan in the interview room thirty years ago that went round and round and round but never, ever got anywhere near to fighting off the sweltering heat. DCI Baldwin brushed the sweat from his forehead so many times it left his cuff stained and discoloured. As the hours passed, the energy appeared to drain from his body and his face turned a jaundiced yellow. But still he persisted, like a boxer that keeps getting back up on his feet.

"I'm not going anywhere," he whispered in my ear, leaning across the table, clammy hands leaving prints on the table. "I can wait all day for you to tell me what you're keeping quiet..."

My eyes fixed on that fan, going round and round, blowing hot, stale air around the room. I said nothing.

I suck in the fresher air from this room, then look down at the photograph. My throat fills with bile. My mouth feels like I am chewing a battery. I shake my head.

"His name is Ken," I say. "He works at the supermarket close to where I moor my boat. He puts the trolleys away."

"He was a good friend of yours, was he?"

"*Was?*"

DCI Reeves' voice softens. "I'm very sorry to be the one to tell you this, Marcus, but Kenneth John Hooper was found dead at approximately 14:40 yesterday afternoon. He was bludgeoned to death with a sharp instrument. Mr Hooper was found in a pathway just away from where he worked, by somebody walking their dog."

Of course, I knew he was dead as soon as I saw his mug shot. I just needed to go through the formalities. It must have been where he took his cigarette breaks, where he'd just come from when I brought him a coffee the last time we met. It was off the beaten track. Why *him?* I barely knew him. In a way, that was a good thing. I already knew he hadn't got to anyone close to me. Of course, I spoke to my dad, Jenny and Emma on the phone straight after I spoke to *him*. Of course, I broke down in tears as soon as I heard their voices. And Erica was waiting for me when I got back to the boat. It wasn't good that Ken had died, but in a perverse way it *was* good that it wasn't somebody else. But then...but then he died because of me, didn't he? Why else? That meek, harmless man would still be alive if our lives hadn't crossed.

"Take a few moments, Marcus."

"Sorry," I say, genuinely confused now, "what was it you asked?"

"How did you know Kenneth Hooper?"

"I didn't," I reply. I stare down at Ken's blank eyes. "I mean, we've met. I just wouldn't say I know him. We've spoken a few times, but only in the last couple of weeks. Come to think of it, we met the day after I came to see you. He was getting picked on by a group of young kids. He wasn't the sharpest, to be honest. He was an easy target. I stuck up for him, helped him out. Whenever I passed by after that I stopped for a chat."

"You must be a much more social being than I am," DCI

Reeves says. "I don't normally stop and chat with the men who put away the trolleys in supermarkets."

I don't respond.

"So you're telling me he had enemies?"

"Listen, he was a sweet, simple guy. Like I said; he was an easy target. He was a victim. I don't know anybody who would have wanted him dead. Certainly not those kids. They were all bravado and no balls. They virtually ran away when I faced them down."

Reeves slowly nods his head. To all intents and purposes, he appears to have given the green light to what I said. "Mr Hooper was stripped of his shirt and he had Roman numerals engraved in his chest..."

He leaves the words hanging. My *jaw* hangs open. Reeves studies my face, scrutinises my reaction. "So he *is* back, then?"

Reeves shakes his head. "Not necessarily. Certainly, that is what whoever is behind this wants us to believe. All we know is that somebody is at least imitating him. We have not yet counted out that he could be a copycat killer. But it is reasonable to assume that whoever called your name in the lift was the same person that committed this murder, or at least an accomplice to the crime."

I start muttering and babbling. "It must be him. You must be able to catch him this time? Things have moved on since he last killed, haven't they? You have CCTV. You must have some DNA. Were there any witnesses?"

Reeves puts his hands up. Things are getting out of control. *I'm* getting out of control. Just like I did in Richard's office. "I'm not able to disclose the exact details of our investigation, Mr Clancy. But I assure you that all the available evidence was gathered and secured in the hour after the officers were deployed to the scene. We are speaking to everybody who may possibly possess information that will be of use to us..."

His tone is deflated. Nervous. I shake my head. "He is still too clever. He is just older and wiser now, probably even cleverer than he was last time. I bet you have nothing, do you?"

Silence fills the room. Reeves changes the direction of our chat. "That is not the only reason I wanted to speak to you, Marcus. The crime scene investigator reported the likely time of death to be around midday. To be around 12:00..."

He dangles the statement in the air like a banana, making me the monkey he wants to take a bite. I nod my head, remain nonplussed.

"I checked my phone and I have two missed calls from the same number. The last call was at 11:59. I dialled the call return number today, and do you know whose voicemail it went to?"

I make a show of acting innocent and naive. "11:59? Hold on. I would have called you at that time..."

"Is there a reason you were calling me at the same time a victim was murdered? A victim you just happened to know?"

"So you are suspecting me of something? You should arrest me. This should be recorded."

"Like I said; you are free to leave at any time, Mr Clancy." Silence. I don't move.

"Where were you at the time you called me, Marcus?"

I have a thought. I act quickly. "I was on my way to you. I was calling to let you know."

I reach into my pocket and pull my blue phone out of my pocket. I slide it across the table. "You must be able to track my phone? Whereabouts? Take my phone. You'll see that I was on my way to you..."

Reeves indicates that he doesn't want my phone. "Why were you on the way to me? Why did you need to see me so desperately?"

"I came to see you a few weeks ago didn't I? The feeling has been building and building. Felt that something terrible was going to happen. It was this insane gut feeling..."

"But as far as I'm aware, Marcus, you didn't see me, did you?"

I consider telling him some story about going to the main desk, that I was told he was out or unavailable, but think better of it. This is the police I'm messing with here. Surely they could check this story out? I opt for a version that is less traceable, possibly less believable.

"I reached your building at just gone 12, DCI Reeves. And then the feeling just vanished. I knew it was too late. I stood outside your building and there just seemed no point speaking to you. I had no evidence. I'd just be wasting your time."

"Who are you - Mystic Meg? We could do with you on the force." It was the stiff taking notes. He'd suddenly recharged his batteries. Reeves glances at him as if to say it was probably best he just kept quiet and continued taking notes.

I push my phone back across the desk. "Check my calls. I was in a mad panic. I made a load of different calls. Just before I called you. My dad said I should call you if I was worried. And so I did. Check later. I called the same people again, to tell them I was fine, that the moment had passed..."

Reeves reluctantly taps away at my phone. He knows he isn't going to find anything, that he is going through the motions. Why would I be so keen to pass him the phone if it contained anything incriminating?

"I appreciate that this has been a difficult time for you, Marcus," Reeves says. This is textbook empathy. I know, because I've taught it in my workshops. The dumb prick *is* falling for it. "And to be honest with you, the anxiety is written all over your face. You look like a shadow of the man who sat opposite me a few weeks ago. No offence. And I know this recent revelation is only going to cause you further stress. But we both know that if whoever this is wanted you dead, then you'd be dead by now. This is a murder enquiry now, so I have a team working night and day on it. You need to tell me straight away if you hear anything. Do you hear?"

"I hear."

"Do you still feel something terrible is going to happen?"

I shake my head. "The grim reality, officer, is that it already *has* happened. I feel nothing now. Just empty. That's why I couldn't get out of bed this morning. Numb."

"Have you heard anything from him since you last saw me?"

"Nothing. I've been looking out for him all the time. I've been a paranoid mess, if truth be told. But nothing. You'd be the first person I'd tell if I thought I was at risk, DCI Reeves. Despite all my false bravado, I'm aware you're the best there is, and I'd want you on my side if I thought I was in danger."

This thaws the ice. I knew he'd like his ego massaged. I also knew he'd be too dumb to realise I'm taking the piss.

"And you promise that you aren't holding anything back? That you are telling us everything you know?"

"Promise."

The stiff puts away his pen, looks ready to go get a coffee, maybe a biscuit, possibly a sugar donut.

"Am I free to go, DCI Reeves?"

"You've always been free to go, Marcus."

DAY TWENTY-THREE
23RD JUNE 1988

Lisa James pulls her wrist close to her eyes and then squints. *Jesus.* 4am. Good girls weren't supposed to be out having an absolutely *fabulous* time at this hour. They were supposed to be tucked up in bed, *wishing* that they could be out having an absolutely fabulous time. This might possibly be the best night of her life *ever*.

The night had started like any other. There had been no signs that this night would be different, would be special. They met at seven on Nolton Street, making the most of the cheaper drinks in the pubs, returning from the bar with two drinks each, spilling most on the floor. Lisa remembered smiling at her reflection in the mirror in the third pub, pouting her lips and blowing a kiss. She looked so much prettier after a handful of drinks, particularly through glazed eyes.

By the time they reached the final pub the handsome barman in a black waistcoat had already told her off for dancing on the table. The leery men didn't seem to mind; they cricked their necks to look up her skirt. Her friends assumed, as they always did, because they didn't take the time to look – not *really* – that Lisa was the life of the party.

Everything was always skin deep; they never talked about anything serious, anything that mattered. Lisa longed to tell them that she often dragged herself out of bed in the mornings, that she drunk buckets full of alcohol just to numb the taunting thoughts, to bring the occasional glimmer of light to the dark clouds that followed her. One particular night, she drank enough to tell her mate that she sometimes stood on the platform in the mornings, surrounded by the same grey faces as the day before and the day before that, and thought about jumping off just as the train arrived. Lisa looked up, ready for the aghast reaction, to be told she needed help, but her friend had her eyes closed, dribble trickling from the corner of her mouth. Lisa never bothered opening up again, never attempted to remove the mask with the curled red smile, just like the Joker.

They were huddled around a large round table in the club when she first spotted him, stood on his own, dressed all in black, blending into the shadows. How could somebody so beautiful be so innocuous? At first, he was merely an interesting outline through her glass. It was only once she'd downed her drink and slammed it down (with a wet splash) on the table that she realised the interesting outline was looking at her. He signalled with his middle finger for her to come over. Oh, that line, Lisa thought. *If I can make you come with my little finger, imagine what I can do with the rest of me.* She glanced around the table to check whether any of her friends had noticed. They'd either mock or patronise; she didn't fancy either option. Luckily, they didn't appear to have spotted him. Lisa told them she was taking a leak, wetting the lettuce. They pointed and laughed, like they were in the presence of that comedian who'd died on stage a few years ago: Tommy Cooper was it? They all said she was the funny one which, Lisa felt, was the same as saying she was the one with a personality as opposed to looks.

Fuck it. Her chair scraped along the floor. She shimmied her hips as she walked up to the guy, still half-expecting it to be a mistake, to be a joke. Lisa was ready for this boy to put her in her place, ready to sneak off to the toilet like they'd never exchanged a look, never uttered a word. At least enough alcohol flowed through her body to make a joke of it, to laugh it off.

"*You* look like you're having a good time," the guy said, widening his grey eyes. His tone was friendly. There was no indication that he was mocking her.

"Girls' night out, isn't it..."

There was adventure in his eyes. Right at that moment, Lisa felt like she'd do anything he asked her to do.

"I'm leaving here. Looking to broaden my horizons. Make the most of my night. Don't like routine. I prefer the unexpected. Why don't you come with me, become part of my evening?"

Lisa brushed one hand through her strawberry hair and the other along the contours of his firm arm.

"That's *outrageous,*" she said, laughing. She let the words linger. She longed for him to contradict them. "I don't know you. I don't even know your name."

The boy smiled. "It is outrageous. I know. And no, you don't. But if you knew my name then I wouldn't be a complete stranger, would I? But you *want* to come with me, don't you?"

Lisa both nodded and shook her head all in one motion. The boy started laughing, and she did, too.

"Where you heading to? How are you going to broaden your horizons? Isn't this all just talk? Cliché? Dare I say it: bullshit?"

Lisa knew her eyes wandered over his body as she spoke, absorbed the long limbs, the narrow midriff. Lisa was aware he noticed, that he smiled.

"Who knows? Maybe I am all talk? Maybe I just want to take you for a curry? But, are you willing to take the risk to find out?"

Lisa glanced around at her friends. They hadn't even noticed her speaking to this boy. They assumed she was still in the toilet, applying an extra layer of soap to her hands. "Maybe."

Moving closer to her now, he whispered in her ear. "Meet me over by Boots in five minutes. If you come then I know you really want to be here, that I'm not dragging you along against your will..."

Lisa began protesting, started telling him that if he wanted her to go then he could damn well take her, but before she could, he was gone.

She did meet him, of course. She wondered how long it took before one of her friends looked for her in the cubicles. He was waiting for her, his reflection visible in the shop window. He took her hand without uttering a word and then they walked the deserted backstreets until her heels clicked on the concrete steps to the park. Lisa was able to look for miles in every direction. She was completely alone with this stranger. And, true to his word, he'd remained a stranger.

"There is a rope swing down there," he said, pointing to the river with the dead fish that floated on the surface, hidden by the overgrowth of trees.

Lisa unhooked the strap of her shoes and ran barefoot towards the river. For once, she felt no urge to jump in the river, see how long she could keep her head under the water before she stopped breathing. The wind blew through her strands of red hair, which gathered in a mess, covered her eyes. She had no idea what he intended to do with this damn rope swing. He was no Tarzan (though she'd like to see him stripped to the waist) and she was sure as hell no Jane. He was damn sexy, though. He could do whatever he wanted with her down by the mouth of the river and nobody (but them) would know. It would be their little secret. She'd even resist telling her friends, not that they'd believe her anyway. Lisa was aware of the dampness that seeped through her knickers as her burning feet moved closer and closer to the mouth of the river.

She turned around, gasping for breath. Leaning forward at the waist, hands on her knees, she could barely make him out in the dark open fields in his black clothes. He walked slowly, in no rush. Lisa glanced at her watch, gasped as she realised she'd been walking for hours with this stranger, that it was four in the morning.

"So where is this mythical rope swing of yours? I hope this isn't some devious ploy to get me down here in the middle of nowhere on my own?"

His face lights like a candle. This guy is full of mischief, she thinks. He'd had plenty of opportunity to take advantage of her, even on the drunken walk down to the park, but he'd chosen not to. He was biding his time, making her wait. He hadn't laid a single hand on her body yet. It could only be a matter of time, though. She looked into his eyes and she knew they weren't innocent, that thankfully they were full of ill-intent.

"I have a better plan," he says. "Let's cross the river."

"You what?" Lisa follows him anyway, grasping her shoes in one hand. It is only when she spots the thick metal pipe running from one side of the river to the other that she understands.

"Ladies first," he says, holding out his hand, his long piano fingers spread wide.

Blowing out her cheeks, Lisa puts her shoes down against the dry riverbank. *Now, this is living!* Placing one bare foot down against the cold pipe, her second foot quickly follows, hands gripping the railings. *This was easy.* Her foot slips. For the first time, she stares down at the shallow water below, barely covering the rocks and pebbles, realises just how high up she is. Her knuckles whiten as her grip tightens. She regains her balance. Dares to take another quick look down. Damn. If she fell then she'd break every fragile bone in her body.

Only, she wasn't going to, was she? She wasn't alone. Not quite. Strong hands nestle around her waist, keeping her steady.

"Careful," he whispers, his breath hot against her neck.

Arching her body, Lisa pushes her buttocks against his crotch. He edges away. *Fucking tease.*

She tenses, startled. Her eyes widen, then narrow. Something wasn't right.

"You see that?"

"See what?"

She wants to point her arm, but she doesn't dare release a hand. "Over there. On the other side of the river. I saw something."

His laugh, over her shoulder, is rasping.

"Darkness does awful things to your imagination if you let it. Relax. You're with me..."

Lisa focuses her eyes. Feels ridiculous. All she can see are dark shapes. Everything is moving. The gentle, constant flow of the river underneath her provides some solace.

He is right. This stranger. There is nothing there. Just the two of them.

She is buoyed with even more confidence. She's had enough of his teasing. It is way past her bedtime and besides, she is a girl with needs. If he isn't going to make a move, then she is. There is no way she can fall from this slippery metal pipe, twenty feet or so from the river bank, not with his careful, considerate and strong hands protecting her. She swivels around on the balls of her feet, ready to welcome his sinewy body into her arms.

All she welcomes, though, is his wide smile reflecting in the razor.

Her only possible escape is the shallow river that lies twenty or so feet below, with the sharp, protruding rocks and pebbles. So what if she breaks every bone in her body? She lunges, but his hands are just too careful, too considerate and too strong to let her fall. After all, they are there to protect her from the water. Her knight in shining armour has a much worse fate in mind for her.

Lisa stands, frozen to the spot, neither hand on the rail, as she realises it is *him*. She closes her eyes and releases a muffled whimper as she allows him to carve lines down her chest with his razor.

She knows that, by the time she plummets to the waiting water below, she'll most likely already be dead.

DAY TWENTY-FOUR
24TH JUNE 2018

Over the last few days and weeks I've been spending less and less time on my boat. There, I'm a sitting target. I know that, by staying away, I'm running. *You can run, but you can't hide.* I know Richard doesn't want me to run. No. He wants me to fight. Easy for him to say, hidden behind the comfort of his mahogany desk. The serial killer isn't interested in *him*. For me, right now, it isn't so much that I need to keep running; I just need to keep busy, to focus and distract my mind. And so I've roamed the streets, sometimes with purpose, mainly aimlessly.

Passing a shop just like any other on the high street, I turn back and enter. Scanning the wall behind the glass counter, the shelves are stacked with an array of gadgets and accessories, such as iPods, headphones and laptops. This is the equivalent of a sweetshop for the modern male. Glancing at a faded white sheet of paper pinned to the wall with Sellotape, I hand the bearded guy behind the counter a quid and he silently points at a vacant computer behind me.

This is only the second time I've been in one of these places. I never anticipated a second time after my first experience. Sure, it ticked most of the boxes. I purchased a lukewarm can of coke from the counter. The monitor was clear and free of glare. At a quid for an hour, I couldn't argue with the prices. So why was I put off? These establishments seemed to attract a particular type of clientele, that's why. I could cope with the punters shouting and arguing with the guys behind the till who didn't speak great English. I can't quite clear my mind of the guy next to me rubbing his dick under the table to some porn, though. I really don't care what goes on behind closed doors, so long as I don't have to see it when I'm checking my emails.

I roll back the blue swivel chair, eyes checking for any unidentified white stains. I smile and nod to the young guy at the computer to my left; he stares at his monitor and rolls his chair further to the left. I click to start my hour, aware that I'm on borrowed time, hoping I won't need the full quota anyway.

What, I ask myself, is the most appropriate search to find what I was looking for? Bowing my head, I close my eyes and thumb my temple. This is the first hurdle, and it seems I'm no Colin Jackson at jumping over them. This was going to be more difficult than I initially anticipated. How could I search for somebody when I didn't know who they are? I'm interested in two people, but I don't have either name. I type in the one name I did know, my only link to the other two.

Jesus. He fills page one and so I click onto page two, then three. Clearly, I'm not the only one interested. I'm momentarily impressed at how popular he is, how much of a footprint he has made in his field. My hand hovers on the mouse. None of the search options fit the bill. I type some specifics into the search engine, then some more.

That's the one.

I glance at the countdown on the bottom right of my screen. I still have fifty minutes. I glance down at the crotch of the young guy to my left, just to make sure he hasn't taken things into his own hand; he rolls even further to the left. I move my eyes from left to right, like I'm at the tennis, as I scan the words on the page. At first I skim-read, skipping the occasional word and sentence to get to the gritty detail. By the second paragraph, my reading slows and my jaw drops. This is worse than I feared. My fingers tap against the edge of the table, then I slam my fist down hard. Eyes burn the back of my head. Glances are exchanged both left and right. I don't care; at least I don't have my cock out.

The evil little bastard.

I keep reading. I can't help myself. My heart is in my stomach, churning my guts, but I have a need. Suddenly, I sit up, press my elbows against the desk. There is a twist. A fucking immense twist. I shouldn't feel like this, but I can't help it. This is personal. The anger seeps out of my body and is replaced by a warm, numb glow.

The evil little bastard got what he deserved.

I wish I could have picked up a shovel and dug his grave myself. I would have used the shovel to smash his face first.

Instead, something strikes me first. A thought. A terrifying thought. I recall our conversation. What he said. I repeat his words. The realisation hits me like a bowling ball to the skull. Pulling the chair back, I nod to the guy behind the counter and then the warm air outside hits my face. I don't even bother to log out, don't care that all and sundry can check my search. Sweeping some crumbs aside, fodder for the birds, I park myself down on a bench overlooking the passing traffic. I stare into space, oblivious to the pedestrians walking in every direction all around me. Have I jumped to conclusions? Richard warned me against this. I search for an alternative conclusion. Can't find one. Come back to my initial, gut conclusion.

He killed him.

DAY TWENTY-FIVE
25TH JUNE 2018

One day. That is all it has taken. One, solitary day and my approach has flipped. Total opposite. I'm no longer staying away from the boat. I don't want this misery to continue till the end of the month. Either I win or I lose, but I don't want it to be prolonged.

You can run, but you can't hide.

The phrase keeps intruding my mind, joining all the others. There is barely enough room. One of them needs to roll over.

And the little one said "Roll over, roll over!"

The simple things are what I miss most from my previous life, the last one. Bedtime stories. Sometimes I'd try to skip a sentence, maybe accidentally turn two pages instead of one, mainly because I was tired, but it was a pointless exercise, for Emma always noticed. She knew the words of the stories better than I did, knew them off by heart.

And so, despite my better judgement, I've followed Richard's advice, although it might be more accurate to say I've done so in spite of Richard. His words have played on my mind more than any others. They can't possibly make sense, can they? They're a paradox. The truth is that I'm not fighting because of Richard. I'm just tired of running. Better he comes to me rather than anybody else, maybe one of my family.

I'm not one for half-measures. Not only am I back at the boat, but I'm literally a sitting target, bare-chested on the striped deckchair, pink shoulders melting like an ice cream in the sun, feet dangling just inches from the discoloured canal water. He doesn't need to stab me. If he really wanted to then he could sneak up behind me, pick up the chair legs and topple me into the water. I dare you. Go for it.

Feet graze the tips of the overgrown grass behind me. The movements are subtle. Gentle. Familiar. I yearn to crick my neck. My eyes stay fixed on the water, on the delicate ripples, but my fists clench and my arms go rigid. I glance to the ground to my right. I can't resist. There is a shadow, the outline of a body. It is moving. Becoming larger. Getting closer.

"Finally caught up with you then..."

I swivel around; turn my pink shoulders to the water. "I made it easy for you," I say. "I'm not exactly hiding, am I?"

I stand up, holding out my hands, feet pressed into the hard ground.

"No need to stand up on my behalf..."

Jenny kisses my cheek. Her face is reddened and shiny. She pulls the other chair from the side of the boat and carries it in her outstretched arm. Brushing aside the cobwebs, she sinks into the chair alongside me. The sun has lightened her hair, dark only at the roots, just as it does every summer. A light sprinkling of freckles on her chest have returned to enjoy the heat, to say hello. She stretches out her legs and she catches me looking.

"To what do I owe the honour of a personal visit, then?"

Jenny narrows her eyes, smiling. There really should be more creases to the sides of her mouth. "Well, I know you aren't too fond of talking on those phones now are you?"

"I've been using my phone much more recently, I'll have you know."

I leave it there. I don't tell her why, and she doesn't ask.

"The truth is, Marcus, I've been worried about you. I know you went back to Wales last week. That call the other day really freaked me out."

Was that really the other day? Ken was alive the first time I called her, just after I spoke to Dad. Ken was dead when I called her the second time, just to check she was safe, only a couple of hours later.

"I'm sorry about that, honest to God I am. I overreacted. It turned out to be something about nothing. Just me panicking. Hope it didn't worry Emma, too?"

I detest the thought of worrying Emma. It eats me up inside whenever she is even remotely hurt. I rubbed the grazes on her knees when she was a kid, just from playing in the garden, asked her again and again if she was okay. Still, now I crave reassurance. I want Jenny to tell me just how much my little girl loves her daddy.

"Didn't tell her. What was the point? She knew something was up, though. You know what she is like. Has a sixth sense. I half expect her to tell me she can see dead people. I managed to make up some ridiculous lie. She didn't believe me, of course, but it was enough to reassure her that everything was alright."

"Thank you."

"So, are you okay? *Really?* You weren't okay at the Bowlplex, that's for sure. You saw something. Looked like you'd seen a ghost.*"

There is no point lying. Jenny will see through it. The best option is to be diplomatic with the truth and then just hope for the best.

"Well, I can't deny I'm going through a shit time right now. You know, with things from my past. You know *all* about my past. But I'm working on it. Don't want you to worry about it. Think I can beat it."

I expect her to tell me I'm talking bullshit, curse me for trying to pull the wool over her eyes, but instead she leans forward and rubs my hand. Her eyes say everything. She doesn't believe me, but she is willing to let it pass just because she doesn't want to make things even more difficult for me.

Her lips quiver, and I know what that means. She's
gearing up to ask a question, but she isn't sure whether she
should. Turns out that she goes for it.

"So have you told Erica about your past life yet?"

I decide to act dumb (which isn't too difficult) just to play
for time.

"About you and me? The responsible, civilised life I lived
before I met her? Of course. She thought it was hilarious.
She doesn't exactly play by the rules, you know. You've met
her, remember?"

Jenny pulls her head back and laughs. I glance at the
crease between her chest. "Not about *us*. About your real
past life, before we met."

I'm sure she knows the answer, which is probably why
she asks the question.

"Not yet," I say, shaking my head. "I found it quite
difficult to raise when we first met. We all have skeletons in
the closet, but I nearly became a skeleton, didn't I? What was
I supposed to say? 'Oh by the way, dear, I was almost killed
by a serial killer? Oh and another thing, Marcus isn't my real
name. To be totally honest, I'm not actually who you think I
am at all...'"

Slapping my wrist with her hand, Jenny laughs louder
now. "Jesus, Marcus, your girlfriend doesn't even know your

real name, doesn't know that you used to be somebody else. Don't you think that's slightly fucked up?"

"Don't you think that I'm generally slightly fucked up?"

"Good point."

Looking up at the cloudless, impeccable blue sky, Jenny thinks about this for a few moments. "I understand why you didn't tell her when you first met. Didn't want to scare her off. But that was then. You've been with her years, though. Why don't you tell her now?"

"That is the point. I've been with her years. Too many days have passed. How can I suddenly drop that bombshell? There just doesn't seem much point. Don't want to needlessly fuck up any more of my life..."

Jenny holds my look. Her eyes are watering. She is trying to suppress something. She gives up. Jenny bursts into hysterics.

"It really is fucked up when you think about it, isn't it?"

I feel like slapping *her* wrist now, but instead I just start laughing, too. "I've never pretended that it was anything other, dear."

I have an urge to hold her in my arms, to feel the warmth of her body close to me, just like I would spontaneously – absolutely without thinking – when we were Mr and Mrs Clancy. But instead, I just tap my fingers on the side of the deckchair, and *think* back to when we were married. Bad decision. The red mist within me stirs.

"Why do you think he asked you to tell me about your affair, Jenny? I mean, he clearly had no intention of making a life with you? What was the point?"

Jenny's face crumbles. She leans back in her chair, makes an effort to move away from me. I know what she is thinking: why did I have to ruin it?

"Very fucking subtle, Marcus," she says.

That evening is crystal clear in my mind. We'd had a stretch of hot days, just like now, and then suddenly, late afternoon, the unblemished skies were invaded by dark, threatening clouds. The heavens opened. My shell of a one-bed flat rattled and shook, like a cardboard box blowing in the wind. Pellets bounced from the windows.

The doorbell rang. My first reaction: did they have the wrong house? Was some poor soul trying to sell me something in this weather? Who had I actually given my address to? Who cared enough to pay me a visit? The doorbell rang again. Maybe somebody was playing a prank? The doorbell kept ringing until I was hit by the thought that something wasn't right. It had rung for minutes and I'd stayed glued to the spot, staring into space, doing absolutely nothing about it. Now I ran down the stairs two steps at a time, desperate to get to the door before whoever it was gave up the ghost and left.

They were still there. *Jenny* was still there. She looked like a more diminutive version of the Jenny I remembered, like she'd shrunk and withered in the rain. Her face was coated in water and her body shivered. My wife looked so fragile and vulnerable, and yet so exquisitely beautiful. Right then the urge to take her in my arms was stronger than it had ever been; I wanted to comfort and protect her because it was my duty and honour to do so as her loyal and loving husband. Only I wasn't, was I? Not really. Now I was only her husband in name; the sheet of paper declaring us to be husband and wife had been stripped of any meaning.

Placing my arm around her shoulder, I shut the door and ushered her inside without asking why she was here. It wasn't until Jenny had stripped off her soaked clothes, showered and dressed again that we sat down in the living room and talked. Jenny sat on the floor with her legs crossed, still tiny in my outsized grey tracksuit bottoms. She took the piping hot mug of coffee I passed her like it was a pot of gold. As I sat down on the sofa a good six feet from her, I noticed that her eyes were still red; her vulnerability reminded me of an albino gerbil. It occurred to me that her face had been wet not just from the rain.

"He doesn't want me," she said.

I looked down at her from the sofa. "Who?"

She scowled at me like a cat warning a dog to stay away. I

pressed my outstretched fingertips together. "*Why?*"

It was a genuine question. I was genuinely perplexed. Why would anybody not want this beautiful, divine woman?

Jenny shook her head and took a long slurp of her drink. She'd clearly been asking herself the same question. Jenny shrugged her shoulders. "I met him in his car, like some sort of secret meeting. Yet, we're not having an affair any more, are we? I told him it had been weeks since I told you about our affair, that you'd moved out, and so wasn't it time we started talking about what happened next? He asked what I meant. I said, you know, with us. He again said he didn't know what I meant. Felt like I was talking a different fucking language. He said there had never been an '*us*'. Hadn't they just had a fling? Wasn't that why it had been so exciting? He'd never said it was anything else, anything more serious."

The mug in Jenny's hand shook and I remember thinking – despite myself, because I really didn't want to think it, not at that precise moment – that she might spill coffee over the pristine carpet.

"You know what the worst part was?" she asked, continuing to glance around the room. I think she was asking herself the question as much as me. "We just sat in his car in silence. The rain was bouncing off his windscreen. He just kept looking at me. He didn't say anything, but he knew what he was thinking: *what you still doing here?* I opened the door and got out of the car without even saying goodbye."

I hated this man – this *doctor* – right then infinitely more than when Jenny had told me about their affair. Sure, he had destroyed our life together, but what had he done it for? For nothing. And he had abused my dear, wonderful wife. Not physically. No, this was much worse. It would have been more bearable had he dislocated her collar bone or blackened her eyes. He had destroyed her emotionally.

"Where does he live?" I asked, jumping up from the seat.

This was not mere bravado or pumped-up male pride; right at that moment I genuinely wanted to find this man and I wanted to kill him. It had been a long time since I had felt this way about anybody. Since *him*.

"I don't know."

"You don't *know?*"

The words were coming from her mouth, but it was like her soul was someplace else. "I don't *know,*" she repeated. "I never went there. He never offered, and I never asked. We always met in different places. There was no routine. He was always mysterious. It was one of the things I liked. Made it exciting."

"*Exciting?*"

I paced up and down the room. Felt like punching my fist through the wall. Felt like saying a whole number of things to Jenny, none of them good. But I didn't. Instead, I let the tension cool down. I made Jenny another drink, and then another. Jenny was drained of energy and I offered her my bed. Not with me in it. I slept on the sofa. In the morning, she left.

We don't tend to talk about the reason our marriage fell apart. It isn't exactly going to end well, is it? We only do so when I can no longer stop the resentment that simmers inside me from boiling over. Only occasionally does it erupt.

"You know I don't know why, Marcus," Jenny replies now. "I'd tell you if I knew. You know I ask myself that question every single fucking day when I wake up on my own, without my husband next to me. I ask myself what possessed me to destroy the idyllic life we had together. And I've never - ever - found a satisfactory answer."

I know she doesn't know. The girl who sat cross-legged on the floor of my flat that night was bewildered and broken. Now, I squeeze her hand. She smiles. I'm sorry I said anything. As far as I'm aware the matter is closed.

"I guess his mind worked in a different way from me," Jenny says. I didn't expect her to keep the subject open, to pursue it any further. "It felt like he looked at the world in a different way, through different eyes. I've wondered whether it has anything to do with his education and training. You know; as a psychiatrist I imagine you view the world differently..."

I think I misheard her for a moment. "A psychiatrist?"

"Yes," Jenny says. "You know. He was a psychiatrist."

"You said he was a *doctor.*"

"He *is* a doctor."

"You never said he was a psychiatrist..."

Jenny looks at me nonplussed. "I didn't?" she says. "I assumed I did. To be fair, it isn't something we talk about much, is it, Marcus?"

We sit in silence, the hot sun burning our reddened, peeling shoulders.

DAY TWENTY-SIX
26TH JUNE 2018

I've been fighting against routine for the last five years or so, viewed it as an enemy ever since I split with Jenny, since I began my latest life; now I hang on to it for dear life. I long for some sense of normality.

It seems bizarre to me that, what with everything going on, I should strive to make the appointment with Richard. Cross that. A week ago, it would have made perfect sense. Then I would have clung to his reassurance like a monkey to a tree, fed off his words. But that was before our last session. Last time I met with Richard he destroyed everything we'd created together over the last ten years or so. He made it all a lie, just like Jenny did with our marriage. Maybe that is why I long to see him? Perhaps I'd misunderstood what he'd said, misinterpreted the meaning? Maybe it was all a test? Part of a much bigger plan?

The door edges open and Richard's arm is outstretched for about five or so steps before he shakes my hand. Turning around, I'm tempted to wipe the dampness of his clammy hand on my trousers; right now, though, I fear that he has eyes in the back of his square head.

"How have you been, Marcus?"

"I can't complain really, not after what you told me last

time I was here, Richard. What was all that about? Talk about throwing me a grenade..."

His wide, bug eyes flicker . Chunky thumbs tap against the side of the desk. It reminds me again of that exercise in my workshops where I instruct the interviewer to deliberately ignore the interviewee. All very well, only I'm paying for this horse shit. My voice slows as I start to lose confidence. Begin to feel stupid. I stop talking, mid-sentence. Deliberately. Richard looks down at his desk. A layer of perspiration seeps from his forehead, down towards his cheeks.

I glance at the clock and wonder whether the cuckoo is at home. I long to wave my hand in his face, see if anybody is there, but then, the last thing I want to do is mock the man. I've looked up to him, secretly idolised him, all these years, through thick and thin. I grip my wrist with my hand to prevent myself from doing anything with my spare hand.

"Richard...?"

He shakes his head as though flicking water from his hair. "Sorry," Richard says, prising heavy eyelids open. Throaty laugh. "It was a late night. I couldn't sleep. Please don't mind me."

I return his smile. It crosses my mind that maybe he is just having a moment. Maybe I've just become embroiled in disproportionate thinking?

Richard starts talking. This is reassuring. Richard loves talking, adores the sound of his own voice. This is more like the Richard I know. "It is like I said last time. Sometimes you need to adapt to the circumstances you are in, Marcus. Sometimes you need to be courageous enough to accept that what you're doing just isn't working. And remember, if you do the same thing again and again you are always going to get the same result. Simple logic. We both need to be strong enough to accept that what you've done has not worked, that we need to try a different approach..."

"I disagree -"

"It is the fight or flight principle, like I said. By ignoring him you have, in effect, been taking flight. I assured you he would get bored but he hasn't. I was wrong. I offer you my sincere apologies for that. He has only got stronger. He wants to fight. You need to fight him back..."

"Richard, if I fight him then I will lose..."

"It is your only chance. You are stronger than you realise. You are the strongest person I know. I wish I was as strong as you..."

Richard keeps on talking and talking. I love hearing him talk. Now, though, I despise it. Now he is a receptionist reciting the same words to yet another faceless guest. I squint. The beads, like raindrops, trickling down his cheek are not perspiration. They are tears. His fingers are no longer tapping away; they grip the edge of his desk. The whiteness of his knuckles contrasts starkly with the darkness of his skin.

Standing up, I start walking to his side of the desk. It isn't *me* who needs help right now. I've never been on the other side of his desk before. There is an invisible line that normally can't be crossed. Richard gets to his feet. I think he is going to thrust out his hands, order me to get back to my side, question what the fuck I'm doing. Taking liberties. He doesn't. His forehead sinks into my chest. My shirt drowns out his sobs, smothers them. He pulls away. Looks up at me. Both eyes are bloodshot now. His teeth glisten with spittle.

"I'm sorry," he says. His bulging eyes look like they are reading my thoughts. "I'm so very sorry."

"Why? You've nothing to be sorry for, Richard. You've always been there for me. I'd never have made it this far without you. This is just a glitch. You're the one who tells me not to take things out of proportion."

Richard shakes his head. "That's what makes it so terrible, so awful. I have always been there. Nothing hurts more than being disappointed by the person you thought would never hurt you. I've lived by that all my adult life. Never did I think I'd be the one inflicting the pain."

I glance around the room from his side of the desk, at the bookshelf, the sofa, the rug. "What are you talking about?"

"You know when you are put in a position where you sacrifice yourself or you sacrifice somebody else? Do you throw yourself in the way of a bullet, or throw somebody else in front of the bullet? Well, now I know what type of man I really am. I threw you in front of the bullet, Marcus."

"*What?*"

Richard moves back a step or two, then straightens his back. His fingers wipe tears from the underside of his eyes. "Don't you get it? Everything I've been telling you the last two sessions. I don't believe any of it. I've told you to do things I don't even believe in myself..."

I nod my head. I do get it. I suspected it after our last meeting. Knew something wasn't right. Knew something was horrifically wrong. He holds his arms up rigid, unsure how I'll react. I want to tell him how sorry I am, that I wish he never had to be put in this position, sorry I'd ever entered his life, just like I was sorry I'd ever entered Ken's life.

"Why?"

"He told me to do it. To say it. He threatened me with my job. I need my job, Marcus. If I don't have my job then I could lose everything I love, including my family. It wasn't what he said, but the way he said it. I know he wasn't just talking about my job."

"Who did?" I ask. "Who made you say it?"

Richard takes a deep intake of air and then blows it out

from his puffed cheeks.

"My boss did," he says.

DAY TWENTY-SEVEN
27TH JUNE 2018

It is no surprise that his mother opens the front door. It *is* a surprise, however, that she breaks into a smile when she sees me standing at her doorstep.

"You two youngsters must really be getting on like a house on fire," she says. "I've never known one of Simon's friends come back for a second visit. Even I think he is peculiar, and I'm his mum. He's in the garden, love. Just go through the house. Don't worry about taking your shoes off. The back door is open."

Has she been popping the Prozac? And what is up with Simon? Admittedly, it is yet another scorching June day, yet I still expected the pasty streak of piss to be holed up in the darkness of his basement, the only light emitting from the flashing computer screens. Pushing open the back door, though, I find him sat on the patio, shoulder blades thrust close together, hunched over his laptop. I wish I'd brought my sunglasses, for he even has his shades on, seemingly soaking up the rays. I'm Mr Popular today; even Simon bares his teeth when he sees me.

Standing up, he moves to pull out a chair, but with a flick of my finger I tell him to sit down. He does so without blinking. Shutting the laptop cover, he slides it across the round garden table. I feel my body tense as I think the laptop might topple over the edge, but it stops dead just in the nick of time. Creases spread from the corners of Simon's eyes: he knows he is in trouble.

"You killed him, didn't you?"

I sit down close and wait for him to act the fool. I'm already prepared with a list of counters. I've been rehearsing on the way here. *Who? What you going on about? You crazy?*

"I did, yes..."

My body deflates. I'd geared myself up for a battle, a boxer psyched before entering the ring. I imagine DCI Baldwin giving me a subtle, impressed nod of the head. Maybe I was a natural at forcing out a confession? Simon momentarily sinks his head in his hands, and when he removes them, his face is flushed crimson. He blows out air, then shakes his head.

"God, it felt good to get that off my chest," he says. "Thanks for forcing it out of me."

I puff out my chest. It does feel like I've achieved something, though I'm fully aware that, really, I did fuck all. Simon glances around. Is he looking for his mother, hiding in the clothes line?

"Nobody else knows. You can't tell anybody. I'll be in serious shit."

"You normally are in shit when you kill somebody,

Simon. This isn't stealing from a sweet shop, you know. You need to tell me what happened. Now. Before I tell somebody else and they make up their own mind. And no bullshit. I need to know who or what I'm working with. I need to know whether you're somebody I want on my side..."

There is no need to tell me the motive. The motive is clear. But I do want to know *how* he did it: the nuts and bolts. I know the outcome. The gory details are freely available on the internet. But I have a compulsion to know the build up, how his brain ticked.

Simon bounces his trainers off the patio slabs, brushes his hand across the garden table. "The case had gone cold. Their idea of time was different from my idea of time. Months had passed since his last murder. Robert Price had gone quiet. Intelligence was that he was unlikely to kill again. The initial thrill of the case had disappeared. He was yesterday's news. He'd only killed three people, and they were all taxi drivers. Who *really* gives a fuck about tax drivers? Price wasn't perceived to be a risk to the general public, either by the police or by the general public themselves. It is a natural human instinct: so long as it doesn't happen to me, then I don't really care. Not *really*. Price didn't cause mass hysteria. Not like Spartacus. Remember I told you about the different categories of killers?"

"Organised and disorganised?"

"Right. You listened. Well, Price was your typical disorganised killer. The police didn't know his identity, of course, but it was fair to say he was likely to be a loner, a loser, somebody who didn't have too much going on up top. A simpleton. They were looking for a weirdo..."

"And he wasn't a weirdo?"

"Oh, he was a weirdo alright!" Simon snaps. "This guy was the stereotypical monster at the bottom of your bed. His motive was simple, and it was deprived. Price had a fixed routine that worked. So far. No reason to change it. No brains to change it. How did he do it? He jumped in a taxi and gave an address that was in the middle of nowhere, that led to a dead end. The driver invariably got lost, because the address led nowhere, and that was when he struck. Leaned forward from the rear seat, used wire to strangle the tax driver. The driver struggled, lost consciousness, crashed the car..."

"Didn't he get hurt, too, when the cab crashed? Wasn't this a risk?"

Simon twirls his finger by his temple. "Probably minor injuries, sure. The cab was most likely moving slowly because - remember - they were driving down dark lanes in the middle of nowhere. Truth be told, he probably got turned on by pain. Anyway, he dragged the dead body out of the cab and then had sex with them in the overgrowth on the side of the road. And he'd just leave them there. Then he'd drive the taxi back and just abandon it closer to home. Remember, it was always the middle of the night...."

Simon rubs his finger over a bloodshot eye. No wonder he is upset.

This is his dad he is talking about.

The monster murdered his dad, had intercourse with his corpse and then just abandoned him on the side of the road. No wonder Simon killed him. I would do the same. I consider telling Simon that he really doesn't need to say any more, that he has said enough, but I figure he wants to, that it will be a relief to tell *somebody*.

"So – sure - I became obsessed with finding him. I searched for clues day and night. Turned into something of a lunatic. All clues led to dead ends. My focus was on where Price was picked up from, and where the bodies were found. He was always picked up within a two-mile radius, so it was fair to assume he lived locally. But the end locations were miles apart, all in different directions. There seemed to be no link at all. But I examined these locations deeper, like only an obsessive could. The only pattern I could find was that, within three or so miles of each location, there was a pond. These ponds were remote and hidden away and you'd only ever know about them for one reason; you fished there.

Something struck me; the murder weapon wasn't just wire, it was fishing line. The murderer knew these three locations because he'd fished at the ponds."

"Why didn't you tell the police your theory?"

"Why didn't you tell the police about your updates?" Simon retorts, not missing a beat. "I didn't want the son of a bitch to be caught, did I? Lock him in a cell, put a roof over his head, keep him fed. I wanted him dead. Anyway, this was where the long hours started. It was a long shot, I knew that, but it was the only shot I had. I waited for hours and days hidden away at each pond waiting for him. And, then, in the blink of an eye, there he was..."

"So you just went over and killed the bastard? Good on you..."

"No. I didn't, even though the urge to do so was overwhelming. Even I knew there was a chance this wasn't my guy. There was a chance I could be killing an innocent man, maybe a father just like my dad, merely out fishing..."

"Fishing might be boring as fuck, but it isn't a crime," I say, smiling. Simon warns away my attempt to lighten the tone with a steely glare.

"So I follow him, don't I? I find out where he lives. Fucking dive, as you'd expect. I wait for him to go out. I break in. I search for clues. I recovered his recently deleted search history on his laptop. You know what I found?

Necrophilia porn. I had to put my hand to my mouth to stop from vomiting. This was my guy..."

I slam my fist down on the table. "This sick bastard watched pornography of dead people...?"

"This sick bastard had *sex* with dead people, so what do you expect? Of course he fucking did. Search histories give a great insight into somebody's character. This guy isn't Mary Poppins, you dumb fuck..."

I hold my hands up. I'm alarmed by the intensity of his words, but I know I deserve every single one of them fired in my direction.

"I'm sorry. It's just...well, you know? I went through his drawers and you know what I found? Photos of the dead victims. Photos of my dead dad. Can you imagine? The stupid idiot had taken photos and printed them and left them in his flat. I trashed the place, stole a few things and then made out it was a burglary. After all, I'd broken down his door to get in."

I nod; avoid eye contact. This is horrific. I fear that even I might break down.

"Then it was just a matter of waiting. I could have just killed him in his flat, but as soon as he saw me he'd know who I was, what I was there for. I wanted to toy with him. Besides, I didn't want to leave any trace. So, I waited. Kept coming back, hiding in the shadows. Days passed. Finally, I watched him put his fishing gear in his car. I followed him. Again. This time I waited a good time before I joined him on the bank of the pond..."

"You went fishing with him?"

"Yes. I was all ready. I had the gear in the car. I asked if he minded if I joined him. He mumbled that he didn't mind, but I could tell he was uncomfortable. He didn't want me anywhere near him. The guy was socially inept. Hell, I was like that Rylan Clark off the TV next to this guy. I asked if he came here often, if he knew the area. I said that my dad came here once. He was a taxi driver. And then I said his name. I watched his eyes bulge and his body tense as the penny dropped. He went to move – to run - but I was already primed. I strangled him with the same fishing line he used to kill my dad. He was found by another fisherman three days later."

I gulp. This is a lot to take in. So the bastard ran. He didn't fight. I glance at Simon, his pale skinny legs shaking, his long slender fingers tapping against the table. The whole thing is fucked up. My overriding feeling, however, is that I underestimated the guy.

"Didn't the police question you? After all, the crime has never been solved. The murderer - *you* - is still out there."

Simon shakes his head. "They came around, of course, to tell me that they'd found a body and that, after searching his flat, they believed it was my father's killer. This was confirmed later, of course. They said it was most likely a revenge killing. The file is still open. I don't think they are pursuing it too actively. The general consensus from the public is that the killer saved taxpayers' money that would otherwise have been spent keeping the monster alive. I'm happy with that consensus."

We sit in silence for God knows how long. Eventually, Simon looks up. His long, greasy hair covers his eyes.

"Do you understand why I did it?"

I nod. "Of course I do, you mad bastard."

His smile is sheepish, embarrassed. "Do you want me on your side, then?"

I lean forward and look him straight in the eye. "I can think of no better person," I say.

DAY TWENTY-EIGHT
28TH JUNE 2018

Rather than making the most of every second I have left till the end of the month, till the 30th, I long for the seconds to pass, to just get on with it, to accept whatever my fate may be.

The phone wakes me. My mouth feels toxic, like my gums are corroding. I have no idea what time it is, but judging by the brightness of the room, it is probably the middle of the day. My duvet lies in a ball at the end of the bed, but still my shirt clings like a second skin to my oven-like, glistening body. With the back of my head still engulfed in the pillow, I extend my arm and pick up the phone.

The red one.

I hold it above my head, my thumb navigating the buttons.

Good afternoon, Jeffrey. Only two days left. How very exciting! You'll find your invite in your boat. Don't make too much of a mess looking.

Fuck that. I just need to know what he has lined up for me, however horrific. I pull open cupboards, sweeping glasses and cups to the side. Glass clatters to the worktop. Blood smothers my fingers. I slam doors shut. Drop papers from files.

Standing in the centre of the boat, with my hands on my hips, I survey the colossal mess I've created. I don't know where else to look. Then I remember the first hiding place I always chose with Luke. I slide my hand underneath the bed, searching for something, hoping I'll know what it is when I find it. My chest tightens. There is something there. I'm reminded of the painting I slid under the bed when there was no room left on the walls. It isn't that. Too narrow. I pull it out. Hold it in my hands.

My jaw drops. I stare at the front cover of the book. I don't need to look inside. Reality has already hit.

I remember, during the early days, Erica sent Jenny messages from my phone. Told her to keep away. Said I'd moved on. Pretended to be me. Deleted the messages. When I found out, as I inevitably did, she showed no regret, only bravado. Reminded me what that woman had done to me, how she had torn my life apart. Told me she was looking out for me, that she did it because she loved me and didn't want me hurt again. I believed her.

Stood here now, book shaking in my trembling hands, it dawns on me that maybe I shouldn't have.

"What the hell is all this mess...?"

I jerk my head over my shoulder. Erica's eyes can't quite take in what she is seeing. "What, have you been burgled?"

she asks.

I'm not interested in her question, barley even hear it, let alone register it. Right now, I'm interested in *her*.

I hold the book out, let her take in the title. "This is yours, isn't it?" I ask. "You know who I am, don't you? Who I *really* am? You've always known, haven't you?"

Erica takes a step back, hands held up to her chest. "What the fuck are you talking about, Marcus?"

I lunge for her, but slip on some broken glass. I look up at her from the floor, crumpled and beaten, like a rolled-up piece of paper.

"This is the last straw, you crazy bastard," she says.

I don't see her leave. I only hear the door slamming. Sucking the blood from my cut hand, I wonder whether I'll ever see her again.

DAY TWENTY-NINE
29TH JUNE 2018

I return to my empty boat late afternoon.

I bend at the knees and pick up a couple of leaflets from the mat. Buy one get one free pizza. I now have a collection of cards for the same taxi firm. Not sure I'll look at a taxi in the same way after recent revelations.

Absent-mindedly running the tap and taking a few slurps of water, I gaze through a crack in the net curtain; my mind wanders. I think back to the last time I counted down the days until the end of the month. As a kid, of course, I counted down the days to my birthday, to Christmas. It wasn't that long ago though, surely? Of course, it was back when payday really made a difference, when it meant something.

With no qualifications or experience, I started in the city right at the bottom of the ladder. Officially I was a Junior Administrator, but unofficially I was the shit on everybody else's polished shoes. It didn't matter. I was there. I could have been cleaning the toilets so long as it was in the city. I was part of the morning stampede across London Bridge, brushing shoulders with men and women dangling expensive leather briefcases. It was exciting to be surrounded by so much adrenaline, so much success, so much money. It was a godsend compared to the lonely nights when I first arrived in London, before I managed to get a job. There was so much of everything in the city, including people, that it was nearly impossible to stand out, and I managed to blend in, just as oblivious as everybody else. Of course, without meaning to state the obvious, that was exactly what I needed at that specific point in my life.

Payday was a big deal. It wasn't like I was hard up. Rent in London was nothing like it is today, when you have to pay a small fortune to live in a shed or a cupboard under the stairs like Harry Potter. Catching the tube didn't eat into your pocket like it does these days. It was so much more realistic – more achievable - for a singleton on basic pay to enjoy London, not just survive. I never went without. But still, I counted down the days from about the middle of the month. I ticked off each passing day like it was a success. Payday was a big deal because, suddenly, I was flush. I had notes in my pocket I could flash between my thumb and forefinger at the bar. Not that the barman took much notice, of course. I could mingle with those who really had money (and not just for a day or two). It felt that, just for a few hours, I belonged in this city of success, extravagance and greed. Of course, I was a pretender, but my whole life was a pretence, so what did one more thing matter? I was hungry to earn more, to live like this all of the time.

And, of course, it was payday when I first met Jenny. It always had an extra special place in my heart after that.

That was nearly thirty years ago. As soon as I earned real money – monopoly money void of any real meaning - I quickly became bored of it. And not only did I become bored of it but, in a perverse way, I became ashamed by it. I resented people who were given outrageous bonuses when others could barely rub two pennies together and, more significantly, I despised the fact I was one of them. Rather than flashing my cash, I tried to hide it; I never openly discussed salaries and, when pushed into a corner, I pretended to earn much less than I really did. I pretended to be an average Joe, grafting just to make ends meet. Only the people who knew nothing about me were taken in by this fallacy.

This is the first month I've counted down the days since I was a fresh-faced teenager in a cheap suit.

June 2018.

Only, this time I haven't felt expectation. I haven't longed for the days to pass, keen to get to the other end, over the line. This time I haven't started counting from the midway point. No. I've counted from the very first day of the month, since my name from my previous life was uttered in that lift foyer. Apart from the last few days, when I've just wanted it over, this time I've longed for the days to slow down, to halt, to never end. I know there is no prize waiting for me at the end of the month. I know that whatever is waiting for me is the most horrific thing I'll ever encounter in my life.

For weeks, I've been looking around for signs, glancing over my shoulder and reading into things that just weren't there. It has become a habit, a nervous tick, and I continued to do it as I walked back to my boat. The sun has been relentless, working overtime, and people of all ages were out, enjoying it. I longed for a cool breeze to dry the layer of sweat that permanently covered my forehead, to blow away the body odour hiding beneath my tee-shirt. I know I'm a hypocrite, just like everybody else – I'm not *really* that different - that as soon as the sun is replaced by grey skies, shoulder to shoulder clouds and constant, relentless drizzle then I'll call for it to come back, tell the sun that all is forgiven, you're not so bad after all. I quickened my pace, lengthened my strides, desperate to get home, to open all the windows, lie on my bed and just wait.

Now I'm here, though, the air is stale and suffocating and I just want to break free and get back outside again. The boat is empty, of course. Erica no longer lives here. I'm not even sure who Erica is any more. The sweat on my forehead doesn't dry; it trickles into my blinking eyes. Kicking off my shoes at the sink, I reach between the gap in the net curtain and urgently push open a window. My big toe stubs against the kitchen surface, yet again. When will I learn?

"You fucking little bastard," I shout, hopping on one foot.

I run over to my bed now, desperate to disappear within the security of the duvet, to hide away and pretend that none of this is really happening.

It is only when the corner of the duvet is in my hand and I am ready to give it a good yank that I see it, lying right in the middle of the bed, just demanding to be noticed. Still, I think about ignoring it, pretend I haven't seen it, but my eyes remain fixed, staring like a madman.

The envelope is crisp, white and unexceptional. My name is written in blue pen across the centre. My birth name! This is no birthday card. It isn't my fucking birthday, for starters. I tear open the envelope and dangle it upside down so that the contents drop onto the bed. I poke my eyes inside like a kid hoping to find a ten-pound note. Nothing. Everything that is important – that, presumably, could determine whether I live or die – lies motionless on the bed, waiting for me to examine it.

I pick up the orange strip of card, already knowing what it is. A train ticket. Just one. A single ticket. No return. London Paddington to Bridgend. My eyes scan the ticket, looking for the date, merely confirming what I already know. There it is. There you go. Right there.

30th June 2018.

DAY TWENTY-NINE
29TH JUNE 1988

Yvette Allen peers over the tip of her third cup of tea, glances at the tepid dregs. Fingertips pressed against the morning's newspaper (Wednesday), her eyes fix on the clock on the kitchen wall, follows the red hand as the seconds pass.

She kissed her husband goodbye over an hour ago. Normally she'd busy herself, pouring tea for Jeffrey, buttering toast, tidying up, making a start on the morning's chores. This morning, though, she remained motionless in the silent kitchen, bare feet pressed down against the cold tiled floor, unblinking eyes focussed on the damn clock.

Pulling sharply on her dressing gown belt, Yvette sucks in air and rises to her feet. She'd given it till ten to see if he came downstairs for breakfast. Still no sound. No sign of life. She has to do this, she thinks, climbing the stairs.

"Jeffrey?" she says, tapping on the door.

Nothing. She knocks on the door again, louder this time. No movement. Pulls down the handle, pushes open the door.

Yvette pulls her hand to her mouth to silence her gasp. *Not this bad. Surely things haven't got this bad?*

Not even the powerful morning sun can bring light to the

room, for the curtains are thrust tight together. The foul air suggests that the window hasn't been opened for days, possibly weeks. Stepping over crumpled cans of coke, flat crisp packets and dirty underpants, her eyes can't help but glance at the faded newspaper clippings covering the walls. Jeffrey's bed is just a tepid mound. It is difficult to tell whether the sheets have gathered together or a body lies underneath.

Drawing the curtains and opening the window, Yvette perches on the edge of the bed. She wonders whether Gordon did the same when he chatted with Jeffrey a couple of weeks ago. She clears her throat.

"It's another beautiful morning, Jeffrey. Aren't you supposed to be studying for your exams? Only a couple of weeks now..."

Nothing.

Yvette pulls the bed sheet from his face, smoothes down his dirty blonde hair with her hand. Jeffrey rolls over, looks up at her. His cheeks are puffy and red, his lips dry and cracked. The eyes are perfect circles, signalling anything but perfection. Slowly, he nods his head.

"I will do," he says.

Yvette squeezes his hand. "Not that exams are that important, not really. We just want to make sure you're okay..."

Jeffrey nods his head again. His dad had already told him this. He knows exactly what she means, needs no further explanation.

"Why don't you jump in the shower, freshen up a bit? I'll cook you some bacon and eggs and we can have a chat in the kitchen?"

Subtle creases appear at the corners of Jeffrey's eyes. "Sounds good," he says, voice expressionless.

Yvette pushes forward her neck, focuses on the newspaper clippings on the walls. Details of the victims. Her head rotates. One victim more than any other.

"Jeffrey?"

"Yes?"

Yvette holds her son's look, tries to recognise him as the fearless young boy with a swagger, taking on the world with his older brother.

"You told your dad about a girl you liked, didn't you?"

His eyes flick to the ceiling. Doesn't say anything.

"She was the girl that was killed, wasn't she? That lovely, pretty girl. Marie Davies?"

Jeffrey still doesn't say anything. His eyes still stare blankly at the ceiling. A single tear rolls down his cheek just moments before he releases a loud, pained shriek.

Yvette pulls her little boy's sobbing face to her chest, tells him that it is fine, that his mum and dad are here for him.

Always.

Jeffrey sits up, rests his back against his pillow. He looks healthier – happier – like he has emptied his soul of pent-up sadness. Yvette thumbs the underside of his chin.

The feeling of impending doom has been growing inside of her the last few weeks. When Yvette was a child, she'd blank out the noise of her arguing parents by closing her eyes and escaping to another world, one where she could walk along hot sand barefoot, or maybe shelter from the rain within a forest. She was reassured that, however awful things got in the real world, she always had a wonderful, albeit imaginary place, to escape to. And then Luke died, and even the brightest sunrise felt drab and grey and powerless. She closed her eyes and thought of her parallel world. But rather than bringing colour and hope to the dark and despair, the alternative world that belonged in her mind terrified her; however desperately she tried, Luke would not join her. She just could not imagine Luke in her fake world. All these years later, Yvette is not sure she has the strength to endure all that pain and suffering again, that she has it in her to come out the other side.

"Just promise me one thing, Jeffrey?" she says.

"Yes?"

"Whatever you are planning, can you promise to please, please be careful?"

Jeffrey glances to the ceiling again for just the briefest moment, before looking his mother straight in the eye.

"I promise," he says.

DAY THIRTY
30TH JUNE 2018

Of course, I considered packing a bag – it felt odd not to –
but then I realised it was futile, utterly pointless, kind of
idiotic. I'd only been given a one-way ticket. I didn't even
know whether I'd be getting off the train alive, let alone
staying the night somewhere. What the hell was I thinking?
This wasn't a holiday, an opportunity for a luxurious night in
a hotel. Packing a toothbrush and a change of underwear
was, frankly, the least of my worries. All month I'd been
crossing the days off one by one, but now there are no more
left I long for a few extra days in June, maybe just a solitary
one, like July and all the others, merely to prepare for
whatever is to follow, possibly just to delay the inevitable.

I shut the door to my boat early, *too* early. I've prepared
for every eventuality that might possibly stop me from
arriving at the platform on time – an explosion on the tube,
getting mugged, wetting my pants – and then I've added
some more minutes just for good measure. Recalling my job
interview in the big city, I arrived at the office so early I set
up camp in a cafe and I was high as a kite on coffee by the
time they called my name (my *new* name). Still, I was
adolescent and virginal (literally), and the experience boosted

my confidence; I took on the big bad wolves with their swanky suits and oily hair, nailed the interview and got the job. There really wasn't much I couldn't take on after that, was there?

What doesn't kill you makes you stronger.

The route I take isn't as the crow flies. Far from it. My thoughts from earlier in the day kept niggling away, a distraction from the real issue at hand. The thought had grown until it was a permanent fixture in my mind. This isn't even a detour. I head in a completely different direction. But I have time. Time to kill. Ironic, really.

"Hi," I say, "I'll try a cappuccino this time, please. With chocolate sprinkles. I like to live each day like it might be my last..."

Catching my eye, she blinks when she recognises me. Glancing over her shoulder, she realises that none of her bulky male colleagues are here to provide back up. There is hardly *anybody* here. It is later in the day than last time . Much later. A red flush appears to her cheeks. She lowers her eyes. Looks down. "Oh," she says.

"Don't worry," I quickly say, keeping my tone soft. "I'm not here to cause trouble. I just wanted to confirm something with you, that's all. Somebody told you to call out that name, didn't they?"

The girl glances in every direction now, checking nobody

is listening. Her cheeks burn pink. She doesn't say anything. Continues to avoid my eyes. Nods her head.

"What did he say?"

"Listen, you need to believe me when I say I'm sorry, okay? I don't even know you and so I have no reason to upset you, do I?"

"But why did you do what he asked?"

"He asked me to call out a name I'd never even heard of before. What was the harm? I had no idea it would freak you out so much. He said he'd tell my manager about the drinks I've been taking without paying. Never felt like a big deal to me, to be honest. Perk of the job. He gave exact times I'd taken the drinks. Knew my manager's name. Freaked me out. He'd been watching me, hadn't he? Said theft was a very serious crime, that prison was no place for a delicate, pretty young girl like me. Asked if I'd ever been raped before. Was it something that appealed to me? I was scared. You know how much they pay me here anyway? I can barely afford to pay my rent as it is..."

"It's fine."

She looks up at me. First time. She is attractive when she smiles. "It is?"

"Sure. No problem."

She makes my coffee in silence. Her cheeks look hot to the touch.

"Keep the change," I say, handing her a note, heading for the door.

"But this is..."

Her protests fade into the background as I leave the coffee shop and enter the warm evening awaiting me outside.

On the train, I press my head back against the cushioned seat and close my eyes. Fuck it. If I'm going to die, then I may as well enjoy my last few minutes of relaxation before I do so. Stretching my legs as far as they'll go, the tips of my shoes tap against the heel of the person in front, so I wind them back in. Resting the palm of my right hand flat on the empty seat next to me, the fingertips of my left hand drum rhythmically against the window. I stop drumming when I sense the person in front shifting in their seat. I've already kicked the back of their shoes and I don't want to be identified as an irritant during – potentially – my last few hours on this planet.

Welcome to the 20:45 Great Western Service travelling from London Paddington to Swansea, calling at Reading, Swindon, Bristol Parkway, Newport, Cardiff Central, Bridgend and reaching Swansea, our final destination, at 00:03.

The voice is warm, syrupy, (presumably) educated and rightly belongs on an aeroplane rather than a train. I glance at the ticket that I'd hidden beneath my flat palm. Only takes me as far as Bridgend. And we're due to reach Bridgend at 23:28.

I lay in bed last night thinking about the monumental significance of the journey. Of course, I had plenty of space to think. Erica hadn't shared my bed for days. She hadn't returned my calls for days, either. My head propped up on two pillows in one corner, my feet pushed against the wall of the boat in the opposite corner, the sheets rolled into a tight ball by my belly. Staring up at the ceiling, my whole body was coated in perspiration. Questions, questions, questions. Why was my ticket only taking me to Bridgend? Was I even going to *make* it to Bridgend? Where was I expected to get off? Of course, I couldn't sleep, but still, I wished that the train was the first out of Paddington and not the last. I just wanted to get – whatever it was – over and done with. Why had he chosen this train? To deliberately taunt me? Make me wait and suffer?

Outside, the guard on the platform theatrically blows his whistle. His moment in the limelight. Any runners, I consider, desperate to get on the train before the doors close, have lost their race. It is probably for the best, I think. Who knows whether this drama will draw in anybody else? Innocents. I lower my shoulders as the train slowly and smoothly leaves the station, gaining pace, gathering momentum. I smooth down my trousers, fingertips running

over my blue phone in my left pocket and my red phone —
his phone — in my right pocket. I glance out of the window
and — once again — stare in awe at the beautiful countryside
visible in the rapidly fading sunlight as we move further and
further out of the big city. I wonder when and how he will
contact me.

I *do* know that I'll need to be ready.

Of course, a couple of other questions have been
relentlessly running through my mind.

Is he even on this train? If so, where is he?

Opening one eye as the train slows to its first stop,
Reading, I conclude that I am still alive.

Stretching my head to the side, I watch the few
commuters on the platform, staring at the square button,
urging it to turn green, hurrying the punters off the train so
that they can embark. Waiting, waiting, waiting - just like me.
Widening and then narrowing my eyes, I study their ages,
their demeanour, determining whether one of them could
possibly be him. Not him. Not him. I discount them, one by
one. I conclude that either he is already on the train (maybe
even just a few feet away) or he has not yet got on (maybe he
never *will* get on). But wait. I'm not even thinking straight.
I'm only looking at passengers boarding my carriage. There
are eleven or so carriages. He could be anywhere on this
train.

Passengers struggle to squeeze their luggage into the overhead spaces. The suitcases are too big, the spaces too small. Everybody is so prepared, with food, drink and reading material. All I have on my person is two phones (red and blue), my train ticket and my wallet. Dismissing the overnight bag, I still considered bringing the odd item. What about a weapon? Maybe a knife? After all, the person who booked my ticket is (almost definitely) intent on killing me. He only bought me a single ticket, didn't he? But I decided against all of it. I decided to just bring myself.

I check both my phones. Nothing. He hasn't contacted me all day. And it has been the longest day of my life yet. I glance around. Maybe he is close? Maybe he is watching me?

The doors slide open and the ticket inspector joins our carriage. He is tall, long-limbed, young and smart in his uniform.

"All tickets from London Paddington," he booms. "All tickets from London Paddington."

Somebody behind me mutters and swears. Glancing around, a figure retreats in the direction of the toilet. I wonder whether the inspector has the time or the inclination to wait for him to come out, or to make a mental note of his seat number and come back for him later. The inspector seems jovial and friendly enough. His smile is just a little too wide, his eyes are just a little too far apart. I hold my ticket out ready, keep glancing up as he edges closer to me.

I make sure I smile as I hand him my ticket. He thanks me just a little too loudly. His fingers are long and slender and covered with fine, sparse hairs. Most significantly, though, they are shaking. He glances at the ticket, glances at me; nods his head.

"Thank you," he says.

"Thank you," I say, taking back the ticket. I hold his eye. The whites are disfigured with blots of red. I start counting. Reach number three.

"You are invited to join the gentleman in carriage F, seat 43, at precisely 22:50."

He whispers the words, slowly and clearly. His instruction must have been to make sure there was no misunderstanding, ensure nobody else overheard.

"Thank you," I say.

My smile is narrow and it is forced, but nevertheless, it is evident. The man nods and then straightens his back. I imagine a weight dropping from his shoulders with a heavy thud. I don't want to keep him here any longer than he needs to be. I know that – whatever his involvement – it isn't voluntary. I have a million and one questions. Who is this man sat in carriage F seat 43? What does he look like?

"Just one thing," I say.

His body rotates slowly. Looks down at me. The cluster

of horizontal lines on the sides of his eyes weren't there a few moments ago.

"Could you please tell me what stop that will be?"

He is eager to tell me. He fires out the words. Relieved that I don't ask who the gentleman is, what threat he made. This is one question he *can* answer.

"Certainly, sir," he says. "We will have just left Newport."

At Newport, just a minute or so before 22:50, there is a scrum to get on the train.

The travellers are loud and excitable. It isn't difficult to ascertain that they've been out in the local pubs in Newport and are now heading to Cardiff – the main event of the evening - to finish the night on a high. A group of young lads fill the table close to me. One of them pulls a crate of Stella from a plastic bag and slams it down on the table. The cans disappear from the middle of the table. I catch an eye, get a thumbs up.

I wait until the aisle has cleared and everybody is seated before I start counting to a hundred. I do so mechanically. I blow out air and then rise to my feet. The train moves fast and there are plenty of twists and turns, and so I grip the tops of the seats as I begin my descent down the carriage. The windows are pitch black and the carriages are illuminated with lights. I sense movement behind me.

The young ticket inspector leans his long angular body

back to let me pass. He stares at the floor, at the ceiling and then – just as I pass – he glances at me. The colour disappears from his cheeks. I nod. I intend it to be reassuring, tell him that I'll be okay. He believes none of it. He knows I'm in danger, knows that he has conspired to lock me in the lion's den. He manages to nod back.

It becomes quieter with each passing carriage. I reach carriage F. I take a moment. Dip my hand in my pocket and pull out my wallet. I glance at the photograph of me with Luke, my older brother. Pumping out my chest, I stand tall and keep walking.

I can only see the tops of a few sporadic heads. The clutter and noise of my carriage has been replaced by peace and calm. I count down the numbers. Try to work out the general vicinity of the seat. That is it. There. It is a table seat. There are no more heads. He has the table to himself.

His face is engulfed in a newspaper. I know from the full hair, black like soot, that it is him. Spartacus. I hover over his chair, twisting and untwisting my hands. Wait. In silence. The newspaper unfolds. The clouds disappear and then his face is clearly visible to me for the first time in thirty years.

"Jeffrey," he says, looking up and smiling. "You decided to come. I am so pleased. Now, just where are my manners? Don't just stand there, sir. Please, take a seat..."

Taking the window seat directly opposite him, I note that

my throat is possibly a foot or two from his open hands. I cannot help but scan his face, a Terminator looking for signs. He knows I'm doing this, of course, and he raises his eyebrows. He looks five years younger than me, possibly more. His cheekbones, though tightly stretched, remain feline and sharp, and his hair parts in an immaculate line down one side. The white shirt is crisp and the grey waistcoat clings to his narrow waist. He looks like an amiable accountant.

"Did I have a choice?"

"Oh, Jeffrey," he says, his voice tainted with mock offence. "Haven't I always given you choices? Let's just say that, in my humble opinion, you've made the right choice this evening. After all, this is a little reunion amongst old friends, isn't it? Oh, and by the way, how *is* the delightful Erica?"

"I know you planted that book. And *you* know she's disappeared from my life..."

"Oh, that was merely child's play. I just wanted to prove a point. Help you, if you like. It was petty of me, if truth be told. We both know she isn't the *real* love of your life now, don't we...?"

"What would have happened if I hadn't come?" I ask, deflecting the question.

Spartacus' sharp teeth glisten with moisture. "Do you

really want to go there so quickly, Jeffrey? We've barely exchanged pleasantries. I don't really want to spell it out; where is the fun in that? Okay, let's just say Bridgend was the final destination for both the tickets I bought. If you decided not to join me then I would have hopped off and paid your dear dad a visit. I do so adore him; don't you? There aren't many good, old-fashioned gentlemen left in this world. Been a few weeks since I last saw him. Isn't he keeping well? It would not have been a wasted trip; just a little *unsatisfactory*, I guess..."

His grey eyes sparkle as he observes the whiteness of my hands, gripping the edge of the plastic table. I decide to go on the offensive, to challenge him. "You think you know everything, don't you...?"

Spartacus digs a hand inside his pocket. I flinch. Push back against the padded seat. Spartacus' face breaks into a jovial smile.

"*You* know me better than that, Jeffrey," he says, sliding the knife into the middle of the table, a foot or so from my hand, a foot or so from his. "Like I said, this is a reunion. Thought I'd bring along another friend of ours. It's been thirty years to the day since you last saw this knife, hasn't it..?"

I say nothing. My eyes widen as he digs his hand inside the other pocket. Watch as he carefully places another item down on the table. Another weapon. Another old friend. This one is a cut-throat razor. His eyes follow mine; he delights in my discomfort.

"We're all hypocrites and sinners, Jeffrey. Just look at *you* and all *your* dark secrets. At least I have the decency to be honest about my trivial inadequacies. Okay, so what *do* I know? Well, I know it was *you* who tried to kill *me*. You and your friend Baldwin decided to keep that one quiet, didn't you? Of course, Baldwin knew I didn't cut you with my usual reliable razor. He knew the knife was yours. He played his part well, didn't he? Went through the motions of interrogating you, but he knew what you were hiding from the beginning. Decided it was best not to tell the gullible society – the poor sheep – that *I* was the real victim, didn't he?"

I look away. He's right. But then, Spartacus killed Marie; he deserved to die. Is it a sin to kill a killer? Simon didn't think so. My only regret was that I failed to finish him off. I knew he killed Marie because I was in the club that night, hiding behind a glass of lager and a concrete pillar, as usual. I watched and waited, bided my time until I'd pumped my body with enough alcohol to numb an elephant. I was terrified. Maybe what I felt between us on the dance floor was all in my imagination? What if she didn't even remember me? I had nothing to lose, though, did I? I just had to be brave and fight through the fear. Finally, after yet another jackass turned away from Marie and towards her friend, I took one final glance at the photograph in my wallet, thrust out my chest and headed towards her. Only, Marie stood up, didn't she? Then, with the briefest of waves to her friend, she headed to the door.

Nothing was going to stop me then, though. I was on a mission. I followed her. Of course, something *did* stop me. *He* stopped me. Spartacus. I was too damn slow. By the time I reached the brightness of the hallway, he was already there. It was the first time I'd set eyes on him. Despite my twisted resentment, I was mesmerised. My feet sunk into the floor as Marie's eyes followed the movements of his mouth. He'd already cast a wicked, evil spell on her. How could I be so ridiculous to think a beautiful girl like Marie would even consider the likes of me – a fat, frumpy, awkward boy – when she could be with a man like *this?* Just as I turned to disappear into the safe, dark obscurity of the club, he looked up. Eyes fixed on me. And I'm *sure* he smiled from one corner of his mouth.

Of course, in the days and weeks that followed, Mum knew I was planning something. She saw me change overnight the week before, on the 24th day of the month, when the final victim died. The girl saw me hiding in the overgrowth on the other side of the river, and it was like my mother could smell the fear the next day on my unwashed body. Naturally, she was terrified that something might happen to me, but she understood why I had to take revenge. Mum knew better than anyone what it was like to love and to lose. She'd lost one of her two angels, through no fault of his, and through no fault of her own. She'd have killed with her bare hands to bring Luke back. She never told me not to do it. That was crucial. She never tried to stop me. Mum only asked me be careful. And I *was* careful. I was inferior, but I was careful.

I wasn't drunk the night of Thursday 30th June 1988. This time, the alcohol I'd drunk couldn't numb a mouse, let alone an elephant. I was so good at *being* the drunk, however, that I was a natural at playing the drunk. My pint glass was primarily refilled with lemonade. Adrenaline killed off the rest of the alcohol. I trawled the usual hot spots until, finally, I hunted him down. Spartacus. Stood on his own, blending into the background like a book in the library. He couldn't ignore me for long. Spilling my drink every time I slammed down my pint, speaking loudly and randomly to nobody in particular, I was ideal fodder. An easy, defenceless target; a zebra enticing a tiger. Up to a point, it was the perfect plan.

"After all this time, Jeffrey, you still don't realise I played along with your little game...?"

My eyes widen, just like his smile.

"*Seriously?*" he says. "Maybe I overestimated you. I saw you, remember? A puppy pining after that young girl. What was her name? Marie, that's it. Pleasant girl. Carried too much weight, of course, and she had absolutely no self-esteem, but then, none of us are perfect, are we, Jeffrey? If it is any consolation, at first I wasn't sure whether to kill her. She was just so easy and willing. *Where* was the challenge? She simply wasn't worth the effort. But then I looked up and there you were, all distraught and pathetic. *There* was the fun. You decided for me. She'd still be alive if it wasn't for you, Jeffrey. Does that make you feel important...?"

My eyes fix on the knife, then on the razor.

"Choices, choices, hey, Jeffrey. Not only can you not decide whether to kill me, but you cannot decide which weapon to use. I don't want to make things any more complicated than they need to be, Jeffrey, but does that gorgeous little girl of yours, Emma, really deserve for her daddy to spend the rest of his life in prison? What did she ever do to *you?* But there again, I guess you've already abandoned her, haven't you...?"

"Whose fault was that...?"

"Now that is more like it, Jeffrey. So you have been using your brain, after all. I applaud you..."

I slam my fist down on the table. Spartacus' smile widens.

"So tell me, why didn't you stay with Jenny?" I ask. "What

was the point of your affair? Why did you abandon her?"

"I never intended to keep her, Jeffrey," Spartacus says, crinkling his nose with distaste. "She wasn't the lure. You were. Again, *you* were the reason I destroyed an innocent life. The challenge was merely to take her from you, to ruin that sickly, idyllic family life of yours. I'll be honest, I expected more resistance, at least a token struggle. I thought she'd have more depth, more commitment to her cause. Yet another disappointment. Yet another hypocrite. I barely had to say hello and she opened her legs, ready for me. Do you actually realise how easy it was to entice her from you?"

I force myself to look out of the window, to not even contemplate the magnetic lure of the weapons.

"Your poor mother was the same. Such a lovely lady. As her psychiatrist, I don't believe I can take full credit for your dear mummy taking her own life. She was already stood on the edge of the cliff, ready to jump, the first time she walked into my clinic. She opened up to me, saw me as a confidant, a kindred spirit, which was *nice*. Told me everything. Just what sort of a man are you, Jeffrey? Your dear mother had already lost one son. She warned you to be careful. But what did you do? You tried to *kill* me. She stayed at your hospital bedside for weeks, and how did you repay her? As soon as you recovered, you left her. Like I said, in my professional opinion, your mummy was ready to jump. You deserve more credit than I do that she took her own life. My words of encouragement merely gave her a gentle push, brought forward the inevitable..."

I dig my nails into the skin of my hand.

"Of course, your mother helped me understand what went on inside that warped head of yours. I owe her considerable gratitude. But my real masterstroke, the one I'm proudest of, was placing Richard as your counsellor. You were his special project. What a wonderful subject for a developing counsellor! I made him believe that if we changed your thoughts and behaviours then we could make a real difference. And what a success, Jeffrey! Together, we completely ruined what little life you had. Lost your wife, lost your daughter, lost your job, lost your home. But despite all of this losing, and because of the thoughts we planted into that tiny brain of yours, you still failed to see yourself as a loser! I'm sure you can laugh at the irony now. Still, you genuinely believed you now had a better life, that you had somehow *seen* the light. But all you *saw*, Jeffrey, was what I had created..."

I stare down at the table, at a blank patch of hard plastic. It feels like something inside me is pushing against my chest, desperate to get out. All I can hear is my own breathing, loud and gasping, like a ball of cloth has been lodged in my mouth.

"Ah," Spartacus says, rubbing his hands together and breaking the silence. "We're coming into Cardiff - the capital city of Wales. Where it all began. We're on schedule. Now the fun really begins..."

*****

Glancing out of the window, trying to avoid the glare and the reflection, a fair number of people disembark at Cardiff. The group of lads from my previous carriage start chanting and clapping, like birds let out of the cage, opening up their wings. The few faceless heads from our carriage leave the train; I only notice one person joining us. Merely a shape, he sinks into the first row of seats of the carriage, to the rear of Spartacus.

"You'll know this all too well, Jeffrey, as you've secretly made this journey numerous times, haven't you? We have twenty-two minutes until we reach Bridgend. Twenty-one. Tick-tock. Tick-tock, Jeffrey. So I'm curious: what exactly do you think the game is here?"

I hold his glare; don't dare to blink. "You've set up a duel. To the death. Only one of us gets off at Bridgend Station alive."

Spartacus raises his eyebrows. "Of course you'd think that. It is a natural human instinct. As a species, we fight for our own survival. Rather *selfish*. Let me ask you something, though: do you think I strive to be like the rest of the human race...?"

"Most humans aren't deprived, sadistic killers, so no, I guess you don't strive to be like the rest of the human race..."

"Don't put them on a pedestal. Most humans are *scared*, Jeffrey. Do you think people are model citizens because they genuinely *care* about other people? Or is this pretence of care merely a means to an end? People crave to be liked. *Very* needy. And then there is the fear. On a primitive level, humans generally don't rape or kill because they fear being locked up in a cell, not because their conscience tells them it is morally wrong..."

He slides the knife across the surface. It stops right on the edge of the table, just short of toppling over. I'm reminded of Simon and the laptop. Simon, the killer. The sharp metal edges of the knife caress my fingertips, seducing me, the Serpent luring Adam. I glance down. The razor lies in the middle of the table. Spartacus couldn't reach it in time. I could end this right now.

Holding my eye, Spartacus drags the razor to his side of the table. Leaves it there. Rests his chin in his hands.

"You've got this all wrong, Jeffrey," he says, shaking his head. "Did I ever say I wanted you dead? Is that all you think of me? I realised thirty years ago how simple it was to take a life. So simple it was utterly futile. They were just numbers, nothing more. Just no satisfaction. Why do you think I didn't kill you the first time...?"

"Believe me, I've asked myself that every day of my life for the last thirty years..."

"Initially I used and abused you for my own excitement, Jeffrey. Something to turn me on. You were a hobby, really, that I dipped into for my own enjoyment from time to time. Over time, and the more I dabbled, the more I created, and then I had the urge to prove a point. You could say that it was a calling-"

"You think you're a Messiah?"

"Don't flatter me. I was more of a scientist, dabbling with an experiment in his laboratory. If anything, I am Frankenstein and you are my monster. Using you as an example, Jeffrey, I was driven to prove - to myself more than anybody else - that life is so pointless and meaningless it really isn't worth living. I wanted to satisfy myself that, rather than being the lucky survivor who got away, you were the *unlucky* one I kept alive..."

Placing the flat of my hands down on the table, away from the knife, I lean forward, close enough so he'll be able to feel the spittle spray from my mouth. "Just kill me then! End this miserable life of mine!"

Spartacus wags his middle finger. "Why on *earth* would I

do that? Were you not paying attention in class?"

We look at each other from across the table, two rams preparing to clash heads. Tugging down the collar of his shirt and releasing a yawn, Spartacus glances at his wrist watch. "23:20. Doesn't time fly when you're having fun? Just eight minutes until we hit Bridgend..."

"Yes, but eight minutes until *what* exactly?"

"Until you make your choice."

"I've already made my choice. I'm going to finish off what I should have done thirty years ago. I'm going to kill you, you sick, twisted bastard. I'm walking off this train with a merry skip in my step, and you're leaving it in a body bag..."

Spartacus pulls back his head now so I can see the sharpness of his incisors. His laugh is the roar of success. "You really think, after all I've just said, that I value my own life? My life is just as futile as yours. I'm not the Messiah, like you suggested. I'm no different from anybody else, not really. I'm finished with this world, Jeffrey. This is my curtain call. My last inglorious performance. I have no intention of leaving this train alive, so you can calm your frightful bravado..."

I cock my head, making sure I look nonplussed. "You want me alive? And we both fucking want *you* dead. So, what's the dilemma?"

Our heads nearly touch. "The first dilemma, Jeffrey," he whispers, "is this. Have I convinced you to join me? Has my little experiment convinced me of your worthlessness as much as it has me? Have you finally come to your senses and realised your life just isn't worth living? Basically, my old friend, after everything I've put you through, are you going to choose to stay alive? Or are you going to prove to me you have an ounce of courage, and take your own life?"

"I have nothing to prove to you..."

"What about the consequences of you being dead? After all, there is a chance it could bring you closer to your mother, and not forgetting your dear brother, Luke..."

I say nothing. Don't move away. Just shake my head.

"I thought not. You don't care about them. You only care about yourself. As I thought; you failed the first test. Then, as time is certainly of the essence, we can move swiftly into the second dilemma. You may enjoy this one. Are you going to leave me to cut my own throat, or are you going to cut it for me?"

Spartacus moves back in his seat, folds his arms across his chest.

"Be my guest," I say, forcing a smile. "I'll just watch. Be a dirty voyeur. Nothing would give me more pleasure than sitting back and seeing you bleed to death..."

Spartacus glances at his watch. "Sixty seconds now. The

train is literally coming into the station. Time is running out. You sure you don't want to do one honourable thing in your life, Jeffrey?"

He stretches out his arm, runs his fingers along the contours of the knife. "Don't you want to kill the man who murdered your first love, pushed your mother over the edge, took your wife and separated you from your beautiful little girl? Don't you have enough spine, enough backbone, to take revenge? It will be our perverted little secret, Jeffrey. Just one more. They'll never even know you were here..."

I take hold of the knife. It rattles against the table.

"Forty-five seconds. Forty-four..."

"I'm going to enjoy killing you," I say.

"Forty seconds. Thirty-nine..."

My reflection stares back at me from his misty, grey eyes. I watch myself raise the knife, high above my head, moving in slow motion. It feels like another being. Only, it is not; it is me. Spartacus releases a deep, relieved sigh. Curls his lips at the edges. Closes his eyes. Waits.

"Do it," he says.

I can no longer see my reflection.

His eyes blink open. His face jerks from side to side. The grey of his eyes disappears, replaced by brilliant, horrific white. His perfect, sculptured jaw is tarnished by saliva, trickling down his chin.

"What is happening?" he asks.

I was wrong. He does *not* know everything.

"Twenty seconds," I say, leaning so close my hot breath makes him wince. "Tick-tock. Tick-tock, Spartacus."

The fishing wire wrapped around his neck tenses and tightens. Cuts into the blue veins. The bulging eyes look ready to pop. They glance down at the knife. At the cut-throat razor. I swipe them away, to my side of the table. Just as before, they almost topple over the edge. *Almost.* His strong, sinewy body deflates. He manages to slam his limp fist down against the table.

"You might think we're the same, but we're not," I whisper. "Your life really *is* meaningless and worthless. The best place for you is to be dead. So I'm not going to let that happen, because that's what you want. Sure, you're smarter than me. But unlike you, I'm not alone. You're not smarter than all of us together, Spartacus..."

The train slows. Ready to stop. Is coming into Bridgend. Spartacus' final destination thirty years ago. *Our* final destination now. Spartacus sits motionless, his body rigid, his wide, unblinking eyes remain fixed on me. I'm certain I notice a smile from one corner of his mouth, just like I'm certain I did in that club all those years ago. This time, though, he does not taunt me; he does not pity me.

Simon's stringy hair covers his eyes. His oily skin glistens.

He only joined our carriage at Cardiff. A quick text was all it took. Simon bided his time, allowed events to unfold, just as we predicted they would. Said there was no way he was going to make his move until we reached Bridgend, that he was going to savour every second, play the game right to the end. Simon reiterated what he said when we first met, in his den. If Spartacus wanted to kill me, then he would have done it already.

So we bided our time. Simon chose the moment to silently strike, just as he did with his father's killer, at the fishing pond. He loosens the grip of the wire, the hold on the neck. He has already killed once before. One more time and he will officially be a serial killer.

"Five, four, three, two..."

Right on cue, a figure casts a shadow over the table. Looking up, I catch his bloodshot, watery eyes. An old friend, or possibly foe, from way back. He didn't have far to travel to Cardiff Central. His face is grizzled, his body is weathered and worn, but his mind is as sharp as it was back in the interview room. Handcuffs click around Spartacus' wrists.

"One."

DCI Baldwin wipes his lip with his sleeve. "You did say I'd finally get my man, Marcus," he says.

We stand in an orderly line to leave the train. The four of

us. Spartacus is cushioned between DCI Baldwin and myself. He follows like a sheep. Exactly like the rest of society that he so despises. The doors open and we step off the train, minding the gap, onto platform 1 at Bridgend Station. The stifling heat, that has been with us since that very first day of June, is suddenly replaced by a cool, refreshing and welcome breeze.

Looking around, hardly anybody has disembarked the train. They all offloaded at Cardiff, didn't they, the cosmopolitan capital city. Bridgend has felt like yet another forgotten town for far too long.

We're not alone, though. Far from it. The platform is packed, much busier even than Cardiff Central. We're surrounded by armed officers in blue: ready, waiting and poised.

Spartacus remains silent. Bows his head. Knows it is all over. But it isn't, is it? He wanted it to be over. Tonight. 30th June, 2018. But really, it is only just beginning. I look over at *DCI* Baldwin. Nod my head.

DCI Baldwin blows from his mouth. Turns to the officers.

"Can you please arrest this man?" he says. "And whatever you do, do *not*, for a single second, let him out of your sight. Keep him alive. We need him locked up for a long, long time. Thirty years ought to do it..."

*****

About the Author

Chris Westlake was born in Cardiff and brought up in Wick, a coastal village seven miles from Bridgend. He now resides in Birmingham with his wife, Elizabeth, and two young children, AJ and Chloe. Irritatingly, he is often told by local residents that he no longer has a Welsh accent.

He has written two previous novels, *Just a Bit of Banter, Like,* and *At Least the Pink Elephants are Laughing at Us.* This is his first crime thriller.

Chris blames the delay between novels solely on the arrival of his two children, and he takes no personal responsibility for this whatsoever. He promises, however, that his next novel, a psychological crime thriller, will definitely - *absolutely* - be finished in 2020.

You can find out more about Chris at his website, www.chriswestlakeauthor.co.uk

Printed in Great Britain
by Amazon